# OUT OF NOWHERE

# OUT OF NOWHERE

*A Yellowthread Street Mystery*

---

# William Marshall

THE MYSTERIOUS PRESS

New York • London • Tokyo

The Mysterious Press, 129 West 56th Street, New York, N.Y. 10019

Printed in the United States of America

First Printing: November 1988

10  9  8  7  6  5  4  3  2  1


**Library of Congress Cataloging-in-Publication Data**

Marshall, William Leonard, 1944–
    Out of nowhere / William Marshall.
        p.   cm.—(A Yellowthread Street mystery)
    I. Title.   II. Series: Marshall, William Leonard, 1944–
Yellowthread Street mystery.
PR9619.3.M27509   1988          88–4091
823—dc19                        CIP
ISBN 0–89296–199–6

The Hong Bay district of Hong Kong is fictitious, as are the people who, for one reason or another, inhabit it.

# WYANG

The cold wet air made his nose run and he sniffed.

He listened.

There was a mist coming in off Hong Kong harbor across the Hong Bay freeway and in the back of his truck he peered hard at the radar screen between his knees and listened. It was a little before 2:49 A.M. and the layers of cold air and the fog turned the screen into a flurry of breaking-up flecks and pulses of green light and he could make out nothing, so he leaned back and opened the rear doors of the truck a fraction and listened.

". . . mà mā . . . *ma* . . ." Out there there was nothing but darkness. He heard the wind across the deserted freeway in amongst the median-strip stanchions and railings. In the back of the van, leaning out, P. C. Kwing of the Traffic Radar Division heard nothing. He had only a thin sweater on over his blue police coveralls and he felt the wind and the clamminess of the mist get into his open collar. He listened.

". . . mā . . . — . . . ma." He cocked his head and it came, like the images on his radar speed-trap screen, in a pulse and then it

1

was gone again. He listened. It was there. He heard it as a sharp sudden sound somewhere off on one of the feeder roads and then, as it turned, the sound was gone again.

". . . Māmā . . . mà mā—*MA!*"

It was moving. It was there and then gone again, then there again as something faint, an echo . . . Then it was there again.

Music. It was not music. Noise. It was not noise. Voices? There were no voices. It was sound. It was moving fast and then slow, and then it was gone again, cutting itself on and off as it passed by the barriers and the overpasses and the interchanges and the exits of the feeder roads. He didn't have to look back at his radar screen: he knew there was nothing there. The cold wet air biting at him had damped out all the circuits. SPEED LIMIT 70. It was on an illuminated sign thirty yards down the highway to the south at a brightly lit interchange. P. C. Kwing called out into the darkness to where the chase car was parked and P. C. Li, who was a sleeper, slept. "Li? Can you hear it? What is it?"

"Mama! Mama! Mà mā mā—*MA!*"

He saw Li's shadow move by the car. He wasn't sleeping. P. C. Kwing said in Cantonese, "Listen! Listen!" The radar screen was useless. Up and down the length of the freeway on both sides—three lanes going south and three going north separated by the straight line of the median strip—he could see nothing. Getting out of the truck, holding his hand to his collar to close it against the mist, he could see only the lights from the interchange. All the cats' eyes in the railings and stanchions were dull. There was nothing.

He heard it. "Māmā mà mā . . . MA!" He saw Li in his knee-length blue-serge greatcoat step out onto the road in silhouette and look both ways into the darkness and the mist. He saw the leather of his Sam Browne belt and revolver-holster glint in the faint light from the interchange as he turned to look. He heard the leather creak as Li laid his hand on it.

There was the sound of a bell, then a drum, then a bell again. It was a long way off, then closer, then far off, then close again.

Then it was gone.

The darkness was full of mist and cold and faintly glowing light a long way off. It was a little before 3:00 A.M. It was 2:50 and 33 seconds exactly. P. C. Kwing, turning back from the open door with his hand still exposing his wristwatch so he could read the time exactly, called out, "Li, can you hear it too?"

For a moment, he lost Li's shadow in the darkness. For a moment . . .

It turned. The sound turned.

*Māmā . . . māmā—*

"Li!" He tried to see his shadow. P. C. Kwing, swallowing hard, finding his mouth dry, said as an order, "Li! *What is it?*"


It wasn't one sound, it was two. Out on the highway, looking south, Li said, "There's a truck out there. I can hear the diesel engine." It was traveling fast. In the moist air he heard it roar as the driver accelerated. The music—the cacophony, whatever it was—was on the other side of the freeway moving in another direction, coming from the north. Li said, "It's two of them. The one coming this way is a truck and the other sound, the music or whatever it is, is from a car on the other side of the freeway going south." Li said, "It's a car or a van. It's turning onto an interchange by the railings." *Māmā mà—MA!* It was coming in pulses. Li said, "I can't hear the engine." Li said, "Can you hear it? Have you got it on your radar?"

"The radar's gone!" He saw Li's shadow back at his car, saw him in shadows as he pulled the driver's door open and lit the interior with the roof light. He listened. Li said, "I can't hear an engine!"

"It's there!"

Li had two POLICE STOP signs under his arm and he was reaching into the car for something else. Li said, "It's probably kids in a stolen car with the stereo up full blast on the southbound side and a truck driver on this side who doesn't think there's a cop around for miles." Li said, "We'll take them both out, one on each side of the freeway." For a sleeper, he looked wide awake. Li, coming over to the radar van, his face gleaming in the light from the flickering radar reflections, ordered him, "You take this side and I'll go over the southbound carriageway and take out the kids." He had his arms full of flares and signs. Li, pushing a sign and a flare into Kwing's arms, said, "Okay? Or do you want the other side and I'll do the truck?"

"I'm just radar!"

"Your radar doesn't work!" Li said as a command, "It's a good one. The truck's at least twenty or thirty miles an hour too fast—it's a good one for us!" Li demanded, "Which side do you want?"

He was radar. He was—

Li said, "North or south side? This one or that one?"

Kwing said, "This one."

"Okay."

"The—the southbound side."

"The other one's the southbound side!"

"The southbound!" Kwing said, "What do I do?"

"Get a few feet out onto the road, pull the flare and hold it in your right hand out from the STOP sign and stop the bastard!" Li said, "You've got the kids. They're probably high as kites." Li asked, "Are you armed?"

"*No!*" He was radar.

"You take the truck then. You stay here. All you have to do is stop him and when I've done the kids I'll come over and—"

"I can do the kids in the car."

"The kids in the car may be armed."

Kwing said, "I'll stay here." He had never made an arrest or issued a ticket in his life. Kwing said, "Okay, you're the traffic cop, you—" He was talking to mist. He heard Li's boots thudding across the highway onto the central reservation and then onto the verge of the southbound carriageway. Kwing yelled out, "I can hear the truck!"

*Māmā qí mā. Mā màn. Māmā mà mā.* Mother rides horse. Horse slow. Mother scolds horse. It was Chinese opera played full blast. It was from an old Han dynasty story called *Night Battle.* In the Toyota Hi-Ace, at full volume, it sounded as if, so far, in the midst of the drums and cymbals, chimes and falsetto screeching, it was a battle no one was winning.

*Māmā qí mā*—mother rides horse. *Mā màn. Māmā mà mā*: it was in Mandarin. It was a play on words, a little comic relief in the wyang, the grand opera, that in Peking in the old days would have been a real aisle-rocker. It played on the four flat tones of the language. It was dross for the groundlings too thick to follow the main part of the plot. It was all incomprehensible. It was too loud.

The van traveled, according to the unlit speedometer to the left of the steering wheel, at exactly ninety-three miles an hour.

Three-point-zero-one exactly on the facia clock.

In the van, there were four people.

*Māmā mā—MA!*

There were cymbals, gongs, drums, flutes.

They drowned out every sound except their own.

He saw Li running toward the lit interchange thirty yards down the highway; he saw him as a blur, as a movement through the lifting mist; he not so much saw him as heard him, knew he was there. Kwing, fiddling with the plastic envelope that held the hand flare, trying to read the directions in the glow from the light in his truck, yelled, "Where? Where do I stand?" There was a roaring noise coming—the truck—and he wrenched at the cellophane with his bitten-down fingernails to get it off and couldn't. There was no zip or catch and he had to put the edge of the plastic in his mouth and pull at it with his teeth. He had never done this sort of thing before. He wasn't in uniform. All he had on was a sweater and coveralls. The truck driver could think he was anyone.

He heard the radar ping. He heard it register something traveling too fast and then it pinged again and again and began making a screaming noise. From the open door he saw the screen fleck white with blips and contacts, not the mist, but a hard target and he had it, he could register it. All he had to do was simply put the machine on to video-record, get the number of the truck as it went by and the whole thing could proceed by summons and he could— Kwing, getting into the truck, yelled, "It's all right! I've got him on radar!" He tossed the unopened flare and the sign out behind him as he got back into the truck to turn the video recorder on. Kwing, shouting back out through the open doors, yelled, "I've got him on radar!" Far down the interchange there was a sound like a giant match being struck and the white flare ignited. POLICE STOP. He saw the sign in Li's hand. He saw Li standing out a little on the highway in his full uniform, his leather and his metal and his badges, and Kwing called out—

He saw what was on the screen.

Kwing said in a gasp, "NO! LI!—LI!"

The brilliant white flare was burning. It lit up the highway on both sides. Kwing, scrambling out of the van, starting to run, waving his arms, yelled, "Li! LI! *Get back here!*" Kwing shrieked, "It's not over there! The car isn't over there!" He heard the music blasting, coming fast, reaching a crescendo, drowning out his words. He heard the truck. Kwing, starting to run across the highway toward the median strip to get to the southbound carriageway, screamed at the top of his voice as the truck, coming out of nowhere, roared at top throat, "It isn't over there! The car isn't over there! It's—they're both—they're both—" The truck was almost upon him. He turned in midstride and the car—the van—was— Kwing screamed, "It's coming south! It's coming south on the northbound lane! It's— THEY'RE BOTH ON THE SAME SIDE OF THE ROAD!"

"Māmā . . . *MA MA—MA!*"

He saw it. He saw for an instant the van with all its lights off thirty yards from him, lit up by the truck's headlamps. Kwing, yelling, running backward, falling over, trying to get away, scrabbling to get up, shrieked at the top of his voice, "They're—they're—THEY'RE GOING TO HIT!"


He was running. On the other side of the highway, on the southbound side, Li, running with the burning flare, yelled, "Get out! RUN!" He saw Kwing on the ground like a crab. He saw him trying to move. He saw him give up and curl himself up on the road with his hands over his face. Li yelled, "Get up! *Get up!* RUN AND YOU'VE GOT A CHANCE!" He saw in the van all the people lit up in a sudden yellow flash. He saw the man or woman driving jolt. The truck was a three-hundred-and-eighteen horsepower white Road Boss with steel bull bars. Its lights turned everything into day. He saw it on top of Kwing. He saw it— He saw— He saw—
*Ma—ma—* It was Chinese opera.
He heard.
He saw—


The van and the truck were traveling at a combined closing speed of one hundred and eighty-five miles an hour. He heard a sound like canvas being ripped violently apart and then he saw the van crumple. He saw it turn into cardboard, into paper. In the lights from the truck a moment before they exploded, he saw people in the van. He saw them as black shapes in their seats begin to move forward and then back like dummies in a seat-belt education film and then he saw the van disappear, be passed over, merge into the steel bull bars. He saw— He saw the truck devour it. He saw—
Then the van was there again, come out from somewhere, and it was coming out of the truck, being disgorged by it, forming itself out of crumpled and concertina-ed metal and it was spinning, turning away, all its tires exploding at once and sending sparks up from the roadway as the rims plowed into asphalt and bitumen and locked. He thought the truck had stopped. It hadn't stopped. The bulbs in its smashed headlamps came on: it was spinning, rocking on its axis. It was a flatbed, three-hundred-and-eighteen horsepower Road Boss with steel bull bars. He saw the bars bend. He saw the truck, like a monster above the falling-back van, rock and then move forward, rear up, and then hit the van again as if it were for the first time.
It was happening in flashes, frames. It was happening in awful, sickening moments taken not from this world but from somewhere else.

The shock wave from the collision hit him and knocked him off his feet.

The truck was slewing, coming back to hit the van again. There was no sound—he heard no sound at all. Li shrieked, "*Kwing!*" He was gone, taken away. The truck was slewing, grinding, coming around again and turning the front of the van into pulp, coming back onto it over and over again and Li, wanting mercy, trying to tell someone, screamed, "Stop! No more! *STOP!*"

Li yelled, "*STOP!*"

He had gotten to his feet. "STOP DOING IT!" There were people inside the van. Li shrieked to the truck, to the monster, "STOP! STOP! There are—" He heard the sound. It was a sudden violent clang, the sound not of two metal objects colliding on a flat road, but the sound of something awful, heavy, unstoppable, leaden, falling from a great height and striking. Thrown back to the ground again, scythed off his feet in the concussion of the air, he saw it all happen again. The truck was unstoppable. No force on Earth could stop it or slow it down. The truck was grinding, rocking above the van like a skyscraper. Again, starting from the beginning, from the moment of impact, he saw it happen again. He saw, as all the lights on the truck came on again for an instant and nothing seemed broken, the van shudder and crush. He saw the van illuminated in a shower of sparks from the wheel rims as they plowed in the roadway. He saw all the people inside like rag dolls with their necks twisting and their heads snapping forward. He saw—

Something else was happening. Whatever was happening, it was happening nowhere in this world, not according to the laws; it was happening somewhere else, eternally, over and over on some awful, darkened hell where— He saw the truck suddenly become unstuck from the van, go backward a few feet, and the van, almost undamaged, start to rock. It was all happening again from the start. He saw it in flashes. But there was something else. This time, there was something else. He sensed it. He knew it was coming.

He saw the van, from the inside, start to convulse.

From the rear doors to barely an inch behind the rear passenger seats, the van was loaded with one-eighth-inch-thick sheets of plate glass. It began to move. It began to shatter. With the recoil of the van going backward at high speed, with nowhere to go, the glass, shattering, being blasted into pieces, began to move.

It began to move forward. In the microsecond from the impact, in the single moment that everything that Li had seen had taken, the glass turned into daggers, into knives, into glittering, spinning, razor-sharp shrapnel, and, inside the van, blown to rain, it moved in a single storm inside the van straight ahead and up—like needles.

"*LI!*" It was Kwing. Somehow, he was in the darkness behind the truck, shouting. The truck had passed over him. In his coveralls and sweater, he was running toward the side of the road, coming around toward the front of the van.

Li screamed, "GET DOWN!" He heard it. He heard whatever was in the van take flight and move in a single buzzing roar and then explode and then— And then the glass tore through everything in the van and, seeking ways out, cut the aluminum body to pieces, rent it, holed it, came out like birdshot in a thousand, a thousand thousand pieces.

It was spinning: all the glass was spinning in the faint light from the interchange, billowing like a cloud, a tornado, falling all around him and slicing through the bitumen. It was an explosion of light and energy; it was all the light and life from the van. In the van, everything that lived had been cut to pieces. He saw holes appear like machine-gun bullets. He saw the truck, moving backward, rocking, become holed. He heard the windscreen on the truck go in a violent bang and then the glass hail into the cabin and, losing momentum, ricochet off the doors and the rear wall. He heard someone scream. He saw Kwing running, passing through the glass like a man running through silver rain. The glass was still coming up out of the roof of the van like fireworks. The van was new; it was being scrapped, destroyed before his eyes. All the paint had gone—it was becoming ancient in an instant. Something thudded past him and he thought it was glass. It was ripped-up, insanely turning sections of tread from the exploded tires. Everything was flying, being exploded, blasting out. He heard a long, single scream. He thought it was his own.

He saw Kwing down by the side of the road. He heard him shout something. He heard him shout that he was alive. He saw Kwing on his knees laughing and shouting as, instantly, suddenly, all the glass was gone and there was silence. He saw—

On the highway, in the light from the interchange, he saw only a single monstrous black shadow where the truck and the van had been. He saw, now, only the truck. He saw Kwing, still shouting at the top of his voice, on his knees in an attitude of prayer, violently, unstoppably, start to throw up.

It was 3:02 A.M. exactly.

On the highway for a distance of a hundred and fifty feet in every direction, to the side of the road, across the verge—everywhere— there was the hard, sharp glitter of a half-inch thick carpet of glass.

*Hong Kong is an island of some thirty square miles under British administration in the South China Sea facing the Kowloon and New Territories areas of continental China. Kowloon and the New Territories are also British administered, surrounded by the Communist Chinese province of Kwantung. The climate is generally subtropical, with hot, humid summers and heavy rainfall. The population of Hong Kong and the surrounding areas at any one time, including tourists and visitors, is in excess of five and a half million. The New Territories are leased from the Chinese. The lease is due to expire in 1997, at which time Hong Kong is to become a special semi-independent administrative region of the People's Republic, with British laws and, somehow, Communist Chinese troops to enforce them.*

*Hong Bay is on the southern side of the island, and the tourist brochures advise you not to go there after dark.*

"Kwing—!" In the van there was no movement or sound at all.

All the glass on the road, like sparks, had gone out.

"KWING—!"

On the roadway there was absolute silence and stillness. On the roadway, in all of Hong Kong, in all of the night and silence, there was only the sound of Kwing on his knees by the side of the roadway retching and blubbering.

"—KWING—!"

Tripping, falling, shouting, Li began running from the van in the terrible, glass-crunching, all-enveloping darkness.

# 1

Who knew what evil lurked in the hearts of men?

A married man with three children sitting alone in the Detectives' Room of the Yellowthread Street Police Station, Hong Bay, did.

On the phone at his desk, Detective Senior Inspector Christopher Kwan O'Yee, staying polite, said cheerily, "Detectives' Room." It was always a pleasure on the first Monday of the month when the new batch of horror videos was due to come out to see who you were going to get.

The voice at the other end of the line said, "Grrr."

It was a mass murderer. The new batch of videos had been reserved a long time ago by the literate loonies. The illiterate ones had to wait. O'Yee said, "How may I assist you?" He sounded meek. They liked meek. It was 5:00 A.M. Meek was the path of least resistance.

"DO YOU KNOW HOW MANY WAYS THERE ARE TO KILL A MAN WITH YOUR BARE HANDS?"

O'Yee said, "Yes. Twenty-three."

There was a pause.

The voice said, "Really?"

"That I know of."

The voice said, "Gosh."

He had a can of Diet Pepsi on the desk beside him. He hoped the mass murderer wasn't the sort who drank blood through straws. O'Yee said, "We've got a special on bare-hand killing this month."

"I use A CHOPPER!"

O'Yee said nothing.

"I USE A CHOPPER FOR I AM CHANG THE TOTAL AN-NIHILATOR OF ALL HUMAN LIFE!"

O'Yee said, "Hi. Christopher O'Yee."

"George Chang (not my real name)."

O'Yee said, "Right."

"I INTEND TO TAKE HER BY THE NAPE OF HER SCRAWNY NECK AND EXPOSE HER WRINKLED THROAT, AND WHILE I BREAK HER BACK WITH MY BARE HANDS—NO, TOO GOOD FOR HER—I INTEND TO DRAW BACK THE GLITTER-ING BLADE OF MY NEWLY HONED CHOPPER AND WITH ONE DOWNWARD SWING THAT STRIKES SPARKS IN THE AIR—"

O'Yee said, "CHOP OFF HER HEAD!"

"Right!"

O'Yee said, "Great!"

Chang said, "AAARRGGGHHH!"

O'Yee said, "Ah . . . !"

Chang said "GRRRRR!"

O'Yee said, "Oh . . . !"

Chang said, "GRZZZ-KUCK!"

New one that. O'Yee said, "Ouch . . . !"

Chang said, "Ahhhhh . . ." That felt better. Even if he was literate it was a long time before the video shops opened. The big one this week was *I Eat Your Eyeballs.* Chang said, "The frustration . . . THE FRUSTRATION!" Chang said, "It's the wife's mother."

O'Yee said, "Hmm."

Chang said, "Chop! Smash! Break! KILL!" Chang said to explain, "She isn't that bad most of the time, but there are times when she—" Chang said, "I know she's getting old and I have to make allowances, but every time my wife and I get rid of the kids and we think we might have a few hours to—to—to you know . . ."

That was why they only used mature men on this detail. O'Yee said consolingly, "I know."

"—she's there! Or she's wandering around somewhere due to be there! She goes out—she says it's going to be for hours . . . she says she's going out to see her friends, but she hasn't got any friends and she—" Chang said, "I know she's trying to be nice pretending she's got friends so we can be alone, but she—but she comes back!"

"Women do get weary."

"I know she's good at heart—"

"Try a little tenderness."

"I have! I try to be understanding! I try to think that one day I'll get old myself, but she just keeps—" Chang said, "So I'm going to kill her! Her life isn't worth anything! I'm ringing you to just check up that the official policy is that her life isn't worth anything!" Chang said, "She's old! Nobody would miss her!" Chang said, "She's a sparrow! Sparrows don't count!"

"Not a sparrow falls from a branch without the police noticing." O'Yee said, "George—not your real name—I tell you: you must not do this thing."

"I can get away with it! I've been watching videos and I can make it look like a thrill killing! I can make it look like something from a grave came up with popping eyes and grabbed her on the stairs and took her into his lair in the basement and—"

He drew a breath. O'Yee said in his best sepulchral voice, "GE . . . ORGE . . . !"

"I can do it!"

"GE . . . ORGE, WHAT-YOU-CONTEMPLATE-IS . . . WRONG!"

"I know! I know! But I—"

"THE-LAW-WILL-PURSUE-YOU-TO-THE-ENDS-OF-THE-EARTH!" O'Yee said, "We always get our man." O'Yee said, "There are twenty-three ways to kill a man with your bare hands and the Hong Kong police know every one." O'Yee said, "She's somebody's mother, boys, you know . . ." O'Yee said, "Peace, George, perfect peace. The peace that surpasseth understanding." He took a sip of his Pepsi.

"I HAVE A SOUL!"

"I know."

Chang said, "Nobody understands!"

O'Yee said,

> "We are a pair of red candles
> Shining at a wedding feast for guests;
> We stand at opposite corners
> Of the table,
> Quietly burning away our lives,

> Companions to their pleasure.
> When they have eaten,
> Our lives will be burned away."

The Annihilator said softly, "Wen I-To. I like his poems."

O'Yee said, "Me too."

The nice thing about Dial-a-Maniac was that sometimes you got a really cultured class of drool. O'Yee said quietly, "I send these poems to you.

> "Even if you do not know all the words,
> It doesn't matter.
> With your fingers you can
> Gently caress them,
> Like a doctor feeling a patient's pulse,
> Perhaps you can detect in
> Their excited pulsations
> The same rhythm as your own heart-beats."

Chang said, "Delmore Ling. I really wouldn't do . . ."

"I know."

"I just . . ."

"Yes."

"Thank you."

O'Yee said, "No trouble at all."

"I just had—I just had to—" Delmore said, "She's a fine, good person my wife's mother and the children love her and sometimes some of the kind things she does . . ." Delmore said, "It's just sometimes—sometimes—"

O'Yee said, "Yes."

"It's just sometimes . . ." Delmore said, "I feel better."

"Good."

"It's a great service you run."

O'Yee said pleasantly, "Open all hours."

"Thank you."

"Okay."

"Thank you, thank you . . ."

O'Yee said, "Fine."

There was a silence. Perhaps he was weeping. Delmore said, sniffing, "Can I call again one day if I need it?"

"Sure."

"Thank you!" There was a scuffling sound in the phone as Delmore must have twisted about.

Delmore said politely, "Um, Christopher . . ." Whatever it was he was scuffling for, he had it.

Delmore, feeling a lot better, taking care of the other side of things, asked respectfully, "Um . . . do you take MasterCard?"


5:19 A.M.

Endless night.

On the highway the Accident Investigation Squad had created an auditorium of light. The walls of the auditorium were their vehicles, their arc-light setups, the lights and flares from the police cars, ambulances, tow trucks, the television camera crews with their trucks and the great spotlights of fire engines. It was a hologram of white and yellow, flashing blue lights on top of the police cars and the ambulances, and the red turning lights of the coronial cars and hearses. The light was alive, contained, pulsing back and forth inside the auditorium, a live sun exploding here and there on the edges with flares and hand torches. The light was turned back on itself, consuming itself like a star—there were people in dark uniforms moving in and out of it like fire fighters in a blaze.

Above the pulsing light—where it stopped, could go no farther—lost power—there was dark, starry, black night.

All the traffic on both sides of the freeway had been diverted miles away to the north and the south and there was only the steady roar of generators and the crack of arc lights. The light slowed movement. Caught by it, contained in it, the dark-uniformed people moving seemed to waver, become disoriented and slow down. Unidentifiable individually from outside the light, they moved like automatons. There was a helicopter somewhere off to the south, but the light was too palpable and it circled away from it in a steady scything sound and went somewhere else.

In the center of the light, Chief Inspector Keith Hansell from the Accident Investigation Squad said, shaking his head, "Christ, Harry . . ." He had his hand out for something: a cigarette. There was no petrol or diesel spill on the roadway. The truck, as it had bounced back from the impact, was intact with only its windscreen broken and its paintwork scratched. The van no longer existed. It was merely twisted metal formed into lumps on the road. Hansell said again, "Christ . . ."

There was the sound of a metal saw starting. It caught in a scream and three of the washed-out radiant figures in the center of the light set themselves up around one of the lumps that could have been part of a door and began cutting through it. It was not a door—it was solid metal. The saw shrieked as it contacted. A shower of sparks flew back and up toward the top of the light dome and then fell back like dying fireworks.

He could not see his own body in the white light to find his cigarettes in his coat pocket. Detective Chief Inspector Harry Feiffer, handing Hansell his own half-smoked cigarette, said as the saw stopped, "Here."

Hansell said, "Thanks." He was looking at the van. He held the cigarette in his hand and did not smoke it.

"What about the truck driver? Is he alive?"

"He was when they got him out." Hansell said, "Hospital." Hansell said, "I don't know. One of my boys said he heard he lost his arm." Hansell said with a curious tone, "It was full of plate glass, the van. It—" Hansell said, "Two of the traffic people, Li and Kwing—" He looked around. "He's still here somewhere, Li. I told him to go, but he's still somewhere." He looked around. Hansell said, "The van was coming down the wrong side of the freeway without lights!"

"Occupants?"

"*It was playing Chinese opera, for Christ's sake!* It was loaded with plate glass and it was coming down the wrong side of the freeway without lights and it was playing Chinese opera, for Christ's sake!" He was shaking. He still had the cigarette in his hand, but it had gone out or burned down to the filter and he looked down at it and threw it onto the roadway. Hansell said, "The Medical Examiner, Macarthur, is over there—he's almost inside what's left of the front section of the van on the other side of the truck. He got his head in through a hole we cut for him and he's in there looking around with a flashlight—" Hansell said, "Harry, to get here on the wrong side of the freeway, that van had to travel six miles from a feeder road, pass two signs that they would have seen—obviously—were pointing in the wrong direction for them!"

"Alcohol?"

"There's no evidence of it so far as we can see or smell."

"Drugs?"

He was not listening. He was staring into the light. Hansell, shaking his head, said, "No. We haven't found any."

"Occupants?"

"Four. We think. P. C. Li thinks. P. C. Li thinks he saw them for an instant before the collision and P. C. Li thinks—" He could not stop his hands shaking. He looked down at them, clasped them, and could not stop them shaking.

Time had stopped, slowed. In the light, there was a kind of nothingness, immortality: the power of still being alive amid death. Hansell's eyes, Feiffer's own, were washed white in the light. The light picked out blood vessels in faces, veins in hands, all the defects and threadbare patches on uniforms. The light was everywhere, blinding.

Hansell said, "We—"

"Have you recovered the bodies?"

"We've recovered a *spine*! We've recovered *meat*!" Somewhere on the other side of the truck, the Medical Examiner, Dr. Macarthur, had his head inside the van searching around with a flashlight. Hansell said, on the edge, "When the two vehicles hit, the glass in the back of the van disintegrated. The sheets broke up into individual shards and moved forward at a speed I estimate to be slightly in excess of a hundred and fifty miles an hour through air. It cut through the metal of the van as if it were tissue paper, and then, of those three or four million spinning bits of it, those that didn't go up or out through the sides—those million or so bits traveling in a straight line—turned the backs of the driver's and passengers' seats to lint and turned the people sitting in them to hamburger!" Hansell said, "Have we recovered the bodies? Yes, we recovered the bodies, some of them. We've got a plastic bag full of them!" He could not stop his hands shaking. "No need to bother the undertaker with them though—why bother? They're just the right size—we could take them home and put them on a saucer or two and just feed them to the fucking *cat!*" Hansell said, "And we recovered a spine. Better for the dog, that one. Pity though, there isn't any meat on it. Pity it's clean. It's a full-length human spine with all the meat and muscle gone from it with glass embedded in it from one end to the other like bullets!" He was being accused of something. He was being accused of nothing. Hansell said as, in a terrible scream the metal saw kicked over again and began cutting, "We're still looking! We're still here and we're still looking— my boys are still looking! Poor bloody Constable Li is still here somewhere and he's looking too! All right? Is that all right with you?"

Hansell said, "Christ, Harry . . ." Hansell said with his eyes white and washed out and confused, the marks on his uniform blood and viscera and God only knew what else, "Christ, Harry . . . I can't . . . I can't . . ."

Hansell said, "I keep trying to get the picture of it out of my mind, but I—but I—" He kept looking around for somewhere to go, but there was nowhere. There were only the lights, "But I . . ."

Hansell said, "But I can't! *I can't!* So help me God, Harry, I keep trying, but I can't bring myself to stop thinking about the last moments when the glass . . ." Hansell said, "I can't bring myself to go back to that van and look in there again!"

Hansell said desperately, a shadow in the endless light and darkness, "Harry, for Christ's sake, we recovered a human spine! Harry, in one of the plastic bags, we've got an *eye!*"

"No, sir." At the truck, speaking Cantonese, one of the ambulance men said, shaking his head, "It was his hand." Above him, towering up into the darkness at the edge of the lights, the bogie-driven white Road Boss's windscreen was a spider's web of cracks. To the side where the driver had sat, there was a gaping black hole. The ambulance man said, "It wasn't glass from the windscreen. It was a piece of spinning plate glass from the van. So far as we can tell, at the moment of impact the driver must have put his arm up across his face to protect himself and the glass lopped his hand off." He was very matter-of-fact about it. Maybe all he had had to deal with was the truck. "We got his name and address in the ambulance when we stopped the bleeding—his name is Fan—and we—" There was a screech from the saw and then a loud bang as it cut through something metallic and freed it. "We considered packing the hand in ice for microsurgery, but it was too far gone. The muscles and the joints were all—"

Feiffer said, "All right."

The ambulance man looked very young. He glanced over at the van and the figures moving near it and had no urge to join them. Maybe he was older than he looked. The ambulance man said, "We've kept the hand for the coroner." He nodded at one of the waiting ambulances outside the light, "If you want to check that we—"

"No, that's all right."

"Thanks." He fell silent for a moment. He did not look at the van. He looked hard at Feiffer. The ambulance man said softly, "Your Cantonese is perfect."

"Thanks."

The ambulance man said, still in Cantonese, "You—ah—" The ambulance man said evenly, matter-of-factly, "To go to heaven after you're dead—according to Chinese beliefs anyway—your body has to be intact. Did you know that?"

Feiffer said softly, "Yes."

He seemed to grin, to giggle. The ambulance man said, "A hand is probably all right, or maybe a leg or some other bit, but if you're—if you're—if you're all chopped to pieces then you haven't any hope of heaven at all!" He looked at the van. He was neither young nor old, he was merely afraid. The ambulance man said, "We've kept the truck driver's hand for the coroner." The ambulance man said, "Sometimes, some people—the very religious—sometimes keep things like that all their lives, hidden somewhere, to be buried with them." He looked hard into the lights. He was merely there, waiting. There was nothing he could do for anyone who had been in the van. He merely, following procedure, waited.

The ambulance man said in a whisper, "We've kept the hand, okay? We've kept it for the coroner."

"Okay." It was a whisper.

Endless night.

It was 5:47 A.M. Above the lights the sky was black and still.

"Good." The ambulance man said softly in Cantonese, "Thank you."

He was a diligent, matter-of-fact man. Turning quickly on his heel he went back to his ambulance and, disappearing behind the wall of lights, got back into the driver's seat to wait diligently until his presence was no longer required.


"Here." At the still-glowing cut the saw had made in the lump of metal in the roadway, Hansell said, "Here. Through there." It was the rear axle of the van and what looked like part of the fender and the wheel rim on the left side. He shone a flashlight down into the hole. Hansell said, "You can just read it on what's left of some sort of stick-on thing on the license plate." Hansell read it for him, "Prudent Car and Van Hire, Icehouse Street, Hong Bay." Hansell said, "License plate 68–0032C." Hansell said, "It's a rental." He stood up and, in the light, wrote it all down on a fresh page in a leatherbound notebook he took from his tunic pocket. Hansell said again, "Here." He tore out the page carefully and gave it to Feiffer. Hansell said tightly in Cantonese so the firemen with the metal cutting saw could under-stand, "P. C. Li said that at the last moment he saw a light in the van as if someone shone a flashlight." Hansell said, "All they ever had to do anywhere along the six miles they came, was stop."

Hansell said, "That's all we poor bastards on the scene can tell you—the van was a rental." It was preying on his mind. Hansell said, smiling, "Here, everything we know is written down here on this little piece of paper. Take it."

P. C. Li had said, in that instant he had thought one of the people inside the van—he thought, the driver—had been a woman.

Endless, endless night.

Hansell said suddenly, loudly in English, as an order, "Here! *Take it!*"

*"Hou jên pu 'hao, lien lei shang jên."* It was a whisper in Mandarin, the language of the north. The television crew could not get any pictures with the lights washing everything out and, on the edge of the dome, they stood in a knot hoping to find someone to interview. The helicopter had probably been theirs. The only pictures it would have got from that height would have been the lights. They had not been able to ask anyone how it felt—a television interviewer on the morning of the end of the world would be there to ask the last survivor how it felt—and so they had fallen back on being philosophic in no more than eight words, not for their news but for their comment programs. They stood together, a sound man, a cameraman, and a girl reporter. One of the men had said it: Feiffer saw the girl nod sagely in agreement.

It was only a whisper, a tryout. The police must have said that there appeared to be no drugs or alcohol involved. Therefore, it was suicide.

Not for it to be suicide meant that it was inexplicable.

For it to be inexplicable meant that it could not be covered in no more than one minute's air-time and eight words of inference.

*"Hou jên pu 'hao, lien lei shang jên."* It was an ancient Mandarin aphorism. It meant, "Bad descendants involve ancestors in disgrace."

They kept looking around for someone to interview.

Feiffer heard the girl translate it slowly and carefully into Cantonese.

They kept looking around to find someone who, on cue, would say it.

"Sir! Mr. Hansell!" Out from the van, on the median strip, P. C. Li, standing up into the light, pointing down at something, shouted, "I've found something!" He was speaking Cantonese, all the words run on together. Li, pointing down, shouted, "Look! Look! Papers! I've found papers!" He ducked down and put his hands together in a cup to kill the light so he could read them. Li, seeming to jump up and down and start to reach for the thing he had found, shouted to anyone who might listen, "Papers! I've found papers!"

He was covered from head to foot in blood.

No one was coming through the light. If anyone was coming through the light he could not see them. He was blinded. Li, getting down on his hands and knees to pick up whatever it was, yelled, "It's part of the cover of a tape cassette! It's the opera they were playing! It's got paper stuck to it and it's—" It was a scrap of gray paper six or eight inches square, jagged and ripped at all the edges and spotted with blood.

It was skin.

He had not gone home. He had been ordered to, but he had not gone home.

It was human skin. Crumpled like paper and jagged, it would be cold and dead and, like everything else, merely wreckage.

He would not go home.

He could not help himself.

On his knees, in an attitude of prayer, with the tears running down his face, he put out his hand to touch it.


Endless night.

Behind the Medical Examiner, Dr. Macarthur, lying full-length on the road with his head and shoulders and arms inside a sliced-out cavity in the front of the van, Feiffer said quietly, "All right."

*Woosung Road Plate Glass Company.* It was the first thing he saw as Macarthur, ahead of him inside the van, turned his flashlight on. It was stenciled on a shard of glass an inch from his face. It was half submerged in a pool of dark, clotted blood. Macarthur, wearing his heavy canvas Morgue coveralls, drew an audible breath. Macarthur asked, "All right?"

"Okay."

"Better crawl in a bit more."

He crawled in a bit more. The front of the van was upside down. It still smelled of the burned metal from the cutting saw. The flashlight, blocked out by Macarthur's body, was only a glow.

He was crawling inside a steel box. There was another, a heavier smell inside the van. It was not the smell of the metal the cutting saw had burned.

It was the smell, in a small place, of pure, unbridled, nightmarish terror.

"Okay. Stop."

Macarthur, working himself out backward from the cavity, opening it, setting it from *Beam* to *Diffused*, held the flashlight up in the cabin section of the van so Feiffer could see clearly what was inside.

*"God in heaven!"*

Endless night.

Endless, endless night. His hands were covered in blood and tiny shards from the van. Everywhere there were lights and vehicles and unhuman, washed-out figures moving about in uniform. Whispers, sounds: everywhere, in the noise from the generators and the sound of the arc lights buzzing and cracking, there were sounds, whispers, echoes.

All they had had to do anywhere along the six miles of the freeway was pull over and stop.

They had had their headlamps off. They had their music going full blast and, at the last moment, maybe, someone in the van had shone a flashlight at the driver.

Maybe the driver had been a woman.

At three o'clock in the morning, four people in a van had gone six miles down the wrong side of the freeway with all their lights out and the back of their van loaded with plate glass.

Whispers, sounds.

5:49 A.M.

At the van, they had fitted chains to two tow trucks and set them fore and aft in opposite directions.

Feiffer heard someone yell in Cantonese, *"Pull!"*

5:51 A.M.

On the floodlit roadway, with whatever was still inside the van still inside, piece by piece, the two trucks began pulling the van slowly, grindingly, carefully apart.

# 2

H e had finer feelings. He wasn't some sort of shambling hairy ape who made grunting noises: he was a person. He could see the russet leaves of Fall as well as any man, feel the chill of Winter on his face, celebrate Spring, he could see the laughter on a child's face—all these things were in Detective Inspector Phillip John Auden's subconscious too, as any other man. He had a good sub.

Unfortunately at the moment, outside Mr. Wah's Chinese Apothecary and Herbal Medicine Shop in Peripheral Street, the sub was lying on the bottom. Putting his finger in his ear to make sure one of those russet leaves hadn't jammed in his lughole, Auden said with a little smile to show as well as everything else, he had a little whimsy, "You're joking? You're not serious? It's a little ho, ho before we get into the serious stuff, right?" He asked Detective Inspector Spencer, who didn't look whimsical in the least, but very serious, "You're not going to do *what* in order to show Mr. Wah what?" He put his finger in his ear hole to check it was still open. "You're not going to do— what?"

It was early in the morning. It was his best time. Spencer said quietly, "We're not going to use lethal force against the poor thing because the poor thing is doing no real harm and, as two intelligent people, we can outfox a dog."

Outfox a dog. It was a joke. Auden said, "Ha, ha." Just so long as they blew the dog to bits. Auden said, "Right." He nodded. Early wasn't his best time. You had to learn to get on with people whose best time it was. You could do worse than old Bill Spencer: at least he didn't try to borrow money. Auden, nodding, smiling, tapping at his coat to make sure his .357–magnum Colt Python was warm and cosy in there, said, "Yeah. Right. Let's outfox the dog."

Spencer said, "All the poor thing is doing is getting into a shop and taking things of no value."

Auden said, "Wind chimes."

"And the odd bag of spice or herbs."

Auden said, "Right."

Spencer said, "All it is is just some poor homeless mutt cast out by the world collecting useless objects on some unknown and ununderstandable canine impulse." He was still going out with the Chinese girl who had wanted to be a nun before she went into sociology. Spencer said, "It's just a poor little Dalmatian dog—"

Auden said, "Firehouse dog, about sixty-five pounds of muscle and teeth."

"Any why it is stealing what it is is a mystery." He was going glassy. Girls who had wanted to be nuns had that effect on you. Spencer said, "The solution to all of life's problems, Phil, is not always a bullet in the head." Spencer said, "A life is a life."

Auden said, "A dog's life!" He got set to go ho.

"You're not going to shoot the bloody dog!"

"Right!" Okay, Mr. Bones. Auden said, "*You're* going to shoot the bloody dog!"

"No one is going to shoot the bloody dog!"

Too early. "Of course we're going to shoot the bloody dog! We're going to shoot the bloody dog because the bloody dog is getting in windows and holes in walls and wrecking shops and business establishments and because Mr. Wah in here has asked us to shoot the bloody dog!" Auden said, making it clear, "The dog is going to be shot!"

"Why does the dog steal things?"

Auden said, "I don't know!"

"It's a mystery!" He must have gotten a good dose of something, and whatever it was, it wasn't what deglassed your eyes. Spencer, starting to get angry, said, "If it was a kid or a person we'd offer it counseling and help—"

No, he wouldn't. He would have shot it. Auden said, "And—?"

"But just because it's a dog all we can think of is killing it like— like—" Spencer said, "Like a dog!" There was a beep.

Auden said, "Are you all right?"

"Of course I'm all right!"

Auden said, "I heard a beep."

He was nodding. Spencer said, "I'm all right."

"Outfox the dog?"

Spencer said, "Right." He looked determined.

"With a—" Under his coat there, he had something. He saw Spencer pat at it. Auden said helpfully, "With a beeper."

"Yes."

He didn't quite hear. Auden said, "Pardon?"

"Yes! With a beeper! Yes!"

Auden asked pleasantly, "Where did you get it?"

"From a social worker I know . . . somewhere. It's . . . it's a little beeper they sometimes put on little kids' wrists in—in kids' homes so they'll know where they are." Spencer said, "Someone gave it to me."

"Oh."

Spencer said seriously, "I'm a kind man, a good man! I have to deal with thugs and murderers and slime all day but that doesn't mean I can't have kind thoughts *and that God still doesn't look on me as one of his children!*" Spencer said, "Phil, Phil—we can't shoot the bloody dog."

"We're going to bell it with the beeper, aren't we?"

Spencer said, "Yes! And then follow it and catch it and take it to a good home where it can be loved!"

Auden said, "I see." He smiled a little. It wasn't a real smile.

Spencer said happily, "Right." He had the keys to the Kingdom.

"Bill, this may have escaped your attention during the prayer meeting, but that dog is a fucking Dalmatian that goes in through windows and turns shops and everything in them to confetti! The only thing that's going to hold a dog like that long enough for anyone to bell it so we can see where it goes is another fucking great dog, preferably with twenty pounds on the Dalmatian and a mouth full of knives like a—" Auden said, "Like a—like a—" His sub surfaced. It stayed there on the surface for a moment having a little look around and a think and then, shot to pieces, it went down like a rock. Auden said in horror, "Oh my God!"

Spencer said, "My friend who does sociology—"

Auden said warningly, "Oh, no, no—"

"See, she's got this dog—"

Auden said, "Oh, no . . ."

"It's an Alsatian, a German shepherd. It—"

Auden said, stepping backward, "Oh, no, no—"

"And it can do it, Phil. It can run the Dalmatian down, dog to dog, and while it's got hold of it—"

"Oh, no, no, no—"

"Phil—!"

"No, no, no, no!" It was what he should have said right from the beginning. Ho, ho, ho, ho was a mistake. Auden, still stepping backward, said, "Oh, no, no, no, no—" He felt ill. Dogs was dogs. Some dogs just weren't. He knew that eighty-pound ball of muscle and steel. He had seen it once. Auden, going down for the third time, all the escape hatches welded shut, doomed to die there in the dark, said in heartfelt, real horror, "Oh, no, Bill, no—not, not *Petal!*"


". . . and then, with my iron grip, squeezing like a vise, I press!" The last one had spoken English. This one spoke Cantonese. "And then, for I am the Strangler, pulling my black cape around me and dissolving into the night with my footsteps silent and ever-present, I merge into the city, into the throngs of unsuspecting people with white necks, my fingers tingling with electricity and blood lust unsated—"

O'Yee said, "Go on."

It was a high voice. It was either a court eunuch from the last Chinese Imperial dynasty in which case he would have been at least a hundred and seven years old or it was a kid with acne. It was a kid with acne. The kid with acne didn't read well. He had lost his place on the back of his video cover, "And then I—" but he watched a lot of television. The Strangler said, "You only want me to go on so you can trace this call! You're tracing this call, aren't you?"

O'Yee said, "Yes."

The Strangler said, "What?"

"I said, we're tracing this call."

That was a hard one. There was a silence. The Strangler said, "Lies! If you were tracing this call you wouldn't tell me you were tracing this call—what you'd be doing is telling me you weren't tracing this call!" The Strangler said, "No one knows where I am for I am too, too clever for the police!" The Strangler said, "Ha, ha."

"You're calling from a public call box just outside the Star Ferry Terminal in Kowloon."

"Wrong!" The Strangler said, "Ha!" The Strangler said, "See? Wrong! I'm calling from outside where I work in Lim's All-Night Bicycle Repair Shop in Khartoum Street!" The Strangler said, "Ooops."

The phone on the other desk rang. It was Feiffer's phone. It could have been something important.

The Strangler said, "With my steely fingers—"

O'Yee said briskly, "Just a moment, please." It could have been something important.

Pressing the button on his own phone to transfer the call, O'Yee said quickly, "Yes? O'Yee."

He put the Strangler, just for a minute or so, on *Hold*.


*Boon-chuen to-jue ji-san-wai.* Seat of the god who is master of this village. Thirty yards back from where the truck and the van had been, set in the median strip, there was a small, chipped, stone tablet. All the traffic on both sides of the freeway had been diverted a long way back and the freeway on both sides of the median strip was still empty. Stepping over the low retaining guard at the side of the strip, Feiffer bent down to look at the tablet.

It was an Earth God tablet, once the protector of a village or a town that must have stood for generations where the freeway now went. There was no name on the tablet, only on the edges chips and weathering where once the inhabitants of that village had come before each harvest and in each time of disaster to pray to the god and affix little red prayer papers on it asking for hope and better times.

It was not even all the tablet. It was merely the foot-square section of what would have been the central stele where the inscription was.

It had been a shrine to a local divinity that appeased demons and the dragon who lived beneath the Earth's crust. It had been a prayer stone, a balm to still just that little part, perhaps that single scale, of the dragon that lay beneath the village.

Once, it had protected the lives of people and known all their names. Once—

Farther up the freeway, maybe out of the god's domain, in the van, there were no people.

In the van, farther up the freeway, there was only meat.

*Boon-chuen to-jue ji-san-wai*: seat of the god who is master of this village.

There had been four of them in the van, one of them, maybe, a woman.

He wondered who they had been and what, what—in the name of God—they had been doing there.

In Mr. Wah's Chinese Apothecary and Herbal Medicine Shop, Auden, getting mad, said, "Don't you understand friendship and loyalty and finer feelings?"

He was a businessman. Mr. Wah said, "No."

"You can't just shoot a poor living creature dead for no reason!"

Mr. Wah said, "Why not? They do it on television all the time."

"This is not television, it's real life!" It was killing him, this reasonableness. Auden said, "In real life, you think up a plan that will avoid bloodshed and mayhem and blowing a mangy mongrel to pieces so you can get back to more important things! In real life, people who carry .357–magnum Colt Pythons loaded with a hundred-and-fifty-grain handcast semi-wadcutter bullets don't just haul off and lay one in right between the eyeballs, what they do is—" Auden said, "How the hell do you intend to recover the value of your stolen property if we don't bell the dog with a beeper and follow him to his lair and the evil person who has trained him to steal?" That was a good one. Auden said in Chinese, "Aye? Well? Answer me that!"

Mr. Wah said, "Put in a claim to the Police Department for negligent loss through incompetent methods."

Auden said, "Right!" Wrong. Auden said, "Wrong!" He wondered where Spencer was. He didn't wonder where Spencer was. He knew where Spencer was. Spencer was in his car getting out Petal. *Petal?* It wasn't even a girl dog. Auden said, "Listen to me, Wah—"

Mr. Wah said, "And assault on a victim."

The place was a mess. The Dalmatian must have come in on a B-1 bomber and forgotten to tell the bomber not to come in too. Everywhere there were broken bottles and phials of what looked like rhino horn and bat blood mixed in with what looked like more rhino horn and bat's blood. It smelled like a mixture of—of the same. Auden, clenching his fist, looking upward to heaven for inspiration and seeing the ceiling looking as if it had been hit by a bomb, shouted, "Love! *Ever heard of it?*"

"For a dog?"

"For anything?"

"For what?"

"For a friend!"

Ooohh . . . Mr. Wah, starting to nod, said, "Ohhh . . ."

"—loyalty, friendship—that kind of love—" He had already been that route. "—understanding, finer feelings . . . the bond between man and mongrel—" Auden said, losing it, going under, "He's got her dog. His name is Petal. Bet you five dollars it's a good dog too—" He could have sat down and wept.

Auden said, "Maybe the Dalmatian has got everything it wants. Maybe it's done three hits on you and got everything from your store its owner wants and maybe—"

Mr. Wah said brightly, "And maybe it'll never come back again."

Auden said, "Right!" Auden, nodding, said, "Right." He knew how to deal with people; allay their fears, treat them fairly before the law. Life was life: it was a precious, fragile gift. He smiled. He felt a good feeling flow over him. It passed.

He heard the beep. He heard Spencer coming.

He saw Mr. Wah's face.

Auden said desperately, "Look, if it doesn't work—look, I promise you . . ."

Auden said tightly, "—I promise, I'll shoot *both the bloody dogs!*"


There had been nobody on Feiffer's phone. It was a direct line, listed in the phone book as his own was, but when he had taken it, there had been nobody there.

There had been a silence. Nobody had spoken. Somebody, for a few moments until they had put the receiver down gently at their end of the line, had merely listened.

In the Detectives' Room, alone, touching his fingers to his mouth, O'Yee wondered who it had been.


*Petal.*

Well, what you were was what you were. Here you stood; you could do no other.

He stood outside Mr. Wah's door with his hand on the knob. He threw open the door.

Spencer said grandiloquently, *"Ha!"*

He looked down at the dog. He looked at Auden. He looked at Mr. Wah.

Spencer, in a tone of authority that brooked no questions, ordered the dog in a stentorian voice, "Fang! —*SIT!*"


He wondered what, like the gone village, what the people in the van, maybe one of them a woman, what all of them, once, had been.

# 3

In the Morgue, the Government Medical Examiner, Dr. Macarthur, speaking slowly and clearly into the microphone of an overhead-mounted tape recorder, said to begin, "Nine thirty-two A.M.: Statement of Preliminary Findings, Form AR7B: Mass Disaster, Aircraft Crash or Similar, Partial Human Remains. Head-On Collision Two Vehicles, Northbound Freeway, Hong Bay." He stood leaning on the stainless-steel postmortem table in the center of the room. The stainless-steel postmortem table in the center of the room had been too small to take all the sections of the bodies and bones. Everything was laid out on white sheets on the floor of the place. Macarthur, leaning up to the microphone to adjust the gain, said clearly, "Number of separate parts and constituent parts of human bodies: one hundred and eighteen." He wore his thick leather autopsy apron over his white Pathology Department dust coat, and rubber surgical gloves on his hands. From the pocket of his apron he took out a single French Gauloise cigarette and lit it with a disposable plastic lighter. Macarthur, drawing in the smoke and looking down at the sheets, said for the report, "The bodies each appear to have suffered cutting and slicing wounds of a random,

29

nonsurgical nature. Three of the heads have been completely severed at the neck or chest, and two of the bodies, both male, are completely limbless." By him Feiffer drew a breath. The smell in the place was awful. It was the smell of rotting meat. Macarthur, still talking into the machine, said, "There are a number of slashed and damaged human organs, including a liver, part of a heart, what appears to be on preliminary examination about eighty percent of a human spleen and intestinal connections, and there are a number of defleshed major bones including a complete human spine . . ." He drew in on his cigarette, "All sections of clothing and what appears to be clothing have been removed by orderly and valuables including watch found on human arm and various small articles logged in DOA book and secured in Mortuary valuables locker." He saw Feiffer watching him, trying not to look down. Macarthur said, "Four heads have been recovered, one female and three male." They were there on one of the sheets, like pig's heads, laid out in a butcher's shop amidst the offerings and offal. Macarthur said, "Wounds sighted in all cases are consistent with police report of a sudden, high-speed impact with a large oncoming vehicle and the forward movement of a large amount of plate glass at high velocity from behind." He drew in on his cigarette. He asked Feiffer out of courtesy, "Harry? Anything else?"

"No."

Macarthur asked, "Three men and one woman, right?"

"Right." It was a charnel house. There was no glass. All the glass they were going to find was embedded in the flesh and would have to be dug out one piece at a time.

"From preliminary examination, each of the bodies is that of a person of Chinese race, from the general development and flesh tone where visible, well-nourished and in the age range of about forty to fifty-five with no unusual features or deformations apparent." Macarthur said into the microphone, "The bodies have not been identified and the orderly notes in the DOA book that no documents, papers or inscribed articles have been taken into safekeeping." He asked for the record, "What about the van?"

"Rental." Feiffer said quietly, "They don't open for business until ten."

Macarthur said into the machine, "Identifications to follow." Macarthur said into the machine, "Each of the four heads has had the face rendered unrecognizable by the impact of the cutting edges of the glass. Suggest follow-up X-ray scan may be required for deeply embedded particles." The woman was the head and part of the right shoulder and breast at the far left-hand side of the sheets in the room.

She had had long black hair with gray in it on the right-hand side. The hair on the left and at the back of her head had been cut to shreds by the glass. Her long hair hung down only on one side of the smashed, semi-bald, bone-white and gray pulpy mass that had been her face. In her hair, when he had checked again for items of value on the laid-out remains, Feiffer had found a black plastic hair clip. The hair clip was in two pieces, sharp with powdered glass. Once, she had been a person. Once, she had stood or sat in front of a mirror and put her hair up. Macarthur said, continuing for the person who would type out his tape, "Form 6: Standard Postmortem Examination and Pathological Report as to Cause of Death."

He looked at Feiffer watching him. Macarthur asked, "No idea at all who she was?"

"No."

He spoke evenly and for the record. Macarthur said, "Nine thirty-eight A.M.. Bodies to be known in order of examination as bodies one through four."

Macarthur said, "Body number one. Female—" Macarthur, dropping the cigarette into the drain on the stainless-steel table and going forward to get the head, said pleasantly, "Okay, we'll start with her . . ."

CURRENT INVESTIGATION. DO NOT TOUCH OR INTER-FERE WITH THIS VEHICLE. The van was in a far corner of the Accident Investigation Squad's impound yard, cordoned off by yellow evidence streamers tied to four empty forty-four-gallon oil drums. What was left of it was in two sections, the rear load-carrying section and what had been the front section for the driver's and passengers' seats. The seats in the front for the driver and the passenger had been bucket seats. There was nothing but twisted tubing with shreds of vinyl hanging off them. All the springs had gone. They were strewn throughout the floor of the front section of the van clotted with blood. The seats had been welded to the floor of the van with a bar across them to strengthen them and then, four feet back from that bar there had been another bar, at floor level, welded side-on as a sort of little buffer to keep the load separate from the seats in the event of a sudden stop. The load had been at least twenty sheets of plate glass packed standing up facing forward. The sudden stop had come at an impact speed of approximately one hundred and eighty-five miles an hour. Behind the bar that protected the passenger seats, between that and the bar that held the load, there had been two other people squatting down. The bars had stopped nothing. At the side of the front half of the van, Chief Inspector Hansell, wearing fresh white coveralls and a plastic yellow hard hat, sniffed for gasoline. He had a long dipstick in his hand and a set of master keys for the cap cover.

There was no cap cover. Where it should have been there was only twisted, wrenched metal where the Fire Brigade and rescue teams had torn the side of the van apart with their power saws and the cap cover lay on the floor of the van burned black and cut in half. He sniffed. He could smell no smell of gasoline at all. His team, going through everything that was left, picking up everything on the road and bagging it, had found no pills or syringes, no thick bottle glass and no twists of drugs. They had not found a box of matches or even a single match. They had gotten the dashboard cigarette lighter intact and they had found on its coil . . . nothing. It had been used to light nothing.

He sniffed. The cap was still on the gas tank and, carefully, he put his hand to it and twisted it off.

He sniffed.

Wiping the clean dipstick with a tissue from the pocket of his coveralls, Hansell carefully, slowly inserted its end into the gas tank to see how much fuel was still left in the van.


"Axe!"

On the phone O'Yee said, "Chop!"

"Blood!" It was a man of few words. He had a voice like a bass drum. He didn't bother with preliminaries: he got straight to the point. He watched videos because he couldn't stand the suspense of the ads between homicides on TV.

O'Yee said, choosing carefully, "Gore!"

"Ha!"

O'Yee said, "Zombie! Gory zombie with an axe!"

"Big axe!"

"Huge axe!"

"Monstrous axe!"

O'Yee said, "Ger-NAH!"

"YAAHHH!"

"Mutilate!"

"Dismember!"

"Eviscerate!"

"Dematerialize!"

"Cannibalize!"

He was another English speaker. He didn't sound Chinese. He sounded Japanese. O'Yee said, "Liver!"

"Heart!"

"Aorta!"

The voice said, drooling, "White snowy breasts!"

O'Yee said, "We don't do sex, just violence."

The voice said, "Sorry."

O'Yee said, "Fear!"

"Trembling!"

"Horror!"

"Pulse!"

"Beat!"

O'Yee said, "Palpitate!"

The voice said, "*Throb!*" The voice said, "Sorry—"

"Warmth!"

"Hemoglobin!"

*Hemoglobin?* O'Yee said, "Country road at night!"

The voice said, "Alone! Tremble! Fear! Sweat! Worry!" The voice said, "Noises! Rustles!" The voice said, "Heh-heh!"

"Forest!"

"Trees!"

"Leaves!"

"Um—hill."

"Hill!"

"Um . . ." The voice said, "Picnic."

"Hamper!"

"Um—" The voice said, "Um—" He was trying to think.

"Checked tablecloth!"

The voice said, "Um—"

O'Yee said, "Fresh white petticoats!"

"Fumiko Onuki's older sister!"

"Tree!"

"Hill!"

"Love!"

"Light!"

"Happiness!" O'Yee said, "Love?"

"Fumiko Onuki's older sister."

"Light!"

"Happiness!"

"Fumiko Onuki's older sister!"

"Tranquillity!"

The voice said, "Fumiko Onuki's older sister!"

O'Yee said, "*Valium!*"

"Calming raft . . . !"

"Unmarried!"

"Fumiko Onuki's older sister!"

"Letter!"

"Fumiko Onuki's older sister!"

"Write!"

"Stamp!"

"Mail!"

"Do it!" The voice said, "I will!"

"Do!"

"I will!"

"Now!"

"I will!"

O'Yee said, "Great!"

The voice said, "Good!"

O'Yee said, "Wholesome thoughts!"

The voice said, "The love of children!"

O'Yee said, "She loves you not!"

"She does! She says she does!"

O'Yee said, "Fine!" O'Yee said, "Go to it!" O'Yee said, "Find happiness, my son, and be fruitful and multiply!" O'Yee said, "Begone!" O'Yee said, "Thus I release you!" O'Yee said, "Don't call this number again!" O'Yee said, "Bye!"

"*Fumiko Onuki's older sister*!" The voice said happily, "Oh, oh, oh—" He had Come Through. The voice said, "Oh, thank—" Real Japanese men didn't eat humble pie. The voice said, "Oh, I want to say—um—"

O'Yee said—

The voice said, weeping, "Oh, what can I say?"

"Fumiko Onuki's older sister!"

"Yeah. Yeah . . ." The voice said suddenly, "*Ban . . . ban . . .*" The voice said suddenly, another soul saved for the cause of goodness, "BANZAI!"

He had a letter to write.

He hung up.


This time, the call was not on Feiffer's line, but his own.

At his desk, with the phone hard against his ear, O'Yee listened. O'Yee said softly, "Hello?" There was no heavy breathing at the other end of the line, no sound at all.

There was something.

It was nothing. It was there. There was not a sound on the line, but he heard it: he heard what was there. "Hello? *Hello?*"

He heard it. It was there.

A moment before whoever it was hung up the phone and the line went completely, utterly, buzzingly dead, he heard—

He heard *terror*.

The tank was full. Someone had rented the van, loaded it with glass, three other people had been picked up or collected, and the van, with its full tank, had gone down the wrong way on the Hong Bay freeway at three o'clock in the morning and they had all died.

They had been playing Chinese opera at full blast and they had traveled at least six miles on the wrong side of the freeway without lights.

They had all been bombed out of their brains on booze or drugs.

There was no booze or drugs. He had seen a lot of accidents and he knew the smell of booze or drugs in a vehicle. He had seen a lot of dead people.

He had never seen dead people the way the dead people from the van had been. He had never seen them hit by exploding sheets of plate glass and torn to shreds. He had never seen anything on Earth that looked the way they did when he first saw them.

He knew when the Chinese committed suicide they kept their bodies intact in the hope of heaven.

He knew—

What had happened was no suicide. Behind the taped-off enclosure, Hansell, looking again at the dipstick, knew only to do his job. He knew that that alone, night after night, kept him sane, kept him from thinking about it.

The gas tank was full. In the impound yard with a vehicle in this condition there was a fire risk.

He had smelled nothing of booze or drugs anywhere in the van. He took a notebook from his top pocket and, leaning it on the dipstick for support, made a note of his preliminary findings for the medical report that he knew would corroborate him.

He shrugged. He thought only of his job. Always, he tried to think of only that.

Nodding, he went quickly toward the tool room near his office to get a pump and container to drain the fuel in the tank and, after labeling the container and measuring it properly, put it in the fireproof fuel store on the other side of the yard for safety.

\* \* \*

It was Mr. Wah's laughing. A fine, proud dog like Fang wasn't used to it. He bowed his head and snuggled closer to his friend Spencer.

For a good, hard, fighting dog like Fang, you had always to set a standard of stoicism in your own life. It was the first rule of man-to-dog bonding.

He swallowed hard. Without a word, Spencer, stoically, pulling gently on the leash, led poor Petal out of there and back toward his car.


On the stainless-steel postmortem table he had to put the head and shoulder in a rubber-backed vise to stop it rolling away as he dug into it with his scalpel and probes.

On the stainless-steel postmortem table Macarthur had to unscrew the vise and turn the head three different ways to get out all the glass.

On the table the glass was forming a little circle laid out exactly on an invisible two-dimensional skull and neck for the exact positioning he would record into the overhead tape machine.

He probed. Each time, the bit of glass he found made a grating sound inside the head until he could get the forceps around it with his other hand and pull it out through the brain matter.

Around him and Feiffer, watching, arranged in no sort of order on the white sheets, there were one hundred and seventeen parts of human beings to go.

In the Morgue, pacing himself, Macarthur, taking a little break on the head, drew a breath and lit another cigarette.


Something in the van glittered. It was not glass, it was something else. It was something solid and opaque and it was not the glitter of glass but of something else: of metal, of nickel or chrome.

At the gas tank with the container almost full, Hansell, leaning forward, looked in through the hole where the cap cover had been and tried to see what it was. He saw only twisted metal and all the glass and the object was gone. He had a picture in his mind of what he thought he had seen, a glimpse, an outline. He had seen maybe part of something and because whatever it was was familiar to him, his mind had filled in all the missing parts and put it together and he thought what it was he had seen had been a—

Hansell said in a whisper, "Oh my God—" On the freeway, a moment before the truck and the van had hit, in the darkness of the van, P. C. Li had thought he had seen, just for an instant, a flash, a

light as someone inside with a pocket torch, in that last instant—
Hansell said, "Oh my God—"

He moved.

He craned his head.

He saw it.

It was silver, glittering.

Hansell said, "Oh my God!"

He knew what the object was.

Pushing, straining, cutting his arm on the twisted, burned metal near the fuel line, Hansell, gritting his teeth against the pain, reached in to get it out.

In the Morgue the tape was still running. In the Morgue Dr. Macarthur, drawing out with his forceps something from the base of the skull, said suddenly, "Oh, my God." In all the time he had been working he had not asked Feiffer anything about the accident he had not needed to know for his report. Virtually, he had asked nothing.

Whatever it was, it was not glass. He held it up in his forceps and looked at it. Once, the thing in the vise had been the head of a person. Once, it had been a woman.

The tape was still running. Macarthur, gazing at the object in the jaws of the forceps, said tersely, "Harry?"

It was a dark, bloody lump. It was unrecognizable. Once, the thing on the postmortem tray had been a person. Macarthur said, again, curiously, "Harry—?" He saw Feiffer's face. Still holding the object in the forceps he reached down to the side of the stainless-steel table and took a linen swab from one of the packets there for wiping off blood and brain matter. He wiped at the object and held it up. Macarthur said, "Harry, it's a bullet." All around them on the floor were all the bits of bodies. Macarthur said evenly, half for the tape, "It's a fired bullet removed from deep in the brain stem." Macarthur said, "Judging by the weight and configuration, it's a soft-lead, small-caliber revolver bullet fired at close range upward into the back of the neck." Macarthur said, "A kill shot."

Macarthur said, looking hard at Feiffer's face, "Harry—?"

It was a gun. It was a nickel-plated gun in perfect condition with a two-inch barrel and it was a gun.

By the van, his arm starting to bleed through the sleeve of his white coveralls, Hansell turned it over and looked at it.

He read the legend on the top of the nickel flat-top barrel: H & R ARMS CO. WORCESTER, MASS., U.S.A. and the line on the barrel's rubber grips and, on the inside of the nickeled frame, at the handgrip, a serial number.

506507.

It was a gun. It was a Harrington and Richardson .32–caliber nickel-plated top-break pocket revolver with a two-inch barrel.

His hand was shaking. Carefully, he broke open the gun and looked at the cylinder where the chambers for the cartridges went.

Five shots. The gun, fully loaded, took five rounds of .32–caliber soft-lead cartridges.

In the gun, all the chambers were empty except for the one that, when he had opened it, had been directly under the hammer.

In the Morgue, with the tape still running, Macarthur, holding up the bullet, said, shaking his head, "Harry . . ."

The one cartridge in the gun, when he pulled it out, had been fired. In that last, final moment on the freeway, the instant Li saw it and thought it was something else, it had been fired in the van.

Hansell's arm was bleeding.

He held the little silver open gun in his hand as the blood dripped down onto it from his arm and looked at it.

## SURGICAL WARD
### St. Paul DeChartres Hospital, Hong Bay

### ACCIDENT VICTIM REPORT (CAS/THEATER/I.C./WARD)

FAN CHI HUNG aka Lewis FAN, Hanford Hill, North Point, H.K., age 51, status MARRIED, occupation TRUCK DRIVER. *Complete severance right wrist at styloid outer radius. Complete severance styloid process ulna inner side. Surgery commenced 6:03 A.M. Surgery completed 6:38 A.M. No complications. Prognosis EXCELLENT.*

*6:53 A.M. Patient awake. Transferred to recovery room. Patient rambling and confused. Speech incoherent.*

*6:59 A.M. Patient fully awake. No additional sedation administered.*

*7:18 A.M. Patient given IV liquid-glucose solution prior to transfer to ward.*

7:25 A.M. *Patient transferred to ward.*

7:45 A.M. *Compresses used to lower bruising on face and neck by Ward Sister. Patient very anxious. Aware of surroundings. Intermittent light sleep.*

8:10 A.M. *Patient seen by surgeon on rounds. Bandages loosened slightly by Ward Sister on surgeon's orders around stump.*

8:12 A.M. *Patient distressed. One ml. Omnopon in solution administered IM for pain in "phantom" hand.*

8:15 A.M. *Patient distressed.*

8:20 A.M. *Intern recommends no further administration of sedatives.*

8:30 A.M. *Patient sleeping intermittently.*

9:05 A.M. *Patient awake. Patient informed of total amputation of right hand at wrist.*

9:10 A.M. *FAN HUEI-MEI aka Alice FAN, patient's wife, informed by telephone by Ward Sister.*

9:13 A.M. *Patient fully awake.*

9:20 A.M. *Hospital Almoner advises patient confused and anxious. Unclear recollection of accident. Rambling and confused. Believes his vehicle struck brightly illuminated fog-warning light. Mild traumatic amnesia. Distressed, pleading with Almoner for information. Almoner advises patient be given available details of accident.*

9:22 A.M. *Admissions telephoned by Ward Sister. Admissions advises four other persons involved in collision, three male, one female. All Dead on Arrival.*

9:32 A.M. *Almoner and Ward Sister advise patient of available details.*

9:35 A.M. *Patient quiet, withdrawn.*

9:40 A.M. *Patient appears calm.*


"Harry . . . ?"

Macarthur said in a sudden, horrified whisper, "Harry, what in the name of God *happened* out there on the highway this morning?"


9:42 A.M.

He screamed.

In the hospital room, on the clean linen, the truck driver, not looking at his bandaged stump, but at all the nightmares and demons rising around him, began screaming.

# 4

There was someone, some-
where, who was training the Dalmatian to steal on order. So far, for
this someone somewhere, the Dalmatian had stolen (by his car,
Spencer had a little list) two ounces of burned watermelon ash; a twist
of coagulated rhino horn; a cake of solid dried sea-sparrow fish
concentrate; three wind chimes made of glass, bamboo and porcelain;
and a small, wrapped packet of domestic spider slough. To anyone
who knew his Chinese medicine, the person training the dog to steal
must have been a little old wind-chime lover with a bad case of dropsy
complicated by a bad cough complicated by the last stages of malaria
with a side helping of suspected tuberculosis. Or, he was extremely
healthy with a mercenary turn of mind and a large circle of well-off
sick friends. And he also knew about smells. And thought he was a
Yugoslav fireman.

He wasn't a Yugoslav fireman. In Peripheral Street, patting Petal
on the head, Spencer said, wagging his finger, "No, I spent the whole
night boning up on it all and the common misconception that the
Dalmatian dog is originally from Dalmatia is totally wrong. Originally,
according to the latest literature, the Dalmatian dog was called the

**40**

Dalmatian dog because in 1770 it was reported by travelers that they were used to run alongside carriages as sentries for travelers, but that's totally wrong." He could see Auden was interested: he stood very still, staring attentively. Spencer said, "It was just that the traveler in question didn't know much about dogs." Stupid fellow. Spencer said, "Because a few years later, it was also reported that the same sort of dogs were seen in, variously, India, Egypt, Denmark and Spain." Ridiculous. You might as well have called it the Iberian Pharoah dog. Spencer said, "And, of course, Dalmatian dogs are originally . . ." He waited for the answer.

Auden said, "Um—"

"English!"

Auden said, "Of course!"

"They were used in England as stable dogs as far back as the seventh century—a full century before anyone ever heard of bloody Yugoslavia!" Spencer said quickly, not wanting to impart incorrect information, "Or Dalmatia, because, of course, Yugoslavia wasn't heard of until 1929 at the Paris Conference." God knows, after the fuck-up over dogs, you could at least get a nation right. Spencer said, "Before that it was Serbia, Croatia, Bosnia and Herzegovina, Macedonia, Slovenia and Montenegro."

Auden said helpfully, "And Dalmatia."

"Dalmatia is just a part of the coast near Dubrovnik." Spencer said, "I've been boning up on it all. The Dalmatian dog, contrary to popular belief, isn't prone to deafness if looked after in the first few weeks of its life and it isn't the best sort of dog to have in a firehouse to run with the engines—also contrary to popular belief"—he saw Auden's face—"In America it's called a firehouse dog because the San Francisco Fire Department had some as mascots—"

"Oh."

"What it is is just a good, bright dog that stands about two feet high, weighs approximately forty to fifty pounds fully grown, is born snow white and doesn't get its spots until two or three weeks later, *and can be run down into the ground and absolutely slaughtered by any decent half-awake German shepherd Alsatian dog on even the German shepherd Alsatian dog's worst day!*"

He sounded defensive. Dog-lovers often did. He was starting to hop up and down.

"The German Alsatian, the shepherd—the wolfdog—the *Wolfhund*—isn't some sort of feeble, half-understood dog from somewhere off the page in the vales of geneology: the German shepherd is the closest living relative to *canine lupis*, the ferocious savage dog of our prehistoric ancestors! Flowing in any German shepherd's veins is the life-surge of a thousand thousand savage creatures who had to fend for themselves in the era of the dinosaurs!" Well, actually, a bit later. Spencer said, "—or a bit later anyway. And it's only years of careful breeding that have kept the purity in the—"

Auden said, "Good dogs, Alsatians."

"They're not vicious and uncontrollable! That's just the bad publicity they get!"

"Like Dalmatians and firehouse—"

Spencer said, "I'm not prejudiced—"

"No."

"—but any German shepherd that couldn't run over a second-rate, half-starved thieving Dalmatian like a tank running over a rabbit just shouldn't be allowed to live!" He put his hand on Auden's shoulder. It hurt. Spencer, leaning closer, still patting the dog with his other hand, said quietly to his friend, "This is a good dog. This is a dog that will die to serve." He looked down at the dog. The dog looked half asleep.

"Bill, maybe we ought to consider calling in the services of the government dogcatcher"—Auden said quickly, "I mean, to save poor old Fang or Petal or—to save the poor sod the ignominy of actually having to perform in front of a man like Wah—that way, we could—" Auden said, "We could call in the old dogcatcher for a piece of mongrel garbage like the Dalmatian and old Petal here could—"

Spencer said, "Smells."

Auden said, "Right!" It was just an idea.

"The smell is how the Dalmatian is doing it! He smells the herbs and medicines his master wants him to steal and then his master puts him out on the street and then he steals that smell and takes it back to get a pat." Such simple, wonderful creatures. Spencer said, "A dog will do anything to keep someone stronger and more powerful and more dangerous happy."

Right.

Spencer said, "Dogs have long memories for smells . . ." He waited.

Auden said mildly, "Do they?"

"They can remember a single smell for up to eight years. But if we put the Dalmatian in the dogcatcher's van and belled him with the beeper all he'd do is go crazy trying to work out which smell would take him home." Spencer said, "He'd be confused. He'd lose his mind worrying about it." Spencer said, "You can understand that."

Sure. Auden said, "It was just a thought."

"It was a good thought." He stopped squeezing and patting Auden. Spencer, looking into his eyes, said clearly, "No, I've boned up on it all. What we're going to do is wait for the Dalmatian to attack Mr. Wah's shop, let it get a good head start, turn Fang loose on it, and then—when Fang runs it down at half speed and jumps on it, rendering it immobile"—he was speaking very slowly and clearly, formally. People who went mad, for some reason, always did that— "then we're going to quietly and calmly put the beeper around its neck, turn it loose, pat our own good dog on the head, and follow it in the car on the beeper receiver to its lair." He patted Auden with his hand. He patted Fang with his other hand. Spencer said, "Simple. I boned up on it all." He wasn't such a bad fellow. At least, he always went to the trouble of working it all out. Spencer said, smiling, "Okay?"

Maybe the nun wasn't so bad. Maybe—maybe they *talked* together a lot. It wasn't such a bad plan. It was all right. It was good. It was pretty good. It was fine. Maybe even it was a great plan. It was the patting. It was lulling him. Auden said, "Wonderful plan."

"Good." He took his hand away. What a friend we have in Auden. Spencer, touched, said softly, "Thanks, pal."

"Okay."

He smiled. Spencer said, never letting a single sparrow fall without knowing it, "When the two dogs hit, when the beeper goes on—" Spencer said contemptuously, "Dalmatians, of course—having absolutely no breeding at all—bite."

"You'll be fine."

"Good." It made such a difference, a little voice of confidence. If he wasn't a man of peace, he could have happily gone into Wah's and, smiling while he did it—

He smiled.

Spencer, smiling, said sweetly, "Don't worry. When you reach in there to get the collar on—"

Auden said, "What?"

Spencer said, "Phil"—he was going to say "my friend," but you had to stay a little manly—Spencer said to encourage him, to strengthen him, "By God, Phil, don't you think for a moment I'll spare myself getting back to the car as fast as I can to get the beeper receiver going!" Spencer said, "Not for a second, not for an instant!"

He had boned up on it all.

Spencer said to Auden, still listening attentively, positively blank with amazement at the brilliance of it all, "Phil, Phil . . ." He gave him a little punch.

Spencer said, heartfelt, true, "Phil . . . *thank you.*"

* * *

Dial-a-Detective.

On the phone the voice, speaking Cantonese, said, "What color gun holster are you wearing?"

*Defuse-a-Dingbat.* O'Yee said, "Black!"

"With straps?" The voice was working itself up into a lather of sweat.

"With black leather straps that go across my strong masculine back and lace and lock together in tight bondage under my rank but manly left armpit." *Discourage-a-Dumbhead. Numb-a-Knuckledragger.* O'Yee said, also working himself up into a lather of sweat, "Creaking ominously as I walk." O'Yee said, *"Drool!"*

It was a small fat person going prematurely bald: he could tell. The small fat person said in a high voice, drooling, "Wow!" The voice said, "What sort of—what sort of gun is in it?"

There was a silence.

The short bald person said, understanding, "I can understand that maybe you can't tell me." The bald person said, "Security."

He was the sort of person who reads *Guns and Ammo* and books on gunfighting and how to kill people. The trouble was, he had never found anyone to kill. Anyone who could find lots of people who didn't mind being killed was going to make a fortune from people who read *Guns and Ammo* magazine and books on how to kill people.

Phil Auden read *Guns and Ammo* magazine. There was a copy of the latest issue on his desk near O'Yee with a full-color front-page photo of something that looked more like a pneumatic hammer than a gun. O'Yee, glancing across at it and reading the legend beneath it said, "A .357 Israeli Desert Eagle automatic with a five-inch barrel." There wasn't any more about it. O'Yee had to look for himself. O'Yee said, "Gray color."

"Hollow-point bullets?"

Hollow-point bullets? O'Yee said, "Naturally."

"They're the best. When your life is on the line, they're the only way to go." He was standing there in a phone box somewhere stabbing at the air with his thumb. "Yeah, sure the Geneva Convention says they're illegal, but when it's just me or one of the effluvium who infest our streets—"

O'Yee said, "It had better be the effluvium."

"Right."

"Bust a cap on the bums!"

"Cut 'em down!"

"Eat lead!"

"My gun is quick!"

"Really?" O'Yee said curiously, "What sort of gun have you got?"

"I've got a little black street-sweeper just right for a bit of slug and bug fumigation." He nodded: O'Yee knew he did. The voice said, "What do you think?"

He thought he read *Guns and Ammo*. O'Yee said, "An Ingram, right?" He had seen one go off on the police range once. It had scared the shit out of him. O'Yee said, "A little .380 auto Ingram with a sound moderator and a cyclic rate of fire of twelve hundred rounds a minute and a cache of spare magazines in a leather pouch." O'Yee said, "A black leather pouch, right?"

"Right!" He was glad he had worked up the courage to call. The voice said, "If the lead doesn't get them the muzzle flash burns their faces off!"

O'Yee said, "Ha! Ha!"

The voice said, "Ha! Ha!"

"Got the little folding stock attachment?"

"Got that."

"Selective fire?"

"Selective fire."

"Hollow-point bullets, right?"

"Hollow-point bullets."

O'Yee said, "Serial number 8976554, right?"

The voice said, "Right!"

O'Yee said, "Wow!"

He must have lit a cigarette. There was a sort of goldfish breathing sound. The voice said, going a lot deeper, "You know, you guys are okay." The voice said, talking out of the side of its mouth where the cigarette was, "Blizz ad ferngutz timffa."

O'Yee said, "Right."

The voice said, "Right."

O'Yee said, "Okay."

The voice said, "See you!" He had taken the cigarette out of his mouth. "Stay cool." It sounded like "Stair newel." He was talking American. He should have left the cigarette in. The voice said, "You can always count on me."

"Thanks."

"A pleasure. You're welcome." The voice said, "Hey, man, hey—" The voice was being friendly, "Don't shoot yourself in the foot with that there big old hog-shooter of yours."

"You too."

"Right."

"Right."

Dampen-a-Doodlebug. Simmer-Down-a-Psycho. Wind-Down-a-Whacko. Neutralize-a-Nut. Put Your Elbow on Your Desk and sigh.

He sighed. O'Yee said softly, earnestly, "Right—" Sometimes he thought it was a hell of a life.

O'Yee, settling in for a long, learned conversation, said, "*Right* . . . !"


The rusted metal fire-escape stairway at the back of Wah's Chinese Apothecary and Herbal Medicine Shop was a swirl of smells. On the landing, down on all fours with his nose a little up from the metal, the Dalmatian sniffed.

The smells came up like colors, moving, merging. Like colors, there were only a certain number of primary smells in the world—seven—but like colors there were tinges, hues, mixtures, tones. On the landing they flowed up and up and around like a cloak.

The dog's nose was sorting them, sifting them. In all of the olfactory cells in the lining of its nose, in each of the one-thousand receptor nerve endings in each of the cells, the colors were being sorted, sharpened, discarded. In the dog's brain they were blurred pictures and shadows being given shape and form.

There were sounds, vibrations, tremors—the dog smelled and heard Wah's from the outside, building a hologram, classifying, sorting.

The dog was half starved. Its ribs were visible against its spotted coat. The dog, not whining at the pain from its shrinking insides, formed pictures.

It waited, listening, sorting the smells.

It smelled, somewhere off, somewhere from a faded smelltime ago, the smell of another dog. Its eyes were liquid brown and glazed, taking in the smells.

From a long time ago, faintly, it smelled the smell of another dog.

It sorted, brought all the smells into focus and found the one it wanted.

There was an open air duct into the brick building at the stair landing, leading to old air-conditioning conduits between floors, and the dog, coming to its feet without sound, jumped up and got inside the duct with no effort at all.


Fun time.

On the phone the disguised voice said, "Do you know what I'm doing?" In the background there was a chop! In the background there was also giggling. It was Indian giggling. He could almost smell the dal and curry. It was an unlonely loonie in a local lentil lopping location. The heavily disguised voice, sounding like a waiter in an Indian restaurant trying not to sound like a waiter in an Indian restaurant, said amidst the giggling, "What I'm doing is—"

O'Yee said, *"Quick! The order! Where's the order?"*

The voice said, "Ah—um—ugh—" The voice said, alarmed, "Um— I— To eat here or go?"

O'Yee said, "Go!"

The lentil lopper said, "Oh!"

He went.


"Take the next elevator, please." In the elevator, going back down to the Morgue, they had the heads and the larger pieces of the bodies under a sheet on a trolley. All the heads and the larger pieces of the bodies had been x-rayed. There were no more bullets, and the heads and the larger pieces of bodies under the sheet looked like cakes set out in a line to be taken to a children's surprise party.

"Take the next elevator, please." Macarthur, leaning out of the car and obscuring the trolley, smiling, said it on each floor on the way down.

It was habit. He had done it many times before. He turned to Feiffer at the far end of the trolley and shrugged.

On the trolley, under the sheets, the dead things were lumps.

"Take the next elevator, please."

It was force of habit. He had done it many, many times before.

He said it, smiling, not as a request, but as an order, at each and every floor on the way.


"Does she have a name, the social worker?"

Spencer said, "Savannah." He looked hard at Auden.

"Savannah?"

Spencer said, kneading his fist a little, "Yes."

Why not? She had a dog called Petal. The dog was back inside the car in the front seat ready by the beeper receiver. The beeper receiver, off, was dormant. So was the dog. Auden said, "I see."

The street was starting to come alive. There were people moving about and shopping. Wah's Chinese Apothecary and Herbal Medicine Shop had opened its doors for business. From where they waited by the car they could see Mr. Wah trying to clean up before the first of his customers arrived. Spencer said, "I know you could get a single shot in, Phil, and"—he kept trying to see Auden's face, but Auden kept disguising his face by smiling—"Or even a tranquillizer dart and you could . . ." Spencer said, "Or we—we could call the SPCA and they could get a dart in or—but—"

Keep smiling. Auden looked in at the dog. It slept with its mouth open. A lot of big dogs slept with their mouths open. Usually, they slavered or drooled. This one dribbled.

Spencer said, "—but—"

Auden smiled.

"Interesting person, is she? Savannah?"

Spencer said intensely, "Oh, yes!" Auden was still smiling. It was a strange sort of smile. It was the sort of smile you had on your face when you had to make conversation while having a desperate urge to find the nearest public convenience. Spencer said, "She hates guns, Phil!"

Well, she would. And probably whiskers, sweat, bad language and tennis shoes. Auden said, still smiling, "Gosh." He looked in at the dog and watched it dribble. He looked down at the hand that was going to go in between the dribble and the Dalmatian's fangs and wondered about microsurgery. Auden said, still smiling, "That must be difficult for you."

"Oh, I never carry my gun when we're together!"

Maybe that was the problem. Auden said, "Oh." He stopped smiling. The dribbling was getting to him. Auden said suddenly, "Look, Bill, the more I think about this—"

"Her father is in the gun trade, you see! He's been in the gun trade for years and all the time she was growing up she saw nothing but guns and—and—" Spencer said, "He's the Hong Kong and Far East main distributor for Colt and Winchester firearms and he holds the biggest store of small-arms sporting and target ammunition in the entire region!" Spencer said, "Guns! She grew up seeing nothing but guns all her life!" He was getting desperate. Spencer said, "You know that really nice Colt Python you got in all the way from the States with the special combat grips—well, you paid a fortune for it and I was telling him about it and he said that if you ever wanted another, why he had a warehouse full of the things and all the ammunition you could ever use in a million years and, why—" Spencer said softly, "Savannah told him not to talk like that."

He had stopped smiling. he had started glazing. It was a strange, dreamy voice that came out. Auden said, "Yeah?"

"Yes!" Spencer said, "He loves his daughter so much, Phil."

Auden said, "Stainless steel? Has he got the new stainless-steel Python?"

Spencer said, "He's probably got hundreds of them!"

"What about replacement ten-inch barrels and frame-mounted Weaver telescopic pistol sights?"

"Oh, he does everything."

Auden said, "Teflon-coated JHP full-load rounds with nickel cases and magnum primers—"

"Yes!"

"—with wide flash-holes."

"Anything! Anything at all!"

"Ingrams!"

"Sure!"

"Uzis! Has he got any sort of private shooting range for full-auto weapons?"

"He's got two! He keeps asking me if I'd like to come out and try one of his new Steyr assault rifles—"

His mouth had stopped smiling. It had stopped moving. It had fallen open. Auden said with his mouth not working but the sound coming out from somewhere deep in his diaphragm or his groin, "And you said—?"

Spencer said, "I said—" Spencer said, "I said—" Spencer said, "I said I wasn't really keen because of Savannah, but I had a good friend who might be a little interested—"

A small boy's voice said, whimpering, "Me? You meant me?" Auden said, "*You meant me, didn't you?*"

Spencer said quietly, "You are my friend."

Auden said, "I am."

"And in your own way, even though you've never met her, Savannah's friend."

"And the dog." Auden, grinning at the dribble, said nodding, "And the dog. I'd do anything for that dog." Hand, schmand. The nice thing about things like Uzis and Ingrams was that you could always still shoot them with one hand. Auden said, "And the dog! Who's doing this for Savannah and the dog? I am!" Auden said, "Anything! I'll do anything!"

He looked at the dog. Really, all you had to do was put it reasonably. He felt something wet on his chin and he put his hand up to see what it was.

Phillip John Auden, friend.

For a friend, anytime, he'd give his right hand off his wrist.

He touched at the wetness on his chin and wondered what it was.
It was dribble.
He looked at the dog.
Nice dog. They had a lot in common really.
There, in Peripheral Street, one inside the car and one outside, both of them, in concert, had started making little panting noises.


He didn't even know if it was a man or a woman. All there was was the silence.
O'Yee said carefully, "Hello, are you there?" He waited.
There was the silence.
On the phone a voice said very quietly and timidly, "Hello?"
It chilled him to the bone.
It was a child.


There was the silence.
He tried to think of what to say.
In his hand, with a gentle click, the line went—irretrievably—dead.


There were whispers, sounds. There were soft voices, questions; there were the sounds of voices and whispers and questions as people, passing by the Morgue, stopped and listened and wondered if they could hear anything in there.
In there, everyone had gone.
In there, in pieces on the sheets on the floor and on the trolley, there were only the dead.
They listened. They wondered.
There were stories, rumors. They were unarguably, clearly, demonstrably, the dead.
They stopped. They listened.
In the hospital, all over Hong Kong, as the news spread with the morning, the living, pausing for a moment, *wondered*.

# 5

———

**H**e was ready. On the wood-veneer counter top there were smudges where, as he waited, he had wiped specks of dust away. He had straightened his tie. It was too tight. In the imitation-paneled one-room reception area and office of the Prudent Car and Van Hire on Icehouse Street, Roderick Chou recited as if he had rehearsed it, "It's a one-man operation. I can't afford a secretary yet. I've been in business for a year with a family loan and some help from the bank. I rent vans and middle-range cars." He looked at Feiffer across the counter and saw a tall, tired-looking man in a fawn suit watching him with no expression on his face, merely waiting for him to finish. He wasn't on trial. He was on trial. He was always on trial. Roderick Chou, twenty-five years old, with glasses and his neutral dark tie knotted too tightly at his starched white collar said, "Toyota Hi-Ace. Our stock number 5V, license plate 68–0032C, rented yesterday at—at—" He had forgotten his lines. His mouth was trembling. He reached under the counter and brought out a filled-in rental form, "—at exactly five-oh-five in the evening." Chou said, "That's the one, isn't it?" On the desk behind him there was an open newspaper. The newspaper had done a double-page spread of photographs of the accident. Chou said, "It's our van, isn't it?" There were no words on the double-page spread, there were only the photographs and the headline . . . OUT OF NOWHERE! The photographs were all of lights and ambulances and glass.

"Yes." On the walls of the office there were printed exhortations to fair dealing and *if we satisfy tell others, if not tell us* mottos. Chou was a Justice of the Peace—there was his framed certificate above his desk. He spoke careful, learned, practiced English. Feiffer said, "Who rented it?"

"The newspaper says there was no identification found on any of the bodies."

"No."

Chou said, "It was booze, right? Or drugs?" He nodded.

"No."

"How do you know?"

"Pathology has done all the tests on the organs of each of the four people. There were no residual traces of alcohol or drugs. They were all sober and—"

"*How do you know?*"

Feiffer said, "I was there."

*This business stands for Honesty and Fair Dealing. We want your repeat business. We intend to be here serving you for a long time.* It was another sign, on the rear wall above a small coffee machine so he could offer his clients coffee in plastic cups. Roderick Chou said tightly, "It was a man and a woman. They were Chinese, respectable—they were married and they—" His hand was on the counter on top of the rental form. He kept kneading it. "They wanted a small economical van for one twenty-four-hour period only and they had current drivers' licenses and ID cards and they—" Roderick Chou said, "They paid in advance by cash and I—" He was blinking, kneading. "—and the woman took the money out of her purse and counted it out for me and I—to put her at ease while I was taking her money—" Lowest rates in town. *Moderate Rentals for the Working Man.* "—I—" Roderick Chou said, "I said that she must have a neater mind than my own wife because she—because my wife wouldn't have been able to just open her purse and count out money: my wife always needs a four-wheeled excavator just to get to the bottom of the purse with everything she carries in it." Chou said, "She smiled." Chou said, "When she handed me the money, her hand touched mine." Chou said, "She was alive. Her hand was warm and moving and—and—and she was alive and I—" He was on the edge of tears.

Chou said, "Now she's dead and he is too and—" Chou said, "The newspaper says no one knows what happened! The newspaper says no one may ever know what happened!"

"What was her name?"

"Her name was—" Chou, putting his hand flat on the rental agreement as if to, somehow, shut it out, said, "She was—" He had rehearsed it, gone over and over it in his mind. He knew someone would come. He had been waiting. He had turned away business on the telephone to wait. He was sick to his stomach. Roderick Chou said, releasing it, "Susan Lau, female, Chinese, age forty-eight, clean driver's license, Apartment 7, 956 Empress of India Street, Hong Bay, and her husband, S. Y. Steven Lau, Chinese, clean license, age fifty-one, same address." His jaw was held tight. Roderick Chou said, "Toyota Hi-Ace van, stock number 5V, license plate number 68–0032C."

He changed to Chinese. Feiffer asked gently, "Is there anything you want to ask?"

"I've photostated the rental agreements. I made a copy for you—"

"Is there anything at all?"

"One each!" He was shaking. "One each! I rented them one van each! They rented two vans! They rented 5V and they rented 6V—both Toyotas! Plates number 68–0032C and 68–0067C! One each!" Chou said, "I watched them both drive out of the parking area and I stood at the door here smiling because they were nice people and I—" Chou said, "And they both waved at me and, just for a moment, I thought because she had touched my hand, Mrs. Lau looked at me with a funny, sad look on her face and I—" Chou said, "I was helpful, I was polite and courteous and I—I—" It was all going wrong. He had dreamed his dreams of how life would be and it was all going wrong and everything he dreamed was not the way things were. "And I—"

He was a cop. Standing there, looking at him, waiting, he was a cop and he listened. He saw a muscle going in the side of Feiffer's face, but he knew nothing about people who were cops and he thought it must have been anger or—he didn't know what it was.

He was sick to his stomach. He could not get it straight in his mind. Susan Lau and Steven Lau. He had joked about his wife's purse. She had smiled. They had waved. They were dead. They had gotten into his vans—into his familiar, known vans—and they had become dead and the vans were no longer his and they were—

"Where's the second van?"

"I don't know."

"What did they say they wanted them for?"

There was a silence.

"Mr. Chou?"

"Yes?"

He was blinking. He was not listening. Feiffer said again, "What did they say they wanted the two vans for? Did they tell you?"

"Yes." He touched at his tie. He was thinking about something. God only knew what it was. Roderick Chou said softly, "Yes. They told me they wanted to transport some glass." He was on the edge of tears. "I thought they might be worried about damage but I told them that I wouldn't worry too much about just a few little scratches. I told them that the place they were going to to get it, the Woosung Road Plate Glass Company was hard to back into from the main road. I told them a short cut. I told them if they went via Benton Lane that it was exactly a mile away and the traffic would be easier." Roderick Chou said, "I don't know where the second van is."

Roderick Chou said, suddenly changing to Chinese, not talking to Feiffer, but to someone else, to explain, "I told them the short cut. I did it to save them money. I thought—they both thanked me."

He was lost, all his dreams gone to nothing.

Roderick Chou said, "I thought . . . I thought, maybe, that was why, when she drove off—that was why she smiled at me."


On the phone from the Samaritans' suicide-prevention service Katy Wing Ho said, repeating it, "What does it mean if someone calls up and doesn't say anything and then puts the phone down?" She made a snorting noise, "Usually, what it means is that a male counselor has taken the call and the sex maniac on the other end is going to call again until he gets a female counselor he can shock to the dimples." She had a warm, easy voice. She was speaking English. There was an edge to it. Katy Wing Ho said, "However, since we don't have any female counselors with dimples—since dimples are definitely out around here and we've heard it all before anyway—we try to convince them to talk about a few other things: like what's gone wrong with their lives." Katy Wing Ho asked, "Is that what you've got, Christopher?"

"The people who ring this number don't want to shock women to their dimples, they usually want to carve them up to the bone." On the phone at his desk, for some reason, O'Yee had his reading glasses on. He took them off. O'Yee said casually, "I was just wondering, you know, if you'd had any of that sort of thing this morning? That maybe someone was doing the rounds of all the call-in numbers—just being a general nuisance and—"

Katy Wing Ho said, "No."

He had taken his glasses off. It had been something to do. Now he did something else. He drummed on the desk with his fingers. O'Yee said as if it were of no importance, "It's the third time in three hours." O'Yee said, "It's a kid." He waited.

"Male or female?"

"I can't tell."

"Young, very young or adolescent?"

"I don't know."

"Make a guess."

"I can't!" O'Yee said, "I can't make a guess! Fucking lunatics have been ringing me all morning telling me how they're going to make Jack the Ripper look like Mary Poppins or turn Hong Kong into Zombie Central or eat eyeballs or, or—and this goddamned kid has called me three times and all he or she has said in all that time is "Hello" and it's scared me more than all the other goddamned whackos, psychos, lunatics and risen dead put together!" Somewhere in there he recalled he had said something he shouldn't have. O'Yee said, "Sorry." By profession, Katy Wing Ho was a vet in private practice. By vocation she was a suicide counselor. O'Yee said, "Sorry, I didn't mean to swear at you."

"How many children do you have yourself?"

O'Yee said, "Three." O'Yee said, "I'm a Eurasian: you know, Chinese-American father and Irish mother—just can't stop that breeding—"

Katy Wing Ho said, "I accept as read, Christopher, that you're a good, compassionate person. I accept that your concern is genuine. I'm just trying to think of something to suggest to you that might have a hope of real success."

O'Yee said, "I want to keep him or her on the line." O'Yee said, "I don't know what to say."

"No." Katy Wing Ho said softly. "No."

"I don't know what the hell he or she or it is even doing calling this number! This number is the cop shop! This number is Sedate-a-Psycho—it isn't for kids, it's for lunatics and maniacs and people who need help—grown-up people!" O'Yee said, wiping away his drumming with a sweep of his hand, "Why the hell shouldn't a kid need help?" O'Yee said, "Katy, what should I say? *What the hell do you say?* What are the usual things people call you about?"

"Christopher, he isn't calling us, he's calling you."

"Do you think it's a boy then?"

"No. I don't know. I just meant—" Katy Wing Ho said, "Usually, people call us in one of three categories. The categories, broadly speaking are either, one, biological crises, like loss of function or menopause or illness or growth crises, or, two, environmental problems like bereavement or marriage problems or—" She was trying, he could hear it in her voice. "Or, three, what are known as adventitious crises, accidents, acts of God like injury or unemployment or—" Katy Wing Ho said, "Or auto accidents, sudden deaths, disasters—people call us because their lives are in turmoil and they think—they think there's no way out." Katy Wing Ho said, trying hard, "Usually, we don't talk at all. Usually, we just listen." Katy Wing Ho said, "I don't know what to suggest to you. He or she wants you, not me."

"Maybe not. Maybe he or she hangs up because they want someone else—!"

"Is there anyone else?"

"No." O'Yee said, "No." O'Yee said, "The third time he or she said 'Hello' to me." O'Yee said, "I didn't know what to say."

"Christopher—"

Maybe it was nothing. O'Yee said, "Maybe it's nothing." It wasn't nothing. O'Yee said, "Jesus!" O'Yee said, "Fucking goddamned bloody maniacs and goddamned bloody lousy horror freaks and stinking, degenerate masturbators and goddamned *lunatics*—what the hell am I supposed to say to a *kid*?"

All the smells. From where the dog waited in the gap between the ceiling of Mr. Wah's shop and the floor of his living quarters on the first floor, all the smells of the shop and of Mr. Wah were coming up through the cracks in the ceiling and filling its nose.

In the darkness the dog sat with its hind legs stretched out against a rafter and the full weight of its shoulders and head on the thin plasterboard. There was dust everywhere. The dog's nose filtered it out and smelled only the smells of Mr. Wah and the shop.

It smelled sharp smells: nitrates and ammonia; softer warmer smells: the flesh and skin of animals and birds ground to powder; earths: yellow clay and roots of ginseng and dark things from the soil; it smelled fading neutral smells of things that had once been something else—glass that had once been sand, paper and cardboard: trees—it smelled the warmth and sweat of Mr. Wah's body. It smelled everything about him. It smelled what kind of man he was.

In the ceiling, looking down at Mr. Wah's balding head, the dog waited, smelling.

It listened as Mr. Wah unpacked boxes that had once been trees, took out bottles that had once been sand, opened bottles and remembered creatures and birds and fish and life.

It smelled.

It listened.

It waited, listening.

It waited.

In the ceiling, resting on the thin plasterboard, hardly breathing, the Dalmatian—infinitely patient, hunting—waited for the wind chimes.


"I am the Masked Avenger Who Stalks by Night and Punishes Evil-Doers Too Clever to Be Caught by the Ordinary Forces of Law and Order!" The voice said, "Got any really difficult, unsolvable cases beyond your limited powers you want me to work on?"

"Not a one." O'Yee said apologetically, "Sorry."

"Oh."

O'Yee said, "Rest today." O'Yee said, "Masked Avenger, just to know you're out there is enough."

"We are all on the Same Side, Detective."

O'Yee said, "God bless you, Masked Avenger."

The Masked Avenger said merely, manfully, "Damn!" Typical. They never wanted thanks, those guys.

He hung up.


It was still there. The second van, number 68–0067C was parked in the street fifty feet from the Woosung Road Plate Glass Company. The Woosung Road Plate Glass Company was an underground workshop in a closed-off alley and the van had been parked on a piece of vacant redevelopment land they owned for when they expanded. It was locked. It was loaded with plate glass. There were no marks on the doors or windows where during the night anyone had tried to break in because, inside the van, except for the sheets of plate glass in the back, there was nothing to steal. Standing behind him, looking impatient, the manager of the glass company, Mr. Luen, said, to get it over and done with so he could get back to his glass, "Two people, a man and a woman, and two vans. The man telephoned yesterday afternoon, told me he had a rush order for plate glass and asked if we'd be open at nine o'clock at night and when I said we're always open, he said he'd bring two vans by. I asked him what sort of vans, he said Toyota Hi-Aces, I looked up the measurements in my transport book, we built two wooden frames to hold the glass, the man and a woman came by, we loaded the glass into the two vans and he paid by check." Mr. Luen said, glancing into the van, "Second-quality sheets of plate glass, altogether forty-four sheets, twenty-two in each van." He wanted to get back to work. He wore a thick canvas apron. He looked down at his hands and wiped them on the apron. Mr. Luen said, "My brother and I own this business. We're working twenty-four hours a day in shifts to get the capital together to build here." The vacant lot had been cleared flat. It was like a bowling green. It had been flattened probably by Mr. Luen and his brother walking it over and over, siting their new factory. Mr. Luen said, "I didn't see them drive off. My boys loaded them, they locked them and they paid." Mr. Luen said, "I knew who they were so I took their checks." Mr. Luen said, "It was a big order at the moment."

"Steven and Susan Lau?"

"Were they?" Mr. Luen said. "They were just employees. The two checks were signed by two people called G. L. Hang and L. K. Tin."

"Are you sure?"

"I don't forget things like that." Mr. Luen said, dropping his voice in the street, "Security. We get a lot of it." He was speaking Cantonese. He said under his breath as an exhortation, "*Fi dee . . . !*" It meant for Feiffer, "Hurry up . . . !"

"Addresses?

He didn't forget money. Mr. Luen said with a sigh, "54 Shantung Street, North Point for Hang and second floor, 789 Victoria Avenue, Yaumati for Tin." He was talking to someone who knew nothing about the glass business. Mr. Luen said, waving his hand as Feiffer took out a notebook to write it down, "Forget it! They're probably both little forwarding agencies or tea shops or lawyers' offices." Mr. Luen said, "It's second-quality glass. It's not for someone's little apartment window, it's security! It's second-quality glass!" Mr. Luen said slowly to an idiot, "It's no good. It shatters. It's for a millionaire's house somewhere. It's glass millionaires get their security people to break up and set into their walls as anti-intruder devices." He had a heavy pair of pliers in a loop on his apron. He took them out and made clipping motions with them. Luen said, nodding to make it clear, impatient to get back, "You break them up into spearheads and set them in concrete all along your walls and when some bastard tries to climb over . . ." He grinned. It was a big seller. Mr. Luen said, "It slashes him to ribbons." Mr. Luen said, "The man and the woman, they had a nice little job going there." He knew people. Mr. Luen said, "They were security, those two."

"Why is the second van still there?"

"I don't know." Mr. Luen, knowing their ways, said, "Who knows?" He saw Feiffer pull at the door handle. Mr. Luen said, "It's locked. My boys locked both the vans and gave the security people the keys."

"Break it open."

"What?"

"Break it open, please. Use your pliers." He could see the speedometer and the odometer. He could see what the figures on the odometer read. Toyota Hi-Ace van, stock number 6V, license number 68–0067C. On the rental sheet, when the Laus had signed for it, the reading was exactly 23,761 miles. It was one mile exactly from the Prudent Car and Van Hire to the glass company by short cut. The new reading read that mile. It read also, just turning on the little dials, unaccountably, more. It read an extra half mile. He stepped back from the window. He saw Luen hesitate.

Feiffer said calmly, quietly, but as an order, "The window: break it open, please, so I can look inside the van."


"Hello?" In the Detectives' Room, O'Yee said evenly on the phone, "D.S.I. O'Yee. Can I help you?"

It was a wrong number. It was a woman. She seemed genuinely embarrassed. She wanted someone called "Ting Lee." She was very sorry to have troubled him.

She hung up.


It was a time capsule. It was the doppelganger of the van on the highway from a moment before the last moment. It was the moment before the glass had begun to move, a moment before the screaming, the impact—it was frozen like an exhibit with the engine cold and only the antiseptic smell of the car deodorant the rental company must have sprayed it with in their valet service.

Twenty-three thousand, seven hundred and sixty-two and a half miles. It was a mile exactly from the rental company. The sheets of glass in the back were cold to his touch. They were locked in securely on a wooden framework. They would not move. In the front seat of the van, Feiffer touched at the roof. It was cold metal. It had become hot. On the other van, on the van in the other dimension, it had become red hot, it had melted, it had twisted and buckled as the glass had exploded upward and outward and it had— *Oh my God!* He had crawled in with Macarthur and then Macarthur had shone his flashlight. *Oh my God!* It was still. It was a van with two rows of seats and glass packed in the back and it was cold and still.

*Night Battle.* They had come six miles down the highway on the wrong side of the road playing Chinese opera and then— He reached over and touched at the cheap cassette player in the dashboard with just his thumbnail and ejected the cartridge inside.

*Night Battle.* It was a Chinese opera in Mandarin called *Night Battle*: he read the characters.

It was a copy. It was a complete, perfect cloned duplicate.

It was still, locked there on the vacant lot, having traveled only, after it had arrived there, one-half mile—maybe a quarter of a mile away and then a quarter of a mile back.

It was—

"Security!" He sounded worried. He had big plans for his business. Luen, holding his fist tight, said as a statement of fact, "Security! They were in the security business!" He had changed, suddenly, to English.

"For Christ's sake, *don't you read the newspapers?*"

"I haven't got time to read the newspapers! I'm not some cop getting people to smash open vehicles without a warrant, I'm a man trying to build up a business!"

He was shaking. He was losing control. He steadied himself. He tried to steady his voice. Getting out of the van, facing the man, Feiffer said in English, "Last night—this morning . . ." He changed to Cantonese, "Early this morning . . ."

"Security! It was a security job! It isn't illegal for me to sell shatter glass, it's only illegal to set it up as a mantrap, but that's not my problem!"

"The people in the other van, the Laus, probably Tin and Hang—"

Mr. Luen said, "He carried a gun! I saw it! He was security! I don't know whether his name was Lau or not and I don't know her name, but I do know he was security! He worked for a millionaire somewhere! He had a gun! I saw it in the pocket of his coat when he reached in to get the envelope with the two checks in it!" He wasn't going to be interrupted. Luen said, "It was a little nickel-plated gun, a .32—I know guns because we get a lot of this sort of thing—a two-incher! A—an Ivor Johnson or a Harrington and Richardson or a—" Mr. Luen said, "A nickel-plated two-inch barreled .32–caliber Harrington and Richardson five-shot pocket revolver!" Mr. Luen said,

"I saw it!" Mr. Luen said, "Millionaires afraid of burglars or kidnappers, that's who they were acting for! They bought second-quality glass to cut people to pieces!" Mr. Luen said, "It's not my problem! I've got a business to expand!" Mr. Luen said as an appeal to someone, "Don't I work hard enough? Don't I do enough to succeed?" Mr. Luen said, "I let them leave this other van here rent-free!"

Mr. Luen said, "Newspapers?" Mr. Luen said, "Who in the name of heaven has time to read newspapers these days?" He had a wife and children. Mr. Luen said, not to Feiffer, but to someone else, someone important, "If I don't work like a dog twenty-four hours a day, just what—just what do you think is going to happen to us all?" He was a man in his early forties. He looked tired, crushed.

Mr. Luen said, patiently, trying to make it clear to the man, "Please, sir—Chief Inspector—all I want to do is get back to work!"


He waited. The Detectives' Room was still and deserted, quiet. He could not even hear the Uniformed Branch outside at the front desk. For some reason, outside his window, he could not even hear the sound of the traffic in the street.

He waited.

At his desk, he took off his reading glasses and rubbed at his eyes.

He looked at the wall clock: 10:37 A.M.

He waited.

By the phone, in the silence—in the stillness—O'Yee waited.

# 6

W ell, he thought he was dead. So there was no point being tidy about the shop because the shop wasn't a real shop, it was just a memory deep in the grave. All he'd done was take a set of best-quality demon-deterring porcelain wind chimes from a box and the roof of the world made of white ceiling plaster had fallen in on him, a spotted dog had appeared in with the plaster, also falling on him, smashed all his jars and bottles on all his shelves and ledges to pieces, hit him on the shoulder and poleaxed him and now, as the wind chimes started to fall down with the plaster—having somehow gone up—there was a gentle chinkle-chinkling as the gentle monks of heaven led him to his rest to have a few words with him about how the world down there was getting along.

Mr. Wah's ghostly self said gently, philosophically to the celestial monks, "Really, the last memory I have of the world is a large Dalmatian dog coming through the ceiling and smashing up all my years of hard work."

The dog was still turning, coming down. It had bounced somewhere. It was going over and over in the air hitting things of great value.

The head celestial monk said, "Such things are sometimes brought upon us by our own actions. Others are merely sent by the uncaring gods to amuse themselves with our pointless earthly actions." The celestial monk smiled. It was a question.

Mr. Wah's ghostly self said, "The second."

It hit side-on on the counter, turned over, crashed onto the floor in a welter of smashing glass and spices, herbs and two extremely valuable—now worth shit—preserved snakes for virility and, hitting the floor in a rain of plaster, got to its feet and, showing a lot of teeth, looked around for the wind chimes.

The monk, puffing on a filter-tip Camel—Mr. Wah's own brand: he was glad he would be able to get them there—said, musing, "It must have come as quite a surprise to you."

"It did."

It was a spotted dog, half starved with eyes that lit up like burning embers. On the floor, looking around, coiled like a spring, it made a low growling noise.

The monk took a puff.

Mr. Wah said, "I always tried to lead a decent life." Heaven was new to him: best to start off right. Mr. Wah said, "He killed me, the dog, but I forgive him. I wish him in his endeavors every success."

It was snarling. It looked around. In the falling plaster, through the whiteness, the eyes burned like coals.

"Doesn't matter."

"Doesn't it?"

The monk said, "No." The monk, puffing at his butt, said, shaking his head, "Total waste of time."

Mr. Wah said, "I got hit by a falling dog. Am I dead?"

It saw the wind chimes in the plaster. Everything in Mr. Wah's shop had been destroyed. The dog, shaking its head hard, got the chimes in between its teeth and looked for the door.

The heavenly monk thought about it for a moment. The monk, deciding, said, "No."

Mr. Wah said, "Oh." He was lying full length on the floor of his shop looking up as a spotted Dalmatian, snarling and snapping, chinkling with the wind bells in its mouth, looked for the door. Mr. Wah said, "Thank you."

The monk had a brand-new Zippo lighter. He flicked it open and lit another Camel. The monk, having a smoke, nodding to acknowledge the gratitude, safe from cancer, said happily, "Okay."

He got up. He staggered a little. Mr. Wah, getting past the dog, smiling, opening the front door a little for him, said with the peace of all-knowingness, the understanding of every tiny thing that crawled or swam upon the land or in the mud, "Here." He opened wide the door.

Mr. Wah said to himself to start learning all about the world again, one word at a time, "Dog."

Mr. Wah said as the dog, glowering at him, went past, "Door."

Street.

World.

Heaven.

Ceiling.

White plaster dust.

Dog.

Everything he had ever worked for destroyed.

Cop.

He saw Auden halfway across the street coming toward him.

He saw the dog with the wind chimes in its mouth turn and look at him with the pathetic surprise only a simple beast who has never been loved could have. He saw, for a single instant, the sad hound wag its tail.

Mr. Wah said quietly, "Shoot the dog."

Dog.

The.

Shoot.

Mr. Wah said a little louder, "Shoot the dog." Mr. Wah said—

He was starting to jump up and down. He was starting to salivate. He was starting to drool. He was starting to make snapping noises with his teeth—Wah, not the dog. Mr. Wah said as a request, "Shoot the dog." Mr. Wah said as an order, "Shoot the dog."

He was alive. He was hurting. Mr. Wah, relearning one word after another, starting to jump up and down, starting to go black in the face, getting all the words out, making a few comments about heaven and hell and hell on Earth and . . . yelled—

"*Shoot it!*" The dog had stopped wagging. It was off and running. Mr. Wah, back from the dead, a new man, shrieking bootless to heaven in exactly the way the old one had done all his life, screamed at the top of his voice as a command, "Shoot it! Shoot it! You stupid, lunkheaded, thick-nosed cop—SHOOT THE DOG!"


In the hospital room Mr. Fan said quietly, "I run a wholesale antique business. I was taking the truck to the border to pick up a consignment of furniture from China. I was on the road early to be first in line for customs clearance." He was lying in bed with his bandaged stump on his chest. He kept lifting it a little to get relief from the pain. There was a well-dressed middle-aged woman in the room at the window, staring out and down into the hospital grounds. Mr. Fan said, "This is my wife." She turned for a moment and nodded to Feiffer. Mr. Fan said in Cantonese so presumably she could follow the conversation, "I didn't see any lights."

"No."

Mr. Fan said, "The radio says they didn't have any lights."

He saw her face as she looked out. She had her lips held tightly together. It was a strong face. Feiffer said, "It's not your fault."

"Do you know who they were?" Mr. Fan asked, knowing it was true, "Are they all dead?"

"Yes."

"Do you know their names?" He didn't wait for an answer. Mr. Fan said suddenly, biting his lip, "My wife and I—we've just been granted a residence permit for America—to start a business there and be with our children and we—and we—" He closed his eyes. Mr. Fan said with his eyes still closed, "Who were they?"

At the window, she was looking down into the grounds where the sliding door to the Morgue was. In the grounds, the police cars with the relatives in them were arriving. They were coming, in groups. Down in the grounds, from where Mrs. Fan watched with her lips pressed tightly together, they were moving toward the sliding door with people in uniforms.

Feiffer said evenly, reading it from his notebook, "S. Y. Lau, male, age fifty-one, marine electrical contractor, Empress of India Street, Hong Bay, and his wife Susan Lau of the same address, age forty-eight; George Hang, male, age forty-six, Shantung Street, North Point, optical-lens grinder and L. K. Kenneth Tin, male, age forty-eight, gardener, Victoria Avenue, Yaumati." Feiffer said evenly, "A firearm has been found in the van and we believe that Susan Lau who was driving was killed by a single gunshot wound to the head just before the collision." Feiffer said formally, "There was no evidence of alcohol or drugs." The relatives were down there, moving across the grounds in the grayness of the day—she could see them. Feiffer said to Mr. Fan's closed eyes, "They were driving on the wrong side of the road and they had been for six miles. There are two police officers who witnessed the whole thing." He got no reaction. Feiffer said firmly, "It's not your fault."

Below, the last of the relatives went inside the sliding Morgue door and, from the distance at which Mrs. Fan watched, there was no sound as the heavy metal door slid closed. Outside, waiting, empty, there were three police cars.

He opened his eyes. Mr. Fan said with difficulty, "Thank you for coming to tell me." He could not think how to frame what he wanted to say. There was nothing to say. Mr. Fan said, "All my life—all my life—" Mr. Fan said, "Alice—? Alice?"

She nodded. She turned from the window.

Mr. Fan said, "Alice—" Mr. Fan said, "They're here, aren't they? All of them? They're still here in the hospital somewhere?"

Mrs. Fan said softly, "No." Going forward to him and putting her hand gently on the bandaged stump to soothe it, to take away some of the pain, she said as if to a small, sleepy child, "It's all right, everything is all right . . ." Mrs. Fan said, looking at Feiffer, "No, they're not here. It's all over. They've all gone now."

"I don't know anything! I can't remember! I heard music and then there was glass and I—" Mr. Fan said to her, desperately, "I don't know anything!"

"Shh . . ."

"I—I—" He looked up, not at his wife but at Feiffer.

Mr. Fan said in horror, "I thought I was dead! I thought I was dead!" Somewhere, somewhere else in the hospital, here, in the building—whatever anyone said—he knew they were still there. He knew they were still there, waiting. He knew they were cold and dead. He knew— Everywhere, in his sleep, there were demons.

Mr. Fan said, "Nothing! Nothing! I can't remember anything at all about it!" Mr. Fan said, "The driver! I must have seen the driver in my lights just before—"

Mr. Fan said, "I can't remember! I can't even remember if it was a man or a woman." He was talking not to Feiffer or to his wife, but to all the times he would be asked, over and over and over again.

He was in pain. He kept trying to move his hand under his wife's gentle touch.

Mr. Fan said to explain, to placate, to send the demons away, "Nothing! I swear, I promise—after we hit—"

Mr. Fan said, "Nothing! *I can remember nothing at all about it!*"


"*Don't shoot the dog!*"

He wasn't going to shoot the dog. Auden, running, chasing after the dog to head it off before it got to the end of the street, yelled back to Spencer, "Let slip Petal!" He turned and saw Spencer at the car door, yanking on it. It was stuck. Auden yelled, "Use your keys!" He saw the rear of the Dalmatian going like hell with something hanging outward from where its mouth must have been. Whatever it was it was making a chinkling sound. Auden, half turning, getting his coat off to wrap around his hand for when he reached down with the beeper, yelled, "It's locked! Use your keys and open the door!" Where the hell was the beeper? Spencer had the beeper. Auden yelled back, "Bring the beeper when you come!"

"It isn't locked! Petal's leaning against it and I can't get it open!"

The Dalmatian made a one-hundred-and-eighty degree turn on the sidewalk. It saw Auden. It turned back. Auden caught his breath. Auden yelled, "Try the other door!" He looked back. He couldn't see Spencer.

The dog stopped. It snarled.

"I'm trying the other door!"

*"Use your keys!"*

"It isn't locked! Petal's leaning against it!"

The Dalmatian was wondering whether it should leap on him and tear his throat out or simply turn back and keep going. Auden yelled, "How the hell can it be leaning on both doors?" He got no answer. There was no answer. Auden yelled, "Bring the beeper!"

"The beeper's in the car!" Spencer, yanking at the car doors, yelled pleadingly, "Petal! Let me in!"

"Go around to the other door!"

"I have!" Spencer yelled, "Petal—no!"

"Try the other door!"

"It's too quick for me!" Spencer screamed, "Petal, it's me: Billy-Poo!"

"What?" Auden, in the street, said, "What?"

"Petal! Petal! PETAL!" Spencer shouted, "It's accidentally leaning on both door locks when I go around to them and I can't get the door open!"

Even the Dalmatian stopped and listened.

Spencer said—

The Dalmatian looked at Auden. He heard Auden make a sniffing sound. He saw Auden, very slowly, unwrap his coat from his hand and put it gently over his arm. He heard Auden make a sniffing sound. There was an expression on the face of the man with the coat over his arm. The Dalmatian didn't recognize it. It wasn't a smile.

"Phil! Phil—!" There were sounds coming from the other side of the car. In the car there was some sort of furry lump leaning on the window.

The man with the coat over his arm slowly looked down at his thumbnail and examined it. There was an expression on his face. It wasn't a thumbnail-examining expression.

The man with the coat over his arm, examining his thumbnail, not exactly smiling, turned.

Chinkle-chinkle. The wind chimes in the Dalmatian's mouth as it trotted away at its own speed and went, a little puzzled, around the corner, went lightly and gaily *chinkle-chinkle-chink.*

In Peripheral Street, still looking down at his thumbnail with a strange, quiet, blank look on his face, Auden began slowly and unhurriedly—taking all the time in the world—to walk back to the car where Fang and Billy-Poo were.


It was him. It was a boy. There was a pause and then on the phone the boy said in Cantonese, "I've got a gun."

He could have wept with relief. They came in all shapes and sizes. O'Yee, lighting a cigarette, smiling, said, "Really? Machine gun, shotgun, sub–machine gun, assault rifle, pistol, revolver or ray gun?" It was the Cantonese comics. Before you were old enough to get the videos, the Cantonese comics got you ready. O'Yee said pleasantly, "Big gun, small gun, middle-sized gun?" O'Yee said, "There are a lot of guns."

There was a pause. The boy said, "Big."

"Cannon, field piece or howitzer?"

He was silent. The boy said in a tight tone, "It's a Luger."

"Oh." Not a cannon, field piece or howitzer. O'Yee said, "Like in No-Prisoners Ping in the comics." He had children. The drawings in the comics were pretty good if you liked color. O'Yee said to help him along, "You can tell that because it's got *Luger* written on it in Chinese characters—right?" For a moment there—

There was a silence.

O'Yee said, "And just below it, *Fill Water Here.*"

"It's got a word on it."

Right. Right. That did it. On Auden's desk as luck would have it— *just as luck would have it*—there was the *Maniac's Guide to Everything Lethal Since A.D. 100.* It had a picture of a Luger in it. It was the page stuck together. O'Yee, leaning over and wrenching at the tome the size of a Manhattan telephone book, said, "Right! Great! I'm all ears! *Tell me what the word on it is!*"

The boy said, spelling it out, "E-R-F-U-R-T."

Wrong! Sorry! Next! On top of the German Luger in the picture there were the letters DWM (they must have stood for something). O'Yee said, "Wrong! Nice try! Send in another coupon next week and—" he ran his finger down the text. O'Yee said, "DWM— Deutsche Waffen und Munitionsfabrikan!" He read words well for a man contemplating crawling down a telephone line and strangling the little bastard at the other end of it with his bare hands. O'Yee said, "DWM, maybe SIMSON, rarely VICKERS and—and ERFURT— that's all you ever get on the usual run of—" O'Yee said suddenly, "You read it somewhere! You read it in a comic!" O'Yee said, "What does it say on the side of the gun where it should say GESICHERT to show the safety catch is on?"

The boy said, "It doesn't say anything."

O'Yee said, "What?"

"It doesn't say anything."

There was a silence. He looked at the book. O'Yee, running his tongue across his lips, asked, "Is there a triangular piece of metal sticking up on the receiver just behind where it says ERFURT?" It was the extractor. If the gun was loaded and cocked the little triangular piece of metal would have read GELADEN. They didn't print that in the comics. If there was no GESICHERT, then it meant—O'Yee said, "On the triangular piece of metal—what does it say?"

"*Geladen.*"

There was a silence. After a moment, the boy said quietly, "It's a big gun. It's heavy."

Fully loaded, cocked Lugers with the safety catch off were. O'Yee said—

The boy said, "I—" He was going to go.

"*Don't hang up!*" O'Yee said, "Don't! Don't! Don't hang up!— please." He thought he heard, for a second, a sob. O'Yee, holding the phone hard against his ear, making opening and closing motions with his other hand, said calmly, "What's your name?"

"Chi."

"Chi?"

"Yes."

O'Yee said quietly and carefully, "Chi, do you have a family?"

There was a snuffling sound.

"Anyone? Anyone at all?" He had a goddamned, rotten, stinking, lousy, fucking loaded Luger with the safety catch off. O'Yee, starting to breathe hard, asked, "Is there anyone who could—"

The boy said sadly, "I don't know how to shoot it."

"*Don't!* Don't shoot it!" He was trying to catch his breath. He was

alone in the office. There was no one who could trace the call. It was a
call box; he thought he'd heard the coins drop. O'Yee, kneading his
hand, begged the boy, "Please! Please don't try to—Where is it? Have
you got it in your pocket?"

"I'm ten."

Right, right. Ten. Small pockets. O'Yee, trying to remember which
tone worked on his kids, said in completely the wrong tone to use,
"Then where the hell is it?"

"It's in my schoolbag on my back."

*Oh, Jesus.*

The boy said, "I got it from the man."

He couldn't think of what the hell to say! O'Yee said, "The man?"
He heard the snuffling sound. He was weeping. There, in the call
box—where?—he had a loaded, cocked pistol in his schoolbag on his
back and he was weeping. O'Yee looked at his watch. It was class
time. He wasn't at school. He was wandering the streets. O'Yee said,
"Chi—Chi—listen to me . . ." O'Yee said softly, "Don't cry. Don't
cry—"

"I'm afraid!"

"I can fix it!"

"I'm afraid!"

"Chi, listen—!"

He wasn't listening. He was sobbing. He was afraid.

"*Chi—!*"

Chi said, "He was dead."

"The man?"

"He was dead." He was weeping, making sobbing sounds, not
listening.

"*Chi—!*"

Chi said, "I'm afraid! I'm sorry!"

"Please! For the love of God—!"

"I'm sorry." Chi said, sobbing, softly, "I'm—"

At his desk, holding the phone, he could almost touch the fear.
O'Yee said coaxingly, "Chi . . ." O'Yee said in a whisper, "Listen to
me, please . . . please, just listen . . ."

He heard it coming, he sensed it: he felt it. O'Yee, on his feet,
shouting, yelled down the line as an order, "No! No! Don't! *Don't
hang up!*"

He heard only a single click.

The line, like the man, went dead.

\* \* \*

"Phil . . ."

At the car, his lips pursed, Auden looked at Petal.

"Phil—"

Petal looked happy. Its tongue was hanging out and it looked happy.

"*Phil*—"

It was a good dog, a clever dog. It was a dog that thought it was going to live forever. It was a dog that could lean on door handles so you couldn't get it out to be torn to pieces by . . . by anything . . . not even a mouse. Auden, looking at it, said, "Hmm." Bright dog, cautious dog, sly dog—new dog, new tricks. Ha, ha. What a bright little dog.

"*PHIL—!*"

Cowardly little dog. Billy-Poo and the nun's little dog. Auden said so softly that only the great god of dogs heard him, "Cowardly little dog."

"SHOOT THE DOG!" There was a wreck of a man staggering about outside Mr. Wah's shop across the street. It looked like it had been Mr. Wah before a dog had fallen on him.

Auden said, "Sure." He reached across his shoulder holster for his magnum.

"*PHIL!*"

"SHOOT THE DOG!"

He had run out of things to say. "Phil . . ." For a long moment he closed his eyes. He had a sad, pained, lost expression on his face. He looked in at the dog. Spencer said, "Phil, I—I—" He looked in at Petal.

He looked at Mr. Wah.

He looked at Auden.

Petal.

Fang.

Billy-Poo.

Spencer said for the last time, "Phil?"

He put his hand to his eyes.

With no trouble at all, there, right out in the middle of the street, with the rush hour starting and all the shops open for the day's business—with no trouble at all—in Peripheral Street, Hong Bay, he could have sat down and, bowing his head, in terrible, utter disappointment, howled.

. . . Like a dog.


In the viewing room of the Morgue there were no bodies laid out and no photographs, nothing. There was only a single table in the room with personal belongings in separate sections that had seemed to someone to fit together.

In the room in front of the belongings, looking down at them, a little away from Macarthur and the police who had brought them there, there were three young men and two young women, all Chinese, all silent, all waiting to be told something.

They were the relatives. Like the belongings, they were arranged, had arranged themselves, in distinct parts of the room: a son and daughter-in-law of the Laus, Tin's eighteen-year-old only son, and, gazing down at the items nearest them, the grown-up son and daughter of G. L. Hang, lens grinder of 54 Shantung Street, North Point.

On the table in the groups of items there were rings and watches, a thin gold bracelet that had been taken from the dismembered female arm, a hair clip, coins, two small pieces of luck-bringing archaic jade, and sliced through with glass and unrecognizable with dried blood, a single train ticket going nowhere.

They were the relatives. In the viewing room lined with insulation panels against the sound of the refrigerator motors in the next room, they looked down at the items and made no sound at all.

They looked.

It was all there was left. It was all that could be shown.

They were the relatives.

In the little, lined, silent room, no one spoke.

"Deep in the woods, three beautiful co-ed students are stalked by—"

Slice and dice.

"—a disfigured maniac with a long, glittering-bladed stag-handled hunting knife honed razor sharp . . ."

On the phone O'Yee said tightly, "Shut up."

"—their clothes all ripped to shreds by thorns, they flee naked through—"

O'Yee said, "Shut up! Shut up! *SHUT UP!*"

He slammed the phone down hard.

In the Detectives' Room, alone, he tried to think of what to do.

He stood watching them. He had come in quietly and they did not know he was there. He stood a little back with the uniformed people and watched them.

They were the relatives.

They were the son and daughter-in-law of the Laus, the only son of L. K. Kenneth Tin, the grown-up son and daughter of G. L. Hang. They looked, not at the items on the table, but in groups, at each other. He saw it. As Feiffer watched, he saw it on all their faces as they looked at the others.

They were the relatives.

They were the relatives of the Laus, of Tin, of Hang. It was on their faces. It could be read there as they waited. Three groups from four dead people, in pieces, frozen like ice a paneled wall away . . . the groups, each of them—

They knew each other not at all.

# 7

$O$n the phone the Commander said incredulously, "Harry, they rented two vans, they bought glass, they traveled six miles the wrong way along a freeway in one of the vans in the middle of the night with all their lights off playing Chinese opera at full blast—*what the hell do you mean you think they didn't know each other?*"

He was in the pathology-records office near the viewing room in the Morgue. He could see them. He could see how they looked at each other. "I think they were strangers to each other. At best, acquaintances." He could see the sons and daughter and daughter-in-law in their groups with the uniformed police who had brought them there, looking at each other. He saw them wonder. Feiffer said softly into the phone even though the door to the glassed-in office was closed and they could not hear, "They don't know each other. Not one of the relatives of one knows any of the relatives of another. Not one of them who lost a relative—not one of them has ever heard the name of any of the other victims before." They were standing there in the corridor in three groups: Tin's eighteen-year-old son, the grown-up son and

74

daughter of G. L. Hang and the son and daughter-in-law of the Laus. Feiffer said, "They're lost, Neal. They can't explain what happened."

There was a silence. The Commander said evenly, "The newspapers are waiting for the police to say they were drunk while in charge of a motor vehicle." He waited.

"No one was drunk."

The Commander said, "Or that it was some sort of kidnapping or crime that went wrong and that the van was being chased and, in order to try to escape—"

Feiffer said, "I've checked with criminal records—"

"And?"

"And they're clean." Behind him, where the rear door to the office opened into a pathology laboratory, he could see Macarthur at a blackboard explaining something to Hansell. He was explaining what he had seen when he had first looked into the van. There was a chalked schematic of the van on the board. Hansell, taking the chalk from Macarthur, made a cross on it where the driver's seat was. Hansell was in uniform. In his hand he carried something small wrapped in plastic. Feiffer said, "What they were was a marine electrical contractor and his wife, a lens grinder, and a gardener, both widowers." Feiffer said, "They came from all over the city."

"One of them has a goddamned bullet in the back of the head!"

"Yes."

"Well, what about the bloody gun?"

"The bloody gun is unregistered. The bloody gun has probably been floating around the Colony since 1911. In 1911 you could buy the bloody gun legally on mail order." He could not take his eyes off the relatives. One of them, Tin's son, was clenching and unclenching his fist. He kept looking at the others for someone to blame. As he caught their eyes, he looked away. Like them, he looked very ordinary. Feiffer said, "No one has ever seen a gun in any of their parents' possession."

"What was the second van for?"

"I don't know."

"And the glass?"

"I don't know."

"*Where the hell were they going in the van?*"

"I don't know."

"*Well, who the hell does?* The relatives of those people are the relatives of those people—they must know something about their own parents!"

"They know they were ordinary. In all their lives—" He looked at them. "—in all their lives all they can come up with is that—" It was hopeless. Feiffer said suddenly, "Neal, they don't know a goddamned thing about them that's out of the ordinary because up until this morning all they or their parents had ever done was exactly what millions upon millions of people do every day! They were born, they married, they had children, their children left home—"

"Didn't any of them live with their parents?"

"No. The youngest is eighteen, Tin's son. He works out in Lo Wu on a construction site, the daughter of Hang is a junior clerk for a shipping line, her brother is an apprentice toolmaker in his last year, and the Laus' son and daughter-in-law run a small rattan and bamboo furniture store in North Point."

"All they need is a bloody dog with floppy ears and a kid with a slingshot and you could put them on the cover of the *Saturday Evening Post*, couldn't you?" He had nothing to tell the newspapers and television. The Commander said tightly, "Suicide."

"All four of them?"

"It's happened before!" No, it hadn't. And if it had, it hadn't been Chinese who had done it. The Commander said, "What about DMV?"

"Mrs. Lau was a licensed driver and so was her husband."

"Traffic?"

"No record of traffic violations. One parking citation three months ago in the name of John Lau, the son."

"*What sort of damn car?*"

"A secondhand Honda Accord." He drew a breath. Feiffer said, "It was theirs, but the son has it on permanent loan to get to and from his job. He lives in Kowloon." Feiffer said quietly, "Neal, they're all nobodies. They're all hard-working, respectable people—"

"And four of them are dead!"

"And four of them are dead."

"Where the hell were they going in the van?"

"The relatives don't know." He had asked over and over. He had put it to them every way he could think of. He had tried everything. Feiffer said, "Each of them belonged to various organizations and clubs, each of them was a member of either a union or a guild, each of them had friends or acquaintances they had in their homes or ate with in restaurants, each of them had debts or loans from banks or finance companies, each of them—" He saw the Tin boy look over at him. He saw what was in his eyes. "—each of them . . ." Feiffer said, "Apart from the fact that S. Y. Lau and Susan Lau were husband and wife, there's absolutely nothing in common between them at all."

"They died together! They died together on a freeway in the middle of the night!" He was thinking hard. The Commander, grasping at straws, said, "The second van, how far had it gone from where it was parked outside the glass factory?"

"About half a mile."

"You mean a quarter of a mile. One-quarter of a mile somewhere and then one-quarter of a mile back to where it started!"

"Maybe." Feiffer said, "Or it could have been a faulty reading or—"

"Or it could have been a goddamned flying saucer traveling at the speed of light and it went backward in time!" The Commander demanded, "What am I supposed to tell people? What am I supposed to tell the media? What am I supposed to tell everyone I've ever known who rings me out of nowhere and asks, for old-time's sake, if I could just let them know the answer to this one because everyone's talking about it? What the hell am I supposed to tell myself? *What the hell happened out there last night?*"

He saw Hansell finish at the blackboard and rub his hands together to get the chalk off. He saw Macarthur ask him something and Hansell shake his head. He was asking about fingerprints in the second van. There were none. There were only smears. Or they might not have been smears, but wipes. Or they were smears.

In the corridor the relatives were waiting. They were waiting for Hansell and the gun. Feiffer said, "I don't know." He saw Hansell straighten his shoulders and, still talking to Macarthur, still shaking his head, take up the wrapped parcel from the table. Feiffer said, "I have no idea at all. All I know is that—" He saw Hansell start toward the door in pathology that led to the viewing-room corridor.

"Is there anything I can do to help?"

In the corridor, he saw them see him come through the door. He saw the Tin boy's hand clench into a fist. He felt with him the feeling the boy had in his stomach. On the blackboard, from the positions and the path of the bullet and the awful remnants of people they had found in the van, Hansell and Macarthur had worked it out. Feiffer said, "I need a court order to get the Central Credit Register opened so I can check on their financial state in case—"

The Commander said, "I'll do it."

"—in case—"

The Commander said, "Leave it to me."

"—in case there's some connection that—" He saw Hansell stop in front of them. He saw Hansell, like some ghastly uniformed executioner, look at each of them in turn and decide which one of them he wanted. Feiffer said, "—in case . . ." He saw all their faces.

They were ordinary people. In the Morgue, on the floor on sheets, they had had all the bits of bodies laid out, one of them a woman. In the hole the metal saws had made in the van, crawling in after Macarthur, he had looked in. Macarthur had turned on his flashlight. Feiffer said, "—in case they—"

"Harry?"

"In case they—" He saw the little silver gun come out of its wrapping. He saw it in Hansell's hand. He saw, one by one, the looks on the relatives' faces as they saw it, as it passed in front of them. Feiffer said into the phone, "The woman—Susan Lau—the driver, the one who was shot just before the impact—"

He had his back to him. He knew Hansell—very softly—said something.

"Do you know yet which one of the passengers did it?"

"Yes." He saw the Laus' son and daughter-in-law. It was them. Hansell had picked them. On the blackboard in the next room, all the positions had been marked inside the little schematic of the van in chalk.

They were all, the living and the dead, nobodies. They were all, the dead and the waiting, *ordinary*. Feiffer said, "Yes." He saw the son and daughter-in-law struck dumb with horror. He saw their faces.

Feiffer said, "It was her husband. He was sitting directly behind her in the van. It was her husband." He saw one of the women constables start to move forward to get the daughter-in-law before she fell. Feiffer said, "S. Y. Lau, age fifty-one, marine electrical contractor, Apartment 7, 956 Empress of India Street, Hong Bay—a fraction of a second before the impact, with a single bullet to the back of the neck, he shot his wife dead." He saw the relatives. He saw all their faces. "And I have absolutely no idea on Earth, why—"

"Stay there. I'll get the court order." The Commander said briskly and efficiently, "Stay there. I'll call you back." The Commander said to the terrible silence, "Harry? Harry—? Are you still there?"


On the phone from the School Truancy Board, Miss Wong said, "Occasional absentee? Short-term absentee? Or long-term absentee?"

He didn't know. O'Yee said, "I don't know."

"Truant? Occasional, regular or congenital?"

"I don't know."

She had a patient voice. Miss Wong, filling out some sort of form as she spoke, said, "Name?"

O'Yee said, "Chi." He knew that.

"Is that a family name, given name, diminutive or nickname?"

He didn't know. O'Yee said, "I don't know."

"Private fee-paying school, government-run school, day school, boarding school, Communist middle school, religious institution, charity-funded establishment, nondenominational or charity-funded establishment, denominational?" She had a computer. She was filling out something to feed into it.

"I don't know."

"Age?"

O'Yee said, "About ten?" O'Yee said, "He carries a satchel!"

"To school?"

"Yes!"

"Is he truant today?"

O'Yee said, "Yes!"

"Then why is he carrying a satchel?"

O'Yee said, "I don't know." O'Yee said, "Maybe he's just absent."

"Parents' names?"

"I don't know."

"Address?"

"I don't know."

"Description?"

O'Yee said, "I don't know."

"Mr. O'Yee . . . ?"

O'Yee said eagerly, "Yes?"

Miss Wong said, "Mr. O'Yee—"

O'Yee said, "What?"

Miss Wong said, "Is this some sort of joke?"

There was a silence.

O'Yee said softly, "I don't know."

He hung up.


He must have been on the pistol range on the top floor of Headquarters because Ballistics put him straight through. Also because O'Yee could hardly hear him at the other end of the line for the gunfire.

On the phone, Inspector Emery of Ballistics said between the fusillades of police combat shooters combating thin pieces of paper with very big bullets, "You want to know what? You want to know the trigger pressure it takes to shoot off an automatic pistol? What sort of automatic pistol?"

O'Yee said, "A Luger."

"What sort of Luger? Standard model, navy model or long-barreled artillery model?"

O'Yee said, "An Erfurt Luger."

"That isn't a model, that's a maker's name." There was an explosion of banging. The pieces of paper were getting exactly what they deserved.

"Give me an average!"

"Can't. With a gun that old, the springs could have gone funny, or the mechanism got gummed up with gook or the surfaces worn." Emery said, "Has it been looked after or is it out on the street?"

"It's out on the street."

"Nice gun." There must have been some gun freak listening to the conversation. Emery said as an aside, "Old Erfurt Luger." Emery said, "They're all pretty old by now, Christopher. Most of them were made during the First World War and some of the Erfurts were even prewar. Whatever they were they were still military and not built to last the way a commercial gun would be, so—"

"What caliber would it be?"

"Nine mill or, maybe 7.63." Emery said, "If it's 7.63 then the main spring is a leaf spring and, over the years—"

"What sort of range?"

"Killing range?"

"Killing range."

Emery said, "A long way." Emery said, "Mind you, the hard part with one of those old guns is to have the strength to cock it."

O'Yee said tightly, "It's already cocked."

It must have been a mass execution of paper. There was enough gunfire in a single mad volley behind him to chop up all the targets you could make in a year from an entire forest of pine trees. Emery said dreamily, "Nice gun, the old Erfurt Luger, very nice. A collector's piece, but too old and brittle to try to fire." Emery said, "Ever had an ant on your desk when you're trying to work?"

O'Yee said, "What?"

"Have you?"

"Of course I have."

"Ever just glanced over and flicked it away with your finger?"

There was a silence. Even the guns had stopped firing.

Emery said casually, "Trigger pressure to fire an old gun like that after seventy years? Oh, about as much as it takes to flick an ant off your desk."

Emery asked curiously, "Why? Do you know someone who's trying to work out how to do it?"

He knew someone who was trying to work out how not to do it. He knew someone who was carrying the filthy thing in his school satchel and walking around the streets.

He knew someone who nobody else knew who kept calling him and talking about dead men and guns.

He knew someone—

Chi. He thought he was probably about ten years old.

He thought maybe it was some sort of joke.

It was no joke.

In the Detectives' Room, willing it, O'Yee said to the phone, "Ring."

Ring.

O'Yee said, "*Ring!*"

Sitting at his desk with his thumbnail flicking hard at his teeth, O'Yee, watching the phone, waited.

On the phone the Commander said, "I've talked to the people at the Central Credit Register."

He was still waiting in the glassed-in office. Feiffer asked, "And the court order to open their records?"

"You don't need one. They'll give you access." The Commander said, "They've got them ready. When I told them the names they said—" The Commander said, "They were waiting for the names to be published so they could look them up themselves." He didn't mean some curious typist. The Commander said, "They were waiting, everyone's waiting. The director asked me, in confidence, if they were drunk." The Commander said, "I told him it was too early to know." The Commander said with a bitterness in his voice, "The director told me that, don't worry, they were probably all drunk." The Commander said, "Had to be, no other explanation. Probably find from their history of traffic violations that they'd all had three hundred drunk-driving convictions. Or, if not that, drugs. Heroin. Coke. He asked me if marijuana would do that to you. I told him I didn't know." The Commander said, "People are talking about it, Harry. The director said we'd probably find they all had horrible credit ratings, were probably all petty criminals, were out on a bank-robbery job or—" The Commander said, "He punched up the Laus' history while he was talking to me." The Commander said tightly, "Must have been one of the others." The Commander said, "He'll give you full access to the records."

"Okay."

The Commander said, "You'll find nothing." The Commander said awkwardly, "You'll, ah—" The Commander said, "the clear-up rate for crime in this Colony is about, on average, fifty to fifty-five percent. That's good. That's not bad at all. That's domestic murders and hit-and-run and theft and the odd extortion or mugging or—that's pretty good, that rate; that's something to be proud of." The Commander asked, "Are the relatives still there?"

"No, they've gone."

"And Hansell?"

"He's gone with them. He's got a few uniformed people and he's gone to search the homes."

"Gum, gum . . ." On the phone the Commander said, trying to be light, "That'll be me in thirty years or so: an old, wizened little man trying to talk with his shrunken gums while his false teeth keep falling out on camera." The Commander said, "'Great Mysteries of the World'—I'll be on that in some leafy garden back home, nodding and dribbling and saying—about *this!*—'Ohh, eee, ahh, it were a strange one that; oo, ee, ah, it were summat we never solved with our best lads on it'—maybe, by then, I'll remember a strange blue light in the sky I never saw at the time or birds flying upside down or bloody frogs falling from trees and I'll say as they cart me back to the asylum to the rose beds, 'The truth! The truth! Only I know the real truth about it all.'" The Commander said, "I don't know!" The Commander said, "People are telephoning me, they're telephoning my wife!" The Commander said, "People are—"

"I'm doing what I can, Neal."

"There isn't anything to do! I've been thinking about it nonstop and there isn't anything to do. Those people—the dead people—aren't people who should be dead! The relatives, according to you—" The Commander said, "*What the hell was the second van for?*"

"I don't know."

"They must have said something! If it was suicide, they must have at least hinted to their children—"

"They talked to the van-hire man about business. They talked about the weather. They made conversation. They drove off and Mrs. Lau smiled at him. At the glass factory they ordered the glass, they oversaw it being loaded, they gave out checks in the names of Tin and Hang and then they went away."

"Where? Where did they go away to?"

"I have absolutely no idea."

"You say they didn't even know each other! Where the hell did they all meet to drive to the freeway?" The Commander said, "The second van, did it have a cassette player in it?"

"It had a second, identical cassette of a Mandarin opera loaded into it."

"*Why?*"

"I don't know!"

"Did the lights—did the lights on the van that hit actually work? Has anyone checked that? Has Hansell? Has Hansell actually thought to check that maybe the lights just didn't go out and they—"

Feiffer said, "The lights were out a long time. The two traffic cops on the freeway—" Feiffer said quickly, "Hansell checked. The lights would have been okay."

"Fingerprints?"

"No."

"Six miles! They traveled six miles down the freeway on the wrong side—into oncoming traffic—and they—" The Commander said, "There must be something! There must be something that doesn't tally, something that—something rational!"

"Tell me what it is."

"I don't know what it is! I just—" All morning, his phone had not stopped ringing. The Commander said, "I just—" The Commander said, "If I wasn't a cop, if I wasn't used to all this—"

There was a silence. The relatives had gone. From the glassed-in office he had watched them go. He had seen how they were. Briefly, as he turned, he had seen the Laus' son's face. He had seen—

The Commander said, sounding like all his own phone calls, "What the hell happened? What the hell happened out there if they weren't drunk or doped or mad or—" The Commander said desperately, "They were all just ordinary people! Where the hell did they surface from? Where the hell did they—" The Commander said, "Harry, I even called Special Branch to see if they were political! They're unknowns, they're people you see on the street, they're—" The Commander asked, "What about the truck driver?"

"He doesn't remember anything."

"The traffic cops?"

"No."

"Hansell?"

"I don't know what else he can do. He found the gun and he's gone with the relatives to—"

"All he'll find in their houses are the same bloody things you could find in any house anywhere in the Colony!" The Commander said, "I know it! I can sense it! I can sense that—" The Commander said, "The world isn't built this way! The world is built logically, rationally, explainably—people like them don't do things like this!" The Commander said, "Like what? What is this? We don't even know what it's called!"

"What happened to the Lau woman is called murder."

"Really? A hundredth of a second before she was torn to pieces by something else? Why? What difference would it make—a gun isn't any quicker than being sliced to shreds—why? Why did it all happen?"

"Neal, I—"

"Find out." On the phone the Commander said tightly, "Find out. I don't care what it takes, but find out. I don't care if it takes you the rest of your fucking life; I don't care if it takes the rest of my fucking life, *find out!*"

"I'm trying to! I've got nothing to work on!"

"Then find something! Find anything! Find something and then something else, but, at the end, in the—" All morning, there had been the calls. After he had had his secretary hold them, before and after he had called the credit people and Special Branch, there had been the silence. In that silence— The Commander said formally, "Harry, four people are dead." The Commander said, "Four people are—" He stopped. In his office, in the silence, he closed his eyes and wondered.

In the glassed-in office, he could see the blackboard with all the crosses and marks drawn in on it in chalk. Macarthur had gone. The corridor outside the viewing room was empty. There was no sound. There was only silence. Feiffer said softly, gently, "Neal . . ."

"For the love of God, Harry! *I'm sixty-two years old!*" It meant something. He had no idea what, but that meant something. The Commander, pleading, said, "Harry . . ."

The Commander said as an order, "Harry, whatever it takes—whatever—*find out what in the name of hell happened on that freeway last night!*"

# 8

In Peripheral Street, Spencer said earnestly, "He likes you, Phil! Look, he's nuzzling up against you! He wants to be your friend!"

He had all the friends he could take. He was at the trunk of the car looking for his Remington .17–caliber countersniper rifle. When he had his .17 Remington sniper rifle he was going to put a Remington .17–caliber twenty-five-grain Power-Lokt bullet traveling at over four thousand feet a second into the Dalmatian, blow him three ways to kingdom come, pack the bits up in butcher's bags, deposit them on the nearest dump, receive Mr. Wah's accolades, admiration and maybe something to restore his sagging virility, and then he was going to go home. At the trunk, Auden, shaking his head, said, "I don't care."

"He's a good dog! He only needs a chance!"

He was a rotten dog. He needed to be taken to the vet and put to sleep. The dog nuzzled up against him and put its nose against his leg. He was trying to make friends. He was trying to drool all over Auden's pants. Auden said to the dog, "Go away." He found his Uzi sub–

machine gun in the trunk. He looked down the street. Too many people. He looked for the Remington. He found a tear-gas gun.

"It wasn't his fault the door handles got stuck! He was ready! The door handles got stuck because he was so ready to go he jammed the door handles in his enthusiasm!" Spencer, starting to plead, tugged at his coat. The dog drooled on his pants. Auden said politely to both of them, "Let go of my clothes, please."

"GIVE HIM A CHANCE!"

"HE'S HAD HIS CHANCE!"

"Give him one tiny chance! Please, give this poor creature the same benefit of the doubt you'd give a useless cur lying in the gutter! Is that so much to ask?"

He *was* a useless cur lying in the gutter. The pants-drooling trick must have been too much for his delicate nervous system; the dog had sat down in the street with its head on its paws. He found a good, big nightstick one of the uniformed men must have left in the trunk. It was oak. Auden slapped it in his hand. It was good oak. He put it near the Uzi and the tear-gas gun.

Auden said, "I'm going down to the Armory at Headquarters and get my Remington. I put it in to Emery for repair and I forgot to pick it up." Auden said, "It's a good gun, the Remington. It's got a good, strong bolt-action that never fails and it's precision-made, lock, stock and barrel, and when you put it up to your shoulder—"

"WHAT THE HELL DO YOU EXPECT FROM A DOG WHO BELONGS TO THE KINDEST, GENTLEST, MOST LOVING WOMAN ON EARTH?" There were people stopping to listen. He didn't care. "THE HOUND OF THE BASKERVILLES?" Spencer, this time not tugging, but wrenching at his clothing, said, "HE'S A CHIHUAHUA IN AN ALSATIAN SUIT! HOW DO YOU THINK HE FEELS?"

He didn't care. Auden, thinking of his good, strong, reliable old Remington, old Kill-Deer, said smiling, "Beats me."

"HAVE YOU NEVER ONCE FAILED? Have you never once lain in your bed alone at night in the darkest hours knowing you were unworthy? Have you never—once—been sick at heart because—"

No. He hadn't. He looked at the dog. The dog looked up at him. Auden said, "Bill, the dog is no good."

"IT IS GOOD! IT'S A GOOD DOG!" Spencer, flinging his arms about, appealing to the crowd, said at the bar of the Old Bailey, "For God's sake, take pity on this poor creature!"

The crowd didn't speak a word of English.

The dog made a whimpering noise.

Spencer said, "Her father, Phil—her father has got his own private shooting range and I only have to ask him and—" He saw Auden's face. Auden's face was stone. Spencer said, "Pistols! Rifles! Kalashnikovs, Ingrams—he's even got a few rocket launchers and—"

"No." He was a man of principle. Auden said, "No." Someone in the crowd said in a whisper, "*Kalashnikov?*" He made a panting sound. He was about to say, "*Roc-ket launcher . . . ?*" He saw Auden's face and said nothing.

"*Don't you have any compassion at all?*"

Auden said, "No." He closed the trunk and looked not at all at the dog.

"At school, didn't you—"

Auden said, "I didn't go to school." He pulled at the door to the car. It was locked. Auden said, "Give me the car keys."

"Everyone went to school!"

"I didn't." He waited for the keys.

"Well, I went to school—"

Auden said, "That's right. So you did. That must have been why I didn't. They thought you were going to get enough love and light and forgiveness and joy for two so they didn't think there was any point teaching me anything so I just went down the mines at nine months and I stayed there digging out coal to keep you warm while you sat at your desk learning all the things they thought I didn't need to know." Auden said, "Give me the keys."

"I was bullied at school! In my first year at boarding school, the bigger boys bullied me and humiliated me and turned me into a terrific little wretch afraid of his own shadow!"

Auden said, "Give me the keys."

"Look at me now!"

Auden said, "Give me the keys."

"I was the victim of bullies. I was the victim of cowards who pretended they were brave because they were bigger than me! Boys without understanding or charity or compassion!" The public reading of *Tom Brown's Schooldays* had the crowd very interested. He could tell by the way they kept looking at each other and shaking their heads. Spencer said, "The head bully was a big, rough-featured fellow . . . a little like you."

"Give me the keys, Bill."

"Give this poor dog a chance!"

"Give me the bloody keys!"

"One shot! Just one shot at it!"

*"Give me the keys or I'll tear your bloody head off where you stand!"*

The crowd said, "Oh."

Spencer said, "Ah!"

The dog made a whimpering sound and started to crawl away.

"If you don't give me the fucking keys I'll take that fucking dog of yours and jam it right down your—"

There must have been someone in the crowd who spoke English. It was the Kalashnikov man. The Kalashnikov man said, *"Language!"*

"Give me the keys . . ."

Spencer said to the crowd, "The bully. The school bully—"

The dog crawled to Spencer and sat down in front of him, groveling.

The crowd said, "Oohh . . ."

"The school—"

"I wasn't the school bully! The school bully where I came from wasn't the school bully—he was the local gorilla who beat the shit out of your father if he didn't pay what he owed the local bookie!" Auden said, "And if he couldn't find your father, he'd beat up your—" He saw the Kalashnikov man start to open his mouth. Auden ordered him, "Shut up! Clear this area!" Auden ordered everyone in Cantonese, "Anyone still loitering here on this street obstructing police in ten seconds is going to find himself breaking up rocks in prison for the rest of his life!" Auden said in English, "I always wanted a dog! I always wanted a dog to tear the gorilla's throat to pieces! I always wanted a dog to rip out his heart! I always wanted a dog—"

He was speaking Cantonese to the retreating crowd. As they looked back over their shoulders, Spencer said to assure them, "He's a good man. He just sometimes gets weary of all the evil and corruption he has to go through on your behalf to keep the streets safe for your children."

He looked down at the dog. The dog had big, liquid brown eyes. Auden said softly, "I always wanted a dog to be my friend."

"A puppy?"

"Yes." He looked at the dog. The dog's eyes brightened. It was a good nuzzler. It wasn't much good for anything else but it was a good nuzzler.

"A puppy wouldn't have been much good against someone like—"

Auden said, "I would have taught it."

"You must have read a lot about dogs." Spencer, touching at his coat, his friend, said, "To even contemplate—"

"I did. I read everything there was to read about dogs, about—"

The dog got up and watched him. It was a fine dog with good muscle development. Well, it would have been; it was a German shepherd.

Spencer said, "What sort of dog did you want, Phil?"

Lovely natures, shepherds. Loyal, true. A shepherd would run over broken glass, fight eight men and slaughter them for you and then, bleeding from terrible fatal wounds, crawl with its last breath to get to you so it could die in your lap and— The dog came over. It tried a little nuzzle. It found Auden's hand. It tried a little lick. It liked the salt.

Auden said, shrugging, "I don't know; some sort of dog—"

Spencer said softly, "I worry sometimes about Savannah. I worry sometimes when she's alone that if something awful happened, that Petal might not—"

"A dog has to be trained."

Spencer said, "Right."

Being licked wasn't so bad. At least it kept the dribble off your pants. He tried a pat. He got a wag.

Spencer said, "Phil, her father shouldn't really have them, but in the range, in a cupboard, there's an actual—" He dropped his voice, "—there's an actual—there's an actual—" He dropped his voice so low it was no longer a voice, it was a whisper. "There's an actual, mint condition, unfired, camel-saddle mounted .58–caliber *Gatling* gun and three hundred rounds that he said I could—"

It wasn't a bad licker.

And it liked a pat.

And it—

He wondered why, suddenly, from a long time ago, he felt—

It was a good dog, a warm dog, and it—

"—that he said I could shoot in the range if I wanted to if I was interested in classic weapons and he said I could—"

Odd. For just a moment there, he felt as if—he felt as if, like a child, he was going to cry.

"—use up all the ammo on the house and that—"

Stupid, that. He patted the dog. Auden said softly, "All right." The dog was wagging itself silly. Auden, patting it on the head, said soothingly, "All right, all right . . ."

"—I wasn't to worry about the cost because since I was a friend of his daughter's and any friend of a friend of his daughter's was a friend of his, why I could ask anyone else in who might want to and that would be quite okay and that—"

Auden said, "ALL RIGHT!" What the hell was a Remington rifle? A Remington rifle was just a pipe and a piece of wood and cold, inanimate bits and pieces of machinery that— Auden said to the dog, patting it, "All right."

He felt a warmth through his hand where it lay on the dog's head. The dog's eyes were shining. It wasn't a bad dog. It was wagging itself silly. If you could walk with the animals, talk with the animals . . .

"Dog . . ." It was a small boy's voice that came out. It was a voice the dog liked. It nuzzled. It came under Auden's hand and stayed there, safe.

Peripheral Street, Hong Bay. It was a long way from somewhere else and a long, long time ago. It felt just right.

So did Auden.

Auden, patting the dog, looking down the street for Dalmatians, seeing none, having time, said firmly, "Dog . . ."

His dog looked up at him.

He had waited all his life to say it. He saw Spencer's face.

Auden said with no hesitation, with utter confidence, firmly, finally—wonderfully—"Dog, now, today . . . I am going to teach you how to be *brave* . . ."


"Wait! Wait!" In the Detectives' Room, he had him on the line. He had a book from Auden's collection of Murder Inc.'s private library called *The Handgun* open at page 417 where there was a picture of a dismantled Luger and, for God only knew how little time, he had Chi on the line. There was something about the distortion of the L-shaped sear and how if it was bent only a fraction— On the phone, O'Yee said, "The safety catch. If you can apply that, the gun will be safe." He hoped. O'Yee, trying to follow the picture with his finger, said, trying to keep his voice soothing and calm, "It's not difficult. You know on the back of the gun where I asked you what was written? Well, there's a sort of knob. At the moment the knob's up. If you push down on it with your thumb, the knob will move and you'll see the word *Gesichert*—you'll see a word—you'll see a word in German that means *Safe*." He could hear the boy breathing. His breathing sounded thick and rheumy. O'Yee said, "Put your thumb on the knob and push down on it."

There was a silence. Behind him, behind the public phone box he was calling from, O'Yee could hear nothing, not even traffic. He was calling from a side street somewhere.

O'Yee said, "Can you do it?"

He heard nothing, absolutely nothing at all.

"Can you do it?" O'Yee said, "Chi?" O'Yee said, "Chi, can you do it?"

O'Yee said, "Chi?"

He could hear nothing at all on the line.

O'Yee said, "Chi—can you do it?"

He heard him cough. It was a dry, racking cough. He was down in the phone box working away at the gun. The phone must have been hanging down or on the telephone-book table or—

He heard him cough. He heard him cough painfully and hard. "Chi?"

On the phone, O'Yee said urgently, "Chi—*can you do it?*"


Auden said, "I'm not rough-featured."

Spencer said, "It was just a figure of speech."

Auden said, "Oh." He had found a nice quiet doorway. The doorway had a nice quiet stone step. It was a high step. It made the dog sitting to attention on it taller. It didn't make him as tall as Auden. Auden, squatting down a little—not that much—said staring into the dog's eyes, "Auden." He tapped his chest. Auden said, "Au-den."

Spencer said, "Spencer." He tapped his chest.

Auden said, "Shut up."

The dog wagged its tail.

Auden said, "Don't wag."

It stopped wagging. It had deep brown eyes. It was in good condition. It got brushed a lot. Auden said, "Dog." He patted the dog on the head.

The dog went pant-pant!

Auden said, "Don't pant."

Spencer said—

Auden said, "Shut up." He leaned over and mussed the dog's fur. Auden said, "Dog." Its right ear was stiff and alert and pointing straight up. Auden pushed it down. Auden said, "*Dog.*" Bright, open eyes. He pushed down on the eyebrows and the eyes went narrow.

Auden said, "*Dog!*"

The dog stared at him. It didn't wag. It didn't pant.

Auden said, "*Dog!*" He slapped it hard on the chest muscle.

The dog quivered.

Auden said, "DOG!"

Auden said, "AUDEN!"

He put his face an inch from the dog's eyes with his hand on the chest area where the heart was so he could feel it beating.

"AUDEN! *DOG!*"

Auden said, "DOG!" Auden said, "Real DOG!"

Auden said, "Rrrrhhh . . ." He bared his teeth.

Starting slowly and softly so the dog would catch every nuance, feeling its heart with his hand, his eyes widening, he began, deeply, horribly, to growl . . .


DID YOU SEE THIS VAN?

DID YOU SEE THESE PEOPLE TOGETHER?

HAVE YOU EVER SEEN THIS GUN BEFORE?

On the front page of all the afternoon editions of all the newspapers in Chinese, there were all the photographs. There was a photograph of the second van from the glass factory, complete with the advertising logo for the Prudent Car and Van Hire Company of Icehouse Street, Hong Bay. It was very good publicity. The photograph was sharp. It showed the van with all the background removed, framed like a tinplate-metal child's toy in thin air. The photograph of the gun was also sharp, showing every line and curve of the nickel-plated revolver and the legend H & R 32 S & W on the side of the short shining little barrel.

The photographs of the four dead people had been taken from snapshots with everything below the shoulders airbrushed out so the faces looked like busts on pedestals.

The names of all the dead were printed below the photographs. The names were S. Y. Lau (the first photograph), his wife Susan Lau (the second in the row), G. L. Hang, and at the end of the row, L. K. Tin.

The pictures had been taken from snapshots. They were blurred, amateurish, slightly out of focus.

DID YOU SEE THIS VAN?

DID YOU SEE THESE PEOPLE TOGETHER?

HAVE YOU EVER SEEN THIS GUN BEFORE?

The pictures of the van and gun were fine. They took your attention straight away.

The photographs of the people, blown up five times for the front pages of the newspapers, were useless.

They were blurred, grainy, out of focus, bad.

Looking at them—

Looking at them, they could have been anybody.


"Who is that?" On the line, he heard a man's voice say something. He could still not hear the boy. O'Yee, pressing his ear hard against the receiver to hear it, demanded, "Chi? Who is that?"

The man was speaking Cantonese. He was angry. He was talking quickly, giving orders, running out of patience. The man said roughly in Cantonese, "Come on, get out of it!"

"Chi? Have you done it?" He could hear nothing. O'Yee, shouting, yelled, "Chi, *are you there?*" He could hear nothing. O'Yee ordered him, "Push down hard on the knob! Push the knob down!"

"Get out of it, you filthy little scum!"

O'Yee said, "Who is that?" He heard Chi coughing. The man was outside the phone booth yelling at him.

"You slime! You're the sort of little slimy bastard who vandalizes all the phones!" The man was working himself up. There was a bang as he must have thrown open the phone-box door. The man, filling the door, making the boy scuttle, yelled, "*Sut ne go tao!* I'll cut your filthy head off!" The man shouted, "There are too many people like you! Where I live there are hundreds of people like you ruining the neighborhood!" He was working himself up to violence. He was screaming. The man, starting to breathe hard, his voice coming and going in the phone as O'Yee strained to listen, yelled, "You little bastard! You little bastard! You little—"

"CHI!"

He was coughing, rasping. He was trying to get away in the booth: O'Yee could hear him.

"—CHI!"

There was a thud as the man must have taken a swipe at him or the satchel hit something or—

On the line O'Yee screamed, "*CHI!*"

There was a thud. It was the phone-box door closing. A man's voice on the phone said, "It was some dirty little kid pestering you." The voice, pleasant, talking to an adult, said, "I'll hang up now. He won't bother you again."

"Hello—"

The man said, "It's the least I can do. I get hell from them too." The man made a sniffing sound. He was going to hang up.

"Don't hang up! Don't hang up!" O'Yee said desperately, "This is the police! Don't hang up!" He had a gun in his satchel and he coughed and rasped and there was no way he could be found. O'Yee, talking to air, said pleading, "Please, please don't—"

The line went dead. He had in the receiver in his hand only silence.

He had only the buzzing dial tone.

He had only—

He had nothing.

In the Detectives' Room, slowly and carefully, O'Yee replaced the receiver of the phone and put both his hands flat on his desk.

GESICHERT. It meant *Safe*.

He had no idea whether the boy had had the time or strength to get it.

He had no idea whether, ever, the boy would call again.

"God Almighty . . ." In the Detectives' Room, in a whisper, O'Yee said, "Jesus . . ."

For a long time, silently, unable to think, he sat looking down at his hands.


DID YOU SEE THIS VAN?

DID YOU SEE THESE PEOPLE TOGETHER?

HAVE YOU EVER SEEN THIS GUN BEFORE?

S. Y. Lau, Susan Lau, G. L. Hang, L. K. Tin. All the names of the dead, in series, were laid out below the pictures. It was so, if you didn't know any of the answers to the questions, at least—to the questions—at least . . .

At least, you could wonder . . .


"Kill! *Slaughter!* Attack! *Destroy!* ANNIHILATE!"

In a doorway on the other side of the street there was a man down on his haunches shouting at a dog with another man standing a little behind him giving off smells of worry and anxiety.

"MURDER! DO IN! TEAR! RIP! VIVISECT!"

The voice was hard, hypnotic, tight—it was a voice that got into the Dalmatian's ears and sparked little electrical impulses in its brain, made smells of fire and lava, animals with scaly tails and the sky sulfurous and dark.

"PRIMEVAL *SLIME!* KILL OR . . . BE KILLED!" It was a voice of something deep in the Dalmatian's stomach, in its muscles, in its teeth.

BANG! BANG! BANG! BANG! The Dalmatian, echoing in its brain stem, heard the sound of great trees in ancient dog-land crashing to the earth in showers of meteor dust and boiling mud pools.

It was Mr. Wah nailing up his shop with big nails and two-by-four hardwood planks.

"FIGHT! DEFEND! PROTECT! GNASH—! *SNARL!*"

Great stuff.

It worked.

At the corner of the street, settling down on its stomach, its eyes narrowing, the Dalmatian, mad with blood lust and folk memory, carefully, stealthily, worked out how to find another way into Mr. Wah's cave and, on the way out, just for fun and the blood of it, tear him to pieces with his teeth.

The Dalmatian, deep inside its guts, growled.

"DOG! KILL! MURDER! NO PRISONERS! *MASSACRE!*"

Fine by him.

At the corner of the street, hidden in a doorway, the Dalmatian waited for its chance.

# 9

In the Laus' third-floor apartment on Empress of India Street, Hansell asked, "Anything at the Central Credit Registery?"

Feiffer said, "Nothing." As the computer operator had punched up the histories, the staff at the place from the director down to the people from the businesses on the other floors who had come up, had stood around the screen to see what he had seen. What they had seen was nothing. What they had seen was the minimum history of a man and his wife whose son had grown up and married, had been at the same address for ten years, lived frugally, borrowed little and what they did borrow—for a washing machine, for clothing at stores, for recarpeting—had paid back on time. In the corridor at the apartment block, there were also people waiting. They were the Laus' neighbors. They knew nothing about the Laus except that they were quiet and respectable. Hansell had stationed a uniformed officer to keep them out, but they were not going to come in. The people in the Credit Register, similarly, had not intruded—they knew nothing, they merely wondered. They knew nothing.

The windows in the apartment were all closed tight. Outside the windows there was traffic and the city. The traffic and the city proceeded with no noise on the other side of the glass. Hansell, in the center of the carpeted square living room, tapping his fingers on the back of an armchair of middle cost and quality, said, "I've already been through the Hang place in North Point and Tin's in Yaumati."

"And?"

"And nothing." On a shelf there were framed photographs of the Laus' son and daughter-in-law at their marriage and, around them, two baby photographs of their child. With all the windows closed the room was airless and still. Hansell, in uniform, looking huge in the room, said, "And they were ordinary respectable people who were, respectively, a lens grinder in regular employment on low to middle income and a government parks gardener who didn't drink, was reliable and never missed a day's work." In the corner of the room there was a dining table and four chairs. On the table there was a bamboo place mat with a little porcelain statuette of the goddess of mercy, Kwan Jin. The statuette, in a Chinese arts-and-crafts store, would have cost the equivalent of about three American dollars. It was middle quality, nothing—something to put on a bamboo mat in the center of a table.

Behind the table there was a small cane bookcase and what-not stand. It held a few books and magazines and the Hong Kong and outlying telephone books. Moving past Hansell, Feiffer picked up the telephone. It was clean, dusted, wiped down, with the vague smell of some sort of disinfectant Mrs. Lau must have used in her kitchen. There was nothing. They were ordinary people.

"I've checked the bedroom." It was a door off to the right of the shelf where the photographs were. He opened the door and stood to one side so Feiffer could see. "It's the sort of double bed you buy when your children have grown up and you've got a little spare money—it's got a carved headboard."

"They bought it three years ago on credit." He looked in. All the cupboard doors were open, but if Hansell had gone through every piece of clothing in all the drawers he had put it all back folded neatly again. The window in the room was closed. It was airless like a museum exhibit. The bed had been carefully made. At the window there were curtains Mrs. Lau had sewn. Feiffer said cautiously, "Any—"

Hansell said, "There's a marriage manual from about twenty years ago." It was the most secret thing they had. Hansell said, "It was in a bottom cupboard drawer."

"Letters?"

"In a rack in the kitchenette, there are two circulars advertising grocery sales, a warranty on a vacuum cleaner and a receipt for its repair by a shop in North Point; there's an electricity bill due to be paid at the end of the month; there's a goddamned shopping list, and there's a clipping from a local Chinese newspaper suggesting that the latest medical theory for the home treatment of hemorrhoids is more fiber in your diet; and there's a notebook used to write goddamned shopping lists given away by the local goddamned supermarket!" He touched his face. Hansell said, "The remnants of two married master criminals! Bonny and fucking Clyde—what this is is the apartment of two people out of five million people who live on this island! What this is—"

"There must be something!"

"There isn't! And there wasn't anything in the Tin place or in Hang's! The most evil object in any of these places is the bloody television set!" It was outside in the main room with a program for the English and Chinese services. He picked it up. Hansell said, "All that's marked is one of the long-running soap operas and a thing about managing your money for people planning retirement!" Hansell said, "There are no guns, bombs, knives, porno pictures, snuff movies, ill-gotten gains, jewels, diamonds, gold, heroin, coke, marijuana—" Hansell said, "There isn't even an ashtray in the place because people like that—people being careful with their money—don't smoke!" Hansell said, "And no booze except a bottle of cheap Chinese gin that looks about five years old and seems to have had a total of about five drinks at Chinese New Year poured out of it!" Hansell said, "Professional criminals—people who really are plugged in—hide their stuff under the floor of their toilet because that's the last place burglars will look." He kept shaking his head. Hansell said, "The floor of the toilet is tiled and there's a little air freshener in there, and Mrs. Lau, with the sewing machine she kept in a cupboard under the work surface in the kitchen, ran up a few nice curtains for it." Hansell said, "Best-quality toilet paper. One of them had hemorrhoids!"

"Money?"

"One hundred and fifty Hong Kong dollars in cash in a drawer; fifty Hong Kong dollars in change in a glass bottle in the kitchen; an envelope in the bedroom in a cupboard with the baby granddaughter's name on it containing eight fifty-dollar bills; Mrs. Lau's handbag—her second handbag—containing a coin purse with a total of four-dollars-fifty in coins and, in what must have been Mr. Lau's best wallet, a MasterCard and a one-hundred-dollar note uncreased and unfolded." Hansell said, "All of it, put together, wouldn't give you one good bet at the races!" Hansell said, "Oh, and in the wallet there's a little Chinese love poem that looks like it was cut out of a magazine about twenty years ago." Hansell said, "This from a man who took out a pistol and a moment before he was sliced to goddamned hamburger shot his wife squarely in the back of the head!" Hansell said hopelessly, "Harry, they're just like the other two, Hang and Tin—they're ordinary, they're nobodies, they're *nothing*!"

They were people who had suddenly, instantly, stopped. With them, their world had ceased and only the artifacts of it were left. In the apartment everything was neat as it would have been after an evening meal before the bed was turned down for the night. It was a glass bowl with the traffic and the city going by it outside and making no sound at all. It was a burial room in a pyramid, somewhere deep and silent and untouched.

"There's no note or . . . ?"

"Do you mean, like a suicide note?"

Feiffer said, "Is there?"

"No."

"The neighbors—"

"Did you see them?"

"Yes."

"And?"

Feiffer said, "Yes."

"Nice people." Hansell said, "All nice people. The sort of people you—" Hansell said desperately, "Harry, these are the sort of people who don't do things, these are the sort of people who react to what's done! In the West, these people would have been sleeping the great suburban sleep! Mr. Lau was a good, honest man who brought up his child, saw his granddaughter born, was saving a few dollars for a gift for her, loved his wife, probably hardly ever went out, bought things on credit and the wife ran up goddamned curtains on her sewing machine for God's sake!" Hansell said, "*And now they're fucking dead and nobody knows why!*"

"What about a diary?"

"The rack in the kitchen is the diary! It says, 'Pick up vacuum cleaner when fixed,' 'Pay electricity bill when due,' 'Try to save money on groceries at new supermarket,' 'try more fiber for hemorrhoids'—it says, 'Go on living as if nothing will ever happen to disturb you!'"

"Keith—"

"I don't know, Harry, I just don't know." He glanced into the open bedroom and at the photographs of the family on the shelf. "I don't know, Harry, I just—" Hansell said, "The other two were the same."

"Lau was what? A marine electrical contractor?"

"He was an electrician who worked for a marine electrical contractor." Hansell said with a shrug, "He was an employee of one of the people you saw out in the corridor." He said before Feiffer could say anything, "Forget it. He was a good, honest employee who kept to himself, was always unfailingly willing and polite, never argued, always did a good, sound job, could be trusted to work alone and here, in his home, always smiled at the neighbors, helped with the trash, never made too much noise, kept to himself and—altogether—was just the sort of person you'd like living next to you and working for you if you didn't want any problems!" Hansell said, "Ditto Hang. Tin, the gardener—well, according to his neighbors, you wouldn't even know he was alive." Hansell said, "He isn't and everyone is very surprised about that." Hansell said bitterly, "The local apartment sage at Hang's told me in great confidence that an old piece of Chinese wisdom that explains it all is that *You can never tell about the quiet ones.*"

Through the closed window he could see the city. Between two high-rise office blocks, if you craned a little, you could see the harbor and, beyond that, the sea. Like the traffic and the city itself, with the windows shut, the sea was silent. There was a cloud coming in from the south, high cumulus with a darkening center that looked like rain. With his hand lightly on the pane, Feiffer tapped at the glass. It was solid, keeping everything out.

"Harry—"

Feiffer said, "What?" *He had no idea at all what had happened.*

Hansell said, "Harry, I—"

It was the *Mary Celeste.* It was sailing silently, airlessly, abandoned, dead, with nobody in it at all left to say what had happened. The apartment was a ship's cabin. It was a ghost ship, gone, uninhabited, silent in an instant with all its secrets lost forever. It was hopeless. No one would ever know.

"Harry . . ."

At the window, Feiffer turned to see his face.

"Harry—" He was looking at the photographs on the shelf. He was not looking at the photographs on the shelf. He touched at his face. All day, he had been looking. He had been looking for something he had not found.

It was something lost. It was on his face. Outside in the corridor all the neighbors and people from other floors in the apartment block had come to wait and listen.

"One more time, Harry." He nodded. It was what he wanted to do. "One more time."

There was something in there lost to him. There was something inside him he could not find.

Hansell said, asking, "Okay? One more time. Together. One more time. We'll go through the entire place one more time." He was pleading, asking. He saw Feiffer nod. Hansell said, "Right!" Hansell said, deciding, "*Right!*"

Hansell said, "This time, you take the bedroom."

On the phone O'Yee said urgently, "Detectives' Room, Detective Senior Inspector O'Yee speaking."

There was a sound at the other end of the line, not so much a voice as a linguistic slobber.

The slobberer, drawing in a breath, said in heavily Northern Chinese–accented English, reading it, "*Vampire Hookers*. Robert E. Waters presents a COSA NUEVA PRODUCTION starring John Carradine, Bruce Fairburn, Karen Stride. Directed by CIRIO H. SANTIAGO. Assistant Director Leo Martinez. Postproduction Supervisor Emmett R. Alstron. SCREENPLAY by HOWARD CO-HEN. MUSIC by Jaime Mendoza! Nueva Liaison Producer Jerome J. Zanitsch! '. . . WARM BLOOD ISN'T ALL THEY SUCK!'" He waited.

O'Yee said, "Yukkk!"

The slobberer said, "Aa-aahh . . ."

He sniggered.

He giggled.

He gloated.

It was the right answer.

He seemed happy.

He hung up.

People passing thought it was a street magician, the street magician's dog and the street magician's dog handler.

Or maybe a pavement artist, the pavement artist's audience and a dog.

No, the audience was holding the dog on a leash, the pavement artist wasn't painting and if he was, he wasn't using paint on the

pavement, he was dripping sump oil (SAE–30) from a car dipstick
onto the white back of a round cardboard sign (STOP! POLICE!).

It was a lunatic and a blind man holding his dog and wondering
what the hell was going on.

No, the blind man wasn't wearing dark glasses.

People wondered what the hell was going on.

The dog was slavering with blood lust, coiled, pulling at the leash.
People didn't stop to find out what the hell was going on. They
crossed over to the other side of the street.

On the pavement, kneeling down with his dripping dipstick,
Auden said with a wink to Spencer, "Psychology. Rorschach inkblot
test? Conditioned dog reflexes—same thing!" He stood up with the
oily, blotted sign. He held it up in front of him and it was a Dalmatian
pattern. Auden said, "Heh, heh." He could tell Spencer was
impressed. Auden, patting the dog with his free hand and turning the
sign away from him, said, "Good dog. Beautiful dog. Loyal and true
dog."

The dog stopped slavering and made a happy panting sound.

Auden said, "Hmmm . . ." The dog looked worried. He turned
the sign around from STOP! POLICE! to Dalmatian sump-oil
pattern. Auden said, "Hmmm, dog—" He sounded dubious.

The dog loved that man. The dog made a sort of whimpering noise
and looked up at Spencer. Spencer bent down to pat the poor thing.

*"Don't pat the dog!"*

STOP! POLICE! Auden said, "Good dog."

The dog didn't purr. Cats purred, not dogs. The dog tried to purr.

Sump-oil Dalmatian side. Auden, holding the coat of many sump
oils up to hide his face, said suddenly, *"Bad!"*

The dog cringed.

Auden leaned his hand around from behind the sign and hit the dog
on the muzzle.

The dog went, "Yiii!"

"BAD!" Hit.

The dog went, "Yii!"

Auden said, "KILL! SLAUGHTER! HATE!"

The dog snapped.

Spencer said, "Steady, Phil—"

Auden—behind the sign—still showing the Dalmatian pattern,
said, "Shut up!"

The dog turned to bite Spencer.

STOP! POLICE! Auden said in his softest voice, "Friend."

The dog didn't bite Spencer.

Sump oil. Auden said, "YAHHH!"

The dog said, "Yiii!" It saw the hand coming out from behind the Dalmatian oil. The hand cracked it over the head. The dog said, "Yip!" It decided to bite Spencer.

"Friend." STOP! POLICE! No bite.

"Face of dog's-best-friend Auden. Face of friend Auden smile. Hand of friend Auden pat." Auden said from the side of the STOP! POLICE! sign, "Auden friend." He was the sort of fellow a dog could trust—no speak with forked tongue. Auden, patting, said, "HURT!" He turned the sign over to show the Dalmatian oil.

Snap! The dog tried to take a bite.

"BAD!"

The dog, confused, said, "Yip?"

"Not you! You good dog! THIS!" He had the sign out showing the Dalmatian pattern. He threw it on the ground. Auden said, "Grrrr!"

The dog said, "Snap!"

"GRRRR!"

The dog said, "Snarl!"

"GRRR—AHHHHHH!"

"SNARL! SNAP! BITE! CHOMP! MUTILATE!" All dog noises. The dog, standing tall, grabbing the edge of the sign, made a sound from deep inside its stomach that sounded like a chain saw starting to warm up.

Auden said, "BAD!" The dog knew what he meant. Auden, taking the sign in both hands and shoving its edge in the dog's mouth, said, "YAAHHH!" He began ripping it apart.

The dog began ripping it apart.

Auden tore at it.

The dog bit a chunk out of it and went for another chunk.

Simple souls, dogs.

Rip!

Tear!

Mangle!

Yank! Jerk! Pull!

Mush!

Confetti!

A very strong smell of sump oil.

Auden and the dog, together, in unison, pals, buddies, two minds with but a single thought, as Spencer strained to hold the dog back a little on the leash so the raging beast couldn't get loose and turn all of Peripheral Street that even vaguely resembled a Dalmatian dog to shreds, they, piece by piece, laughing as they did—without an iota of pity between them—tore the sign to bits.

At the end of Peripheral Street, the Dalmatian, its head just poking around the corner, tried to see whether the way was clear.

It couldn't see anything for people milling around a safe distance away watching a man and a dog excavating the street so they could bury a bone.

It must have been a big bone. They were fighting hard to see who got it.

The Dalmatian craned its head a little farther around the corner and sniffed long and hard.

In its brain a little electrical synapse sparked a memory.

Mr. Wah's shop was boarded up.

The Dalmatian sniffed.

The man and the dog were battling hard. No one was winning. That was the way things often were in the old cave and dinosaur and great-dog days.

The dog sniffed hard.

Its synapses sparked a little, simple plan. Withdrawing behind the corner again, the Dalmatian, moving quickly and silently, went around to the back lane behind Mr. Wah's to find, maybe, a little air duct Mr. Wah might have forgotten to board up.

On the phone O'Yee said to his wife, "Emily?"

Emily O'Yee said, "Hello, Christopher. Quiet day?"

"Yes." It was a little after four o'clock, long after all the schools had finished for the day. O'Yee said pleasantly, "Hi."

"Hi yourself." Emily O'Yee said, "It's nice of you to call during the day. Is anything wrong?"

He was using Auden's phone. He looked at his own on the desk by the opened schematic of the Luger in Auden's book. O'Yee said, "How are the kids?"

"The kids are fine." Emily O'Yee said pleasantly, "How are you?"

"I'm fine too."

"Good." Emily O'Yee said, "This is a truly fascinating conversation. Are you sure you've got the right number?"

"Are the kids home?"

"Of course they're—"

"Are they all right?"

"Of course they're—" Emily said, suddenly anxious, "Christopher, what's the matter?"

"There's nothing the matter! *Can't a man call his own home to see how his children are without being asked what's the matter?*"

Emily O'Yee said, "Christopher, what's the matter?"

There was a slience. On the desk, his phone was silent and dead.

"Christopher—?"

On the phone, waiting, worried, Emily O'Yee said softly, patiently, "Christopher, has something happened . . . ?"

In the street Professor Auden said, "It's ready." Today Peripheral Street and the Dalmatian, tomorrow the world. He looked down at the snarling, snapping beast tugging at Spencer's leash. He was Auden's to command. He commanded. Auden said, "Shhh," and the dog, instantly, shhhed.

Auden said, "He's a killer. I have created him in my own image." It was a shot at nuns. The nun freak didn't even notice. Auden said, "He won't hurt you unless I tell him to." Better than people, dogs. Give them a simple task and they do it without a murmur.

The simple task he had in mind was a little sinew-tearing, ligament-ripping, viscera-eviscerating Dalmatian murder in the middle of the street.

He had a simple command.

The simple command was, "KILL!"

He stood back with his hands on his hips looking down at Conan the Destroyer and awaited only a Dalmatian with sinews, ligaments and viscera to put it all into operation.

Auden, happy, said, "Good."

He patted the dog.

The dog didn't wag or pant. It snarled.

It was the sort of dog that would take your hand off at the wrist and smile while it did it.

Auden said, "Good dog."

The dog couldn't have cared less.

Auden said to Spencer, "Good dog that." He was pleased.

He didn't try to pat the dog.

No air ducts. At the back of Mr. Wah's shop, instead, the Dalmatian found, almost as if it were waiting there for it, a nice, half-open window to the upper floor and, just within leaping distance, a nice, rust-smelling fire-escape ladder with a broken mechanism that just happened to be within jumping distance of the half-open window and, coming from that half-open window—just faintly—a nice, warm smell of—

It reflected on its luck.

In the lane, gauging the distance perfectly, the Dalmatian made it to the first rung of the fire-escape ladder in a single, silent leap.

In the Detectives' Room, as he waited, there was no sound at all except the single electric click of the wall clock as it moved another, a single extra minute.

He waited.

By the phone, with the picture of the awful, huge gun laid out open on the desk in front of him, O'Yee waited.

He waited.

He waited.

As the clock moved, he waited through all the minutes.

There was nothing.

All he could do was wait.

In the Laus' apartment, there was nothing. There was nothing at all.

In the Laus' apartment, with the windows all closed, there was no air and the rooms were still and deserted like the cabins of an abandoned ship.

They were, like Hang and Tin, good, decent, ordinary people. They were nothing exceptional.

Exceptionally, on a road at night in a storm of glass they were all dead.

They were good, decent, unnoticable, ordinary people going about their business, making plans.

Small dreams—it was what they had had, all of them.

In all of their homes, among all of their possessions, in everything they seemed to have done, there was nothing. Everything they had was merely a component part of what they were: what they had always been.

There was nothing.

There was nothing in any of the places where they lived to show what, suddenly, for no reason at all, in an instant, they had become.

*There was nothing.*

He searched. As he looked, Feiffer could not read the look on Hansell's face at all.

# 10

It was him.

On the phone O'Yee said urgently, "Did you do it? Could you get the lever down on the gun?"

"No." There was a pause and then Chi said brightly, "There was a button on the handle of the gun—" it was the button that released the magazine—Chi said, "It was stuck."

It wouldn't have done any good. It was only in movies that people shucking the magazine out of an automatic pistol thought it was then unloaded. It was the round in the chamber that killed you and that didn't come out with the magazine. O'Yee said, "Are you hurt? Did the man in the phone booth hit you?"

There was a silence.

O'Yee said, "Did he see the gun?"

Chi said, "No." He sounded pleased.

"Did he hit you?"

Chi said, "I tried very hard, but I couldn't move the button or the lever."

"Have you got anybody to help you?"

Chi said, "No."

**107**

"Bring the gun in, Chi. Bring the gun in to me and I can fix it."

Chi said, "No." He was afraid.

O'Yee said, "Nothing will happen to you." O'Yee said, "I've got children too. I know how things are. Nothing will happen to you." Somewhere out there there was a dead man. O'Yee, trying hard, dropping his voice said—

"I can't, mister."

He was about to say, "Call me Christopher." The boy was ten years old. O'Yee said quietly, "Why not?"

There was a silence.

"How old are you?"

Chi said, "I'm ten—or eleven."

"Have you got a mother and father, Chi?"

Chi said, "Yes." Chi said, "Everybody's got a mother and a father."

"I haven't. My father died."

There was another silence. In the background O'Yee could hear traffic, muted. He was calling from a side street somewhere. He was not coughing. He was calling from somewhere safe.

"How old are you?"

Chi said, "Ten."

O'Yee said easily, "Where's the man who was shot? Do you know the address?"

Nothing.

It would have been easy to let go. If he had let go, the boy would stay on the line. O'Yee said tightly, "Do you go to school?"

"Everybody goes to school."

"Which school?"

Chi said, "That's a secret."

"What class are you in?"

There was no reply.

O'Yee said, "Tell me, what's twelve squared?"

There was a silence. Outside the phone booth, the man had taken one look at the boy, pulled the door open, clipped him around the ear and thrown him out. The man had not hung on; had not wanted to know who the boy was speaking to, had not believed he was speaking to anyone at all. O'Yee said, risking it, "Twelve multiplied by twelve is twelve squared. What's twelve multiplied by twelve?"

"I don't know."

"My children did at age ten." O'Yee said, "Eight multiplied by eight?"

He heard the boy hesitate.

"Six times six?"

Chi said, "Thirty-six!"

O'Yee said, "My children knew that when they were eight." O'Yee said, "Seven times eight?"

Nothing.

O'Yee said, "It's fifty-six." O'Yee said, "Seven times three?"

Chi said, "Um—"

"It's the same as three times seven."

"Twenty-one!"

He said nothing at all.

Chi said, "Mister, are you still there?"

In the Detectives' Room O'Yee said nothing at all.

"Mister—? Mister?"

"What class are you in at school, Chi?"

Chi said, "I'm in school!"

"Do you have anyone? Do you have a mother and father?"

"Everyone has a mother and father!"

O'Yee said, "You don't. I don't either. I'm like you. I'm alone." O'Yee said gently, "Man to man; like me, you don't have anyone."

Chi said, "They died."

"Do you have anyone at all? An uncle? Aunt? Grandparents?"

He sounded a long way off. Chi said, "Um—" Chi said, "Do you?"

"No. Are you afraid?"

Chi said, "Yes."

He knew not who he was, but what. In the Detectives' Room, his mouth twisted in concentration, O'Yee said gently, "Were you sad when you had to leave school when you were eight?"

Chi said softly, "*Yes.*"

"Are you crying?"

Chi said, "I never cry!"

O'Yee said, "I do, sometimes."

"When?"

O'Yee said, "Sometimes, when I feel helpless." O'Yee said softly, "Did he hit you—the man in the call box?"

"Yes." Chi said abruptly, maybe not caring, "I get hit a lot because I'm in the way or I—"

"Did your mother and father die?"

Chi said, "Yes."

The school satchel he carried was from a long time ago. In it, he probably carried all he owned. He had no one, nothing. All the time he was afraid. He had nothing. He had the gun. O'Yee said in a whisper, "Chi—?"

# 110 · WILLIAM MARSHALL

He was crying. He could hear it. He was sobbing. At the other end of the line Chi said brokenly, "Mister, I—"

"Chi—?"

"Yes?"

O'Yee said tightly, evenly, willing him to stay on the line after he asked it, "Chi, *are you a sleeper?*"


He was a trained diagnostician. In his shop Mr. Wah, packing up all his goods on his counter for an inventory, diagnosed without any trouble at all that, any second now, the dog was going to leap over the counter and kill him. He was going to die, gnashed to pieces. He was amazed how calmly he was taking all this, but that was the way you got after a brief spell in heaven the first time you were killed and after a lifetime of people's ailments and maybe just after a long life and . . . well, you got philosophical.

The dog was at the bottom of his stairs, looking up. The dog at the bottom of the stairs was making low growling noises. It had eyes like coals. Philosophical was probably best.

Mr. Wah, his hands glued to the counter, tried a little smile. Dogs reacted to smiles. This one didn't or maybe the look he made wasn't a smile. It didn't feel like a smile. Mr. Wah said to the dog, "Good afternoon." The door to his shop was boarded up from the inside. The dog looked like it was looking into a cave full of dinosaurs and wondering which one to tear apart. It made those sort of noises. Polite was good. Mr. Wah, rubbing his hands together—he thought he did, they didn't quite make it and stayed up in the air in front of him in an attitude of prayer—said, "And what can I do for you this fine afternoon?" Mr. Wah said, "Ha, ha." Maybe it wasn't a Cantonese dog. Mr. Wah said in English, "Hmm?"

The dog had eyes like embers. Did dogs have pupils? This one didn't. This one had a bonfire burning on a hill to shed a little light onto the Dark Ages. They must have been very dark ages—the light in its eyes kept throbbing and enlarging and then going back to pinpricks and then throbbing again.

Mr. Wah said in a small voice, "Hello? Are you there?" It was his soul. His soul was thinking about leaving his body. His soul, halfway to heaven, looked around for the chain-smoking monk. His soul said politely, rubbing its hands together, "I think Mr. Wah on Earth could do with a little intercession—Hello? Are you there?"

He wasn't. On Earth, in his shop, Mr. Wah said in a whisper, "Oh, shit."

Mr. Wah said to the dog grinning (the dog, not Mr. Wah. Mr. Wah was still trying to smile), "Well, doggie, you took my wind bells last time and that other little doggie couldn't catch you and—" Mr. Wah said not through his mouth but somewhere through his nasal passages, "Oh, *shit!*—and now, and now—" Mr. Wah said, "Ha, ha. Well, I suppose you've come back for something else to steal from me." Mr. Wah said, chortling (it didn't really sound like a chortle, but it was the best he could do for Christ's sake!), "Well, well, well . . ." Dogs will be dogs. In front of him on the counter there was a pile of boxes, bottles, phials, twists, jars, packages and more bottles, all labeled. Mr. Wah said, "Now, I wonder what ails you and what I could give you—free of charge—to make you feel better?" From heaven, when he was properly dead, he was going to make the two cops out in the street suffer the way no one in history had ever suffered before. Mr. Wah said, "We've got things for—oh—just about everything that could ail you." He smiled. He wished he had a .44 magnum. A .44 magnum would be good. He glanced at his hands. Empty. No monkly intercession. A .22 would be okay. Mr. Wah said, "Oh, Chinese traditional medicine goes back such a long way. We've had remedies for things for a thousand years the West is only just starting to appreciate now." Take acupuncture. Take a bullet between the eyes. Mr. Wah said, touching—very slowly—at one of the packets, "Dessicated sea horses for liver complaints."

The dog tensed. It coiled. It set itself like a spring. It had a great liver.

Forget the sea horses. He thought he was wetting himself. Mr. Wah, touching at a twist, said, "Manchurian ginseng—the best— great for long life and virility." He was out of strychnine, arsenic and cyanide. Mr. Wah said, "Bottles of black squid ink—for the heart."

He saw the dog's eyes flicker to whatever was behind him on the wall. There was nothing behind him on the wall. Behind him on the wall was a list of the properties of ash-burned lotus flowers. The qualities were mainly contraceptive.

Mr. Wah said, "Sign. Just a sign." Mr. Wah, starting to gabble, said, "It's funny, isn't it, how we progress? Thousands of years ago, people would have looked at a sign, at writing, at a drawing, and somehow attributed the properties of whatever the words or the pictures were about to the sign itself. Totemism." Mr. Wah said encouragingly, "Like killing for fun, we've gone past that." Mr. Wah said, "Haven't we?" He wondered where his soul was. Mr. Wah said in his nasal passage to his soul, "Do something!" His soul had fled. Mr. Wah said to the dog, "Now, I wonder why you have this funny urge to rob my shop . . . ?" The dog's eyes were going throb, pulse, flicker. The dog was also making sounds in its nasal passages. They weren't the same sounds. Mr. Wah said, "I'd appreciate it if you didn't kill me." The direct approach.

It wasn't the eyes that were throbbing. All they were was a reflection. In the dog's olfactory mucus, the little sparks and smells were ticking, aching, making something inside its head twitch. It was the smell of something. It was in one of the bottles or the packets or the phials. It was there. It magnetized the dog. It made its eyes throb with longing.

He'd never owned a dog. He'd heard they wanted to get out a lot. Fine by him. Mr. Wah, starting to move behind the counter, said, "Good dog, I'll let you out now." There was something dimly remembered that when a dog went out you had to wind a clock. All he had was his quartz wristwatch. Mr. Wah, moving toward the door, tapping at his watch, said, doggishly, "Hmm, well, well, time to get out."

The dog took a single step.

Mr. Wah didn't.

His soul was up there having a good yak to the monk and puffing on celestial cigarettes. His soul had never been any good. If he got through this he was going to make his soul suffer. Mr. Wah, standing stock still, said politely, "The door's been boarded up." Mr. Wah said, "Ha, ha, how silly of me. But all I have to do is undo a couple of wing nuts and—why!—the whole door will just open and you can—" Mr. Wah said, "Don't look at the crushed dinosaur dust!"

It smelled it. It was from mountains and lava and burning trees and—

Mr. Wah said, "That dust cost me two thousand dollars an ounce! There's ten grand's worth of crushed white dinosaur dust in that bottle! It's for millionaires' bones." He saw the dog's eyes pulse. Mr. Wah ordered it, "Take the squid ink! Forget the dust!" He wasn't going to go to heaven ruined. Mr. Wah, taking two steps back to the counter and reaching for the bottle, said, "Forget the dust. That stuff came from the Urals and a lot of people smuggle it in at great personal risk and I—" His soul came back. No luck with the monk. His soul said, "Give it the dust." It was a no-good soul.

Mr. Wah said to the dog, "Even think about going for the dust and you'll have me to contend with!" Mr. Wah, putting both his hands on the bottle and pulling it to his chest, said warningly, "I've got a .44 that I'll use if you—"

"*Give it the dust!*" Maybe things weren't that hot in heaven this week. Mr. Wah's soul said, "Give it the dust and live!"

"I'd rather die!"

The dog said softly, from somewhere deep in its stomach, "Arggg—grrrr. . . ."

"Give it the dust!"

"This dust is *mine!*"

Outside, the two cops were playing happily with their rotten dog, probably throwing it sticks. First them, then their dog, then his soul. Mr. Wah, clutching the boottle, said, turning, becoming a man, making his stand, *coming through*, his voice all strong and masculine—*fighting back*—"Take this bottle and I'll break it over your head and you'll have to come through a torrent of squid ink first and then you'll have to get me and I won't let go and then you'll have to break the door down with me still hanging on to you and then you'll have to get outside and then you'll—" It was a tall order. Mr. Wah picked up his phial of black squid ink. Very tall order. He'd never had a dog. He didn't like them. His soul said—

Mr. Wah said, "Okay—COME AND GET IT IF YOU CAN!"

"*OH, SHIT!*"

It wasn't Mr. Wah.

It wasn't Mr. Wah's soul.

It wasn't even the dog.

It was the monk. The monk, out of cigarettes, popping down to the corner store to pick up a pack, thinking he might drop in on old Wah to see how he was, materializing in midair between dog, Wah, a snowstorm of white dinosaur dust, a rain of black squid ink, glass, ginseng, lotus ash, door splinters and wing nuts, the monk, instantly, again—

Dematerialized.

He heard a crash. In the street, Auden, still mashing signs and SAE–30, heard a crash.

"Fang!"

He was ready. He coiled. He tensed. Far off there, on some rocky tor before the dawn of time, Fang the Magnificent snarled.

His eyes stayed on Wah's door to see what came out.

He was ready.

He growled.

"*Fang!*"

Somewhere deep in his doggy soul, Fang, ready to go, tasted blood.

He sniffed. He waited.

He was ready for whatever came out of the boarded-up cave.

* * *

In Hansell's car outside the apartment block, he had the Laus' address book in a glassine envelope bag. There was no diary. People like the Laus kept no diary. The address book was written in Chinese and like all Chinese books, working from the Western back page toward the front, the characters in columns read right to left. The book had been sealed in the envelope to be taken to the Government Translation Unit to be transferred to English.

In the car Feiffer tapped at the book. Beside him, on the seat were the two other address and telephone-number books Hansell and Uniformed had taken from Hang's apartment in North Point and from L. K. Tin's room in Yaumati. They were all due to go to the Translation Unit.

In the car Feiffer tapped at the Laus' book. He had lived in Hong Kong all his life. He had been born there.

Susan and Steven Lau, marine electrical contractor and his wife. G. L. Hang, lens grinder; L. K. Tin, gardener.

He opened the Laus' envelope and glanced through all the characters on all of the pages, then through all the pages of Tin's book and all the pages of Hang's.

Names. Altogether, in all the books, leaving aside the addresses of the utility companies and their phone numbers or work numbers or the numbers of relatives, there were—altogether, between the three books—no more than one hundred names.

LAU.

TIN.

HANG.

In not one of their books did the names of any of the others appear. They knew each other not at all.

Names.

All they were, themselves, were names. They were nobodies. They were all dead.

They had known each other not—*they had known each other not at all*.

What came out of the boarded-up cave that had once been Mr. Wah's shop in a shower of splinters was a pure white dog covered in ancient dinosaur dust and a man covered in ancient dinosaur dust who wasn't quite so pure white because he was also covered in a sort of spotted Dalmatian pattern of black squid ink, smelling vaguely of SAE–30.

Old Fang/Petal didn't need things explained to him twice. Pure white creature with four legs running off down the road with string of lotus leaves, ginseng root, rhubarb leaves and dried sea-horse liver paste in mouth. White creature with two legs with black pattern on body standing there shouting abuse at good friend Auden and friend of mistress Spencer and smelling of SAE–30.

Kill.

Bite.

Attack.

Rip.

Slice.

ASSASSINATE!

Fang/Petal, happy to do his job, his sole reward merely a pat from a friend, at top speed, the dog of steel, going straight for Wah the Dalmatian pattern's throat, obligingly, wagging as he went at the cries of encouragement from his friends Auden and Spencer and listening not at all to the plaintive shrieks of his victim, going straight for Mr. Wah's throat, obedient to the end, a new dog, went ferociously, unstoppably, drooling, slavering, *serving* to do his job.


In Hong Kong, with a population of over five and a half million, the government annual figures said that there were probably no more than one thousand street-sleepers, people with no hope, people— men, women and children—alone, who had no one and nowhere and who lived in doorways and in alleys and on roofs and, often, died where they slept.

The figures were not accurate. Accurate figures said there were no fewer than four thousand, and they, too, were not accurate. In percentages, out of five and a half million, the accurate figures came to approximately some meaningless statistical figure under point-one percent—nothing.

The figures were all lies. The figures were all lies because each time the figures were about to be due, temporary government shelters appeared the day before and, for those who were too far gone for the temporary shelters, the ambulances appeared, and for those who were too far gone for the ambulances, the nuns and the social workers and the people who did good works appeared and the near-dead were carried off to die somewhere else.

He was a sleeper.

He was ten years old.

He had a gun and a school satchel and that was all he had.

And always, always, he was afraid.

In the Detectives' Room O'Yee said softly, coaxingly, "Chi . . ." O'Yee said, "I've got children. I know what it is to be alone. Come in. Come in and we can—"

"No!"

"Why not?"

There was a silence.

O'Yee said, "Please, please, Chi, come in and we can—" On the other end of the line, he heard nothing.

O'Yee said gently, "Chi, anything that's wrong, I can—"

"*No!*"

"*Why not?*"

"Because I'm afraid!"

"Of what?" He was losing. Any moment the boy was going to hang up and that was all he would ever hear of him and if he ever did hear of him again, it would be when— O'Yee said, "*Why not?*"

"Because I'm afraid!"

"You haven't done anything wrong!"

"I have!" He was sobbing. Chi said over and over again, "I have! I have!"

"I can make it right!"

"No!"

"Goddamit, I'm a cop! I can make any goddamned thing right! I can make it right for you!"

"It's wrong!"

"I don't care!" O'Yee said, "I don't care. I don't care what you've done—I swear to God whatever it is, I'll make it right!" He sounded so lost and little. O'Yee said, "Please, please, Chi—let me make it right!" His own children were nearly grown up. They needed their daddy no longer. O'Yee, gripping the phone, said as a pledge, "Whatever it is—whatever it is on Earth—I can fix it!"

"The dead man—the man near the gun—"

"I swear I can fix it!"

"He—he—" Chi said, "Mister, I—I—"

O'Yee said desperately, "What? Please tell me. Tell me and I—"

"I—"

"What?" O'Yee, begging him, said, "What? What?"

"I—"

"Please, Chi, please tell me—"

Chi said, "He had money in his pockets and I took it!"

"It doesn't matter!" O'Yee, his hands twisting and untwisting on the phone, willing himself down the wires to come out into the call box and take the boy in his arms and hide him, said, "That's nothing! That's nothing at all—in God's name, you have to *eat!*"

Chi said, "All the money's nearly gone. I've only got a dollar in coins left." Chi said in his own, strange, unknown, unstatistical world, "I didn't use the money for food. I did wrong. I used it for something else." He was sobbing, tired and frightened and alone and lost.

"Chi . . ."

Chi said, "I used it to call you on the phone! I used it and I used it and I used it and now all I've got is a few coins left and I—" Chi said, "I didn't even use it for food! He was dead and I took it and I didn't even use it for—" He was weeping because he did not understand it himself. Chi said, "And I took the gun—I took the gun so—" Chi said, "I took the money to call you and I took the gun because—"

He was ten years old and on the streets. He had been on the streets, in his life, for a very long time. He had no one. Chi said, at the end, weeping, desperate, alone, lost, "And I took the gun because I knew that if I had that you'd have to listen!"

He was silent. In the Detectives' Room there was only the sound of the wall clock. There was no other sound in the room at all.

It was the voice of a ten-year-old boy. It was the voice of an old, old man.

On the phone, Chi said, sadly, all his life teaching him nothing else, "All you want—all you want, mister . . . All you want is the gun."


Well, there wasn't a lot to say. It wasn't like Las Vegas where you could just stroll along to the next store on the block to buy a machine gun, or even Borneo where you could pick up a decapitation sword for a song, not even a gravel quarry where you could always lay your hand on a good rock. It was Peripheral Street, Hong Bay, where no soul ever resided, where no god ever ruled, where, lying half-eaten outside your own shop with a held-back Alsatian still dripping saliva on your chest, you just had to put up or shut up.

He could have cried.

Mr. Wah, looking up at Auden's and Spencer's faces, thought he might say something.

He could have cried.

He looked at Petal.

He could have cried.

It was almost dusk. Soon, he could go home. He thought he might go home now.

He could have cried.

On the sidewalk, with absolutely nothing to say, playing with a few little splinters of what had once been his shop, smelling of SAE–30 and squid ink, Mr. Wah—

Oh, he could have just lain there and *cried*.


It was becoming dusk.

In the growing darkness, looking down at the three glassine envelopes on the seat beside him in the car, sometimes glancing up at the building where the apartment was—where the empty, still, uninhabited rooms were, where the rooms of the dead were—Feiffer waited for Hansell to finish and come back down to the street.


It was a nightmare.

It was how he lived his days and nights.

At the other end of the line, at near dusk, having to find shelter for the night, knowing things he should not have known for years, knowing them all too early, Chi, getting no answer to his accusation, without another, single word, hung up.

# 11

**H**e breathed.

He simply stood at the opened window of the darkened living room of his second-floor apartment above the restaurant and *breathed*. Outside, in the sky, there were faint night clouds moving away from in front of the few stars—Mr. Leung filled his lungs with the cool clean night air and breathed.

After his restaurant downstairs had closed, he and his wife had cleared up, climbed the two flights of stairs to their apartment, and now, showered and in his pajamas—his wife asleep in the bedroom with the light still on waiting for him—Mr. Leung put the palms of his hands onto the sides of the window frame, glanced down into the street, and breathed.

In a week, he would be fifty years old.

The streets were empty, the sidewalks gray in the illumination of the widely spaced streetlights, the road itself with its white-painted lane marking deserted and wet-black as if after rain. In the bedroom his wife was asleep. He had worked, man and boy, since he had been fourteen years old. In a week he would be fifty.

He wondered what he thought of that.

He was bald and rotund.

He had always wanted to learn a few magic tricks to amaze his grandchildren.

He looked down into the empty street.

Somehow he had always had to work and he had never found the time.

Once, not on their birthdays, not on any special occasion, he had bought both of them brand-new bicycles and had them delivered to his son's house wrapped in bright red paper. He had done it on impulse.

He had known once how much the bicycles and the delivery had cost. He had forgotten now.

He was glad he had done it.

Once, not for anyone but himself, he had wanted to learn the names of all the stars, but he had had to work. He had bought a book about it.

He had given it to someone—he could not remember who.

He was doing all right. The restaurant was almost paid off and he was doing, if not well, then all right.

He shrugged. He was doing well. It was two-thirty in the morning and in a week he would be fifty and his wife of twenty-eight years had fallen asleep in the bedroom after work waiting for him. He was doing pretty well. He was almost fifty, he was no longer young or struggling—he had no need to be slim. He could be what he was. He touched at the window frames with his palms and drew in the night air.

He wished he had learned the names of some of the stars.

Somewhere in one of the buildings or rooms opposite there was a dog barking.

He looked, but there was no moon in the sky and the street and the alleys where a dog might be were deserted.

He breathed.

He breathed in the cool night air.

The dog stopped barking and there was absolute, utter, wonderful stillness.

At the window, like God, Mr. Leung looked down almost contentedly into the street.


No moon. In its wrecked and ruined room the Dalmatian stopped barking and moved in darkness toward a targeted pinpoint of smell and instinct by the fallen-in side door. Wood; it smelled wood and paint and, from the outside, a finger of cold air moving low that it sifted, sorted into place where the alley was where the door was where the instinct was. It padded softly, stopping from time to time, moving slowly, flexing to drop to its haunches, its tongue touching at the back of its teeth—it avoided obstacles on the darkened floor without knowing they were there; it avoided them because they were all living and emanating auras and smells and its brain sorted them, classified them like sonar, made them places where the dog should not go.

It heard a faint sound, a scraping, and stopped. Beneath its paws, against the pads, there was a gritty feel—dust and splinters—and the dog became part of it and did not move.

It breathed only lightly, all its metabolism slowed down.

It listened.

It waited.

In the destroyed dark room, there was a swirling of myriad smells, pulsing and throbbing, heightening and lowering in intensity as their sources decayed or changed. There was the smell of spice, of bone, of wood, metal, glass that had once been sand, of earth and rare earths, of warmth and life and hunting—the smells were swirling in the room, invisible, full of color, humming and ticking with life.

Still in the room, on the wood splinters and dust, the Dalmatian listened.

Its guts ached with hunger.

It listened.

There was a faint breeze coming in from one of the broken planks in the door, coming in from the alley where the sound was. The breeze, so softly that nothing on Earth heard it but the dog, set the finest leaf on a porcelain wind-chime tree moving. It moved only once. In the room, barely heard, it made a little, soft ringing sound.

Poised by the door that led to the alley, the dog heard it.

The sound in the alley was gone.

In the room, looking around in the blackness, for a moment lost, the dog made an involuntary whining noise.


He had worked hard for his success. He had worked hard for the restaurant and now it was almost paid off and it would be something to leave when he was gone. If he died first, it would be something substantial for his wife. She was no longer young either and she also was getting fat, and she worried, sometimes, whether he still loved her.

He wondered. He wondered if he did. He had a feeling for her that was part of the same feeling he had for himself and he supposed that was what romantic people called love. They had worked together all their lives getting somewhere—he did not think he could have the same feeling for anyone else now because anyone else would think that all he had ever been was the man he was now.

When they had first been married he had not been able to keep his hands off her. She had always responded. Now, it was a conscious effort because he thought, had been brought up to believe, that women needed affection in their lives. He was almost fifty. He wondered if it were true.

He thought about her—

He thought—

He thought he could not believe truly that they had been together that long.

He thought of how his feelings were hurt when she disapproved of him.

He thought that when they laughed together or shared something, it was as if—

He thought the thought of not dying first, of being alone without her, was more than he could bear. He thought— He thought all this stuff about romance was probably made up, but he thought when it was time, if it was possible, it would be right if they could go together. It did not seem as if they had been married twenty-eight years. She was asleep in the bedroom with the light on. She had fallen asleep waiting for him. It surprised him she was not sick of him after all that time.

He touched at the window frames with his palm. He was who he was. He could think what he liked.

In the street, coming quickly, furtively out of an alley, he saw a shadow, a person.

The street was empty and still and deserted.

It was 2:30 A.M.

At his window, standing in darkness, Mr. Leung looked down to see who it was.


Smells. In the center of the room there were all the wonderful smells, the smells of warmth and love and tail-wagging.

The breeze from the broken door had stopped and the wind chimes made no sound at all.

Late, dark, safe night.

In the center of the room, the Dalmatian, turning three times in a little circle around the center, the exact base and sense-point of the smells, settled itself down, breathing deeply and easily.

There was an object just at the tangent from the center of the smells, smelling of trust and safety and warmth, and the Dalmatian laid its muzzle across it and closed its eyes.

It smelled all the smells of its home.

Like a puppy, it closed its eyes and slept.


It was a kid about ten years old carrying a black plastic school satchel on his back. From his window, Mr. Leung watched him. He was carrying something heavy in the satchel; from time to time he stopped to pull at the straps and settle the load. He was some sort of petty thief or street-sleeper; his clothes were rags and he also carried in his hand what looked like a bundle of rags that probably served him as his blanket. He was a long way off, not under the lights, and Mr. Leung could make out nothing about him except what he was.

The streets, these days, were full of them. The government said there were hardly any, but even around the back of his restaurant when it got cold, Mr. Leung, on any night in winter could count four or five of them, men, women and children.

He was probably stealing something.

Across the street, in the alley he had come from there was nothing but the sides of buildings and a few back doors to shops or small offices and there was nothing there to steal. Mr. Leung had the only restaurant in East Peking Road and there was no food across the road.

The kid was probably looking for somewhere to sleep for the night. He probably had in his satchel everything he owned—it was probably not much. He had grandchildren himself; you could not do everything in the world for everyone in the world. He saw the kid stop near a streetlamp and look around. He seemed to be looking for something on the street itself.

Mr. Leung looked. There was no traffic coming and nothing on the street. It was not trash-collection day and there were not even any bins. There was only a public telephone booth with the light long ago smashed by vandals.

He saw the kid look at it.

He must have had money in his hand. He saw the kid stop, looking at the booth, and then open his hand to see how many coins he had.

He wondered who on Earth someone like that would have to call.

He watched.

He saw the kid try to decide.

He heard, abruptly, just once, the sudden sharp bark of a dog. He saw the kid tense.

He saw the kid, suddenly, deciding, close the hand the coins were in into a fist. He saw him thrust the fist and coins into the pocket of his shorts. He saw him, for some reason, look up, but in the darkness, he could not see Mr. Leung. He saw—

Mr. Leung at his window, said abruptly, aloud, "I'm too old for this. I have to work in the morning."

In the bedroom, his wife had fallen asleep waiting for him.

He drew a deep, final breath of the good, cool night air and, padding across the room in his bare feet, straightening the buttons on the shirt of his striped pajamas, thought he might glance at last night's newspaper in bed for a few minutes and then, because even fat, balding, near-fifty-year-old men needed their eight hours too, take a pill and get a good, deep, restful night's sleep.


It whimpered.

In the room, all the smells were wrong and the dog, sitting with his head down, whimpered because all the smells were wrong.

Earth. Sand. Wood that had been trees and spices and powder and white bone and the faint smell of black squid ink and the leaves from lotus plants and the man-root, ginseng, and splinters and the smell of the air and the night—they were all, all wrong and the dog whimpered at it.

It could not understand.

It was where it should be.

It was somewhere else.

It shook its head to clear the smells from its nose.

It whimpered.

It was wrong.

In the wrecked and ruined room, a thing of simple responses, the dog, making noises softly at first from the back of its throat, lost, helpless, confused, to everything that was in the room, to the room itself, began making begging noises.

Like a puppy, alone, lost, in the darkness, it laid its head on its paws and cried.


The streets were all empty and wet-black as if after rain and there was a coldness in the air. All the buildings, all the windows dark and unlit, towered up and he was in a dark hole between them feeling so small and, all the time, afraid of everyone.

His satchel and everything he had in it was everything he had in the world.

Mr. O'Yee: he was a voice. He was a policeman. He was a voice he could hear with the coins—he wondered if, on the street, he had ever walked past him.

Chi. The voice at the other end of the telephone knew his name.

He had almost none of the coins he had stolen left.

The light in the booth was smashed and if anyone came to get him he could not see them first and he would be trapped inside there while they hit him or killed him or— He felt the weight of the gun in the satchel on his back. It was heavy, pulling him down. It was all he had.

All the time, he was afraid.

He looked up and across the road to where there was a single light on at a window above a restaurant and he wondered if, around the back of the restaurant—

DID YOU SEE THIS VAN?
DID YOU SEE THESE PEOPLE TOGETHER?
HAVE YOU EVER SEEN THIS GUN BEFORE?

Lying in bed beside his sleeping wife, Mr. Leung glanced down at her and smiled. Twenty-eight years. He could not believe it. He looked at her face and tried to see how she had aged, how she had changed, how, when he had first married he would have thought someone like her old and unattractive and running to fat.

He felt good. He was not sure why, but he felt good and happy and maybe, just on an impulse like the bicycles he would wake her up and kiss her and tell her how good he felt and . . .

Silly. He glanced at the photograph of the car wreck on the front page of the newspaper and then, idly, read the names of all the dead under their photographs.

Silly. It would be silly and too silly to explain. Take a pill and get some sleep. Silly.

He didn't think it was silly. Maybe it was romance. Maybe it was—

On the front page there were photographs of all the dead. He looked at their faces.

DID YOU SEE THIS VAN?
DID YOU SEE THESE PEOPLE TOGETHER?
HAVE YOU EVER SEEN THIS GUN BEFORE?

He froze.

In bed, staring at the photographs, frozen, Mr. Leung said aloud in Cantonese, *"Name of heaven!"*

DID YOU SEE THIS VAN?

DID YOU SEE THESE PEOPLE TOGETHER?

HAVE YOU EVER—

Mr. Leung said, "Name of—"

He froze, paralyzed.


He heard the dog, suddenly, viciously, violently begin to bark, and he ran.

He heard sounds, voices. He saw lights come on and he ran.

Mr. O'Yee—he wondered where he was now.

He was nowhere. In the street, he was alone. He knew his name: *Chi.*

In the street, afraid, Chi ran.


DID YOU SEE THIS VAN?

DID YOU SEE THESE PEOPLE TOGETHER?

HAVE YOU EVER SEEN THIS GUN BEFORE?

*"Name of heaven!"*

His wife was awake, staring at him.

DID YOU SEE THIS VAN?

DID YOU SEE THESE PEOPLE TOGETHER?

He stared at the photographs of all the dead and he knew them.

It was 2:45 A.M.

Frozen, staring at the photographs next to his wife in his bed at night, Mr. Leung knew them.

He knew who they were.

# 12

"*Is there any point to which you would wish to draw my attention?*"
"*To the curious incident of the dog in the night-time.*"
"*The dog did nothing in the night-time.*"
"*That is the curious incident,*" *remarked Sherlock Holmes.*

It was a bright new day. Outside, in the street, the traffic was humming, the dust was rising, the inversion layer was stifling, people were working, hurrying, crowding, going about their business, and, in Mr. Wah's case, inside their shops nailing up their doors. They were good big nails. He whistled as he worked. Spencer said, "He did nothing because he was at home with his master!" He handed Mr. Wah a nail. Spencer said, "Cherchez le maître!"

It was a good, big hammer. Mr. Wah, nailing, hammering, nodding, said, "Right." He nailed and hammered.

Spencer said, "The Artful Dodger."

Mr. Wah said, "Hmm." He had lashed out on the best nails money could buy, but what the hell, you only died three or four times. Mr. Wah said, "Where's your idiot friend and his useless dog?"

"Outside in the car keeping watch." Spencer said, "The Dalmatian steals to order. His master orders him to steal. He steals what his master needs!" It was a three-cigarette problem. Spencer lit a cigarette and waited for the flash of understanding.

There was the flash of a six-inch nail going six-inches deep into a doorjamb.

"His master, poor and sickly, on his last few grams of medicine, lets the Dalmatian get the scent and then turns him loose to find that scent and bring back the thing that smells of that scent." Spencer said, "His master has a disease!" "Excellent!" *(Dr. Watson)* cried; "Elementary," said he *(Holmes)*.

Mr. Wah said, "Huh."

Spencer said, "Don't nail up the door. Let your door be always open. The dog is filling a prescription for his ailing master, and to know the full elements of the prescription, the laudanum, the secret formula, is to know all!" They talked a lot better in 1896.

Mr. Wah said, "The dog stole spiders' skins."

Spencer said, "Which is the antidote for what?"

Mr. Wah said, "It's for malaria."

He perceived he had been in Afghanistan. Spencer said, "Ah." Spencer said, "He is a man who has lived in hellholes. He is a traditional Chinese or he would have used quinine." Spencer said, "What else did the dog take?"

"Crushed ginger and onion essence."

"For?"

Wah said, "For skin eruptions."

"Ah. A man who has lived in hellholes, distrusts Western medicine and is hideously pockmarked." Wah had stopped nailing. Spencer said, "What else?"

"Dried mulberries—for a hacking cough."

"Ah."

"Rhino-horn powder. Dessicated monkey testicles taken on a full moon while the heart of the monkey is still—" Wah said, "For loss of erection."

"We may hear his history from some poor fallen woman in Limehouse."

"Lotus leaves."

"For?"

"For prevention of pregnancy."

What a sorry lot the criminal classes were. Spencer said, "He hopes, he hopes." Spencer said, "And for a limp?"

"Does he have a limp?"

"Does he? What would be the first thought of your traditional Chinese if he had a limp? What would he seek?"

"Corrective surgery." He had put down the hammer. Wah said, "Pig's liver. The dog got a bit of that. It's good for asthma." He put down the nails. He saw. Wah said, "I see him as a pockmarked not-young man in pain limping down the street coughing and swaying and touching at his useless crotch while his dog—" Wah said, "Mulberry leaves: he talks in a laryngeal whisper!" Wah said, "My best ginseng and dinosaur dust—for strength in his quest!" Wah said, "The poor bastard is dying!" He hit it. Wah said, "What he does is let his dog sniff the last remaining few grams of whatever medicine in his life of criminal prosperity he was able to afford in bulk and his dog—" Wah said, "His chickens are coming home to roost! He's being punished for his excesses and all he can get to alleviate his pain is what his dog can steal for him!" Wah said, "His dog smells the stuff out!" Wah said, "Spiders' skins, crushed ginger and onion essence, mulberries, monkey balls, lotus leaves"—Wah said, "Ha, ha, no, he's finished with all that!—nothing for a limp. And, and pig's liver, ginseng, rhino horn and dinosaur dust!" Wah said, "The man is a walking monument to an evil life!" Wah said, "Why am I afraid of him?"

"His dog is nought but his loyal and slavish factotum!"

Mr. Wah said, "Right!"

Spencer said, "A factotum is a servant."

Mr. Wah said, "I knew that."

Holmes said, "Sorry, old chap."

Mr. Wah said, "It never bit me, the dog."

"No."

"Your dog was the one that bit me."

Spencer said, "A mistake."

Mr. Wah said, "He sounds like some sort of lieutenant of crime."

Spencer said, "A general."

Mr. Wah said, "An emperor."

"A czar."

Mr. Wah said, "There must be a large reward."

Spencer said, "Probably."

"Where did a man like that get a Dalmatian dog?"

Ah. Where did such men get anything? Spencer said thoughtfully, "Ah, Hong Kong, that great cesspool into which all the loungers of the empire are irresistibly drained . . ."

Mr. Wah said, "Yeah . . ."

"He may well be the Napoleon of crime . . ." He wished he had his violin and his slipper of shag tobacco.

Mr. Wah said, "Too true . . ."

Spencer said, "Unnail your door. Let us see this through together. I have only ever had one problem that beat me and that was to do with The Woman."

Wah said, "There could be a lot of cash in something like this." He looked hard at Spencer.

Spencer said, "The solution, that is my only reward."

Mr. Wah said, "My life is ruined anyway."

"This may be the ruination that builds you your country mansion and regains you your lost fortune."

Right. Mr. Wah said, "Right." Heaven wasn't that hot. All you did was stand around and smoke cancer-free cigarettes and feel smug. Mr. Wah, taking up the hammer and balancing it in his hand, said slowly in Cantonese, "When you have eliminated the impossible, whatever remains, however improbable, must be the truth."

Spencer said, "Right!"

Mr. Wah said, "My Uncle Wing used to say that." Mr. Wah said, "He worked for the Weather Bureau." Mr. Wah said, "I'll do it!" Mr. Wah said, "Smells—clever! Smells—" He nodded. He turned the hammer around to use the claw to get the nails out of the door. Mr. Wah said, "Smells—" Mr. Wah said, "For a detective, you're pretty bright."

Spencer said, "Thank you."

Mr. Wah said, "Do you ever . . . *consult?*"

## INTERNAL

### St. Paul DeChartres Hospital, Hong Bay

PATIENT'S NAME: Fan Chi Hung (Lewis Fan) SEX: Male AGE: 51 yrs. OCCUPATION: Wholesale Antique Dealer. NEXT OF KIN: Wife. PROCEDURE: Simple amputation Right Hand. COMPLICATIONS: None.

### REPORT OF NIGHT WARD SISTER

*Following surgery and a restless night interrupted by intermittent episodes of postanesthesiac pain and anxiety, the patient appears to have settled down well. Several visits by wife during the day and interviews by the police seem to have relieved much of the anxiety, and patient took an evening meal. Swelling on stump of right hand shows first signs of going down. Stump was rebandaged twice during the evening after slight bleeding from sutures. Patient warned not to lie in bed with arm crooked behind head. Claimed it relieved pain.*

*Conversation lucid. No medication given after mild tranquilizer of 4 mg. Valium administered orally at 9:30 P.M. by evening sister. (See Drugs Book.)*
*Patient expected to be moved from private room to intermediate ward today.*
*Patient noticed to be in semi-waking state from time to time during night, but did not call for nurse. No other medication or treatment requested by patient.*

*Signed:* K. Y. Lin, RN, Ward Sister.          *Time:* 7:05 A.M.

He hurt. In the bed, he hurt. It was a little after 8:33 in the morning and through his window as he tried to raise himself in bed with his left hand to get the throbbing stump up above his head, he hurt. His arm was on fire and he felt the pain in his eyes and in the muscles of his neck as he strained to hold his body tight so it did not hurt when he moved.

Through the window, high up, he could see the city. He could see over some of the roofs and the towers toward the harbor and there he could see, along the shoreline, the blurred line of warehouses and offices in a light morning mist: he could see them as faint blue outlines like the faint outlines of an alien city seen from a transiting aircraft at an airport at night.

He could see the sky, but it was not a sky he knew. It was a faint, washed-out sky seen from a different angle and it was alien.

The pain got through his tightened body and, as he moved, he grunted.

The pain was not a pain: it was an ache. It was constant. It was not something like pain that peaked, abated, and then was gone; it was pain that stayed with him and would never stop.

He needed to pass water.

All he had to do was press the bell push-button and a nurse would come and bring him a stainless-steel bottle.

The nurses were all eighteen years old.

He pushed to get himself higher in the bed, somehow to relieve his bladder, to hold himself forever, and the pain washed over him and almost made him faint.

All through the night, he had dreamed of demons and dead people. Each time he awoke—

He pushed.

In his bed, Fan pushed at the mattress with the heels of his feet to get himself higher.

The nurses were all eighteen years old. They were children.

All he had to do to get a stainless-steel bottle so he could piss in his bed was—

Suddenly, silently, trying to get his arm above his head to relieve the pain, he closed his eyes and wept.

He was fifty-one years old. He was a grown man. All the nurses were smiling children.

He hurt.

He wept.

Alone, lost somewhere in a place he did not know, afraid of the nights and the days, Fan Chi Hung, a man who had been someone, needing desperately to piss in private, closed his eyes and wept.

He wasn't a person. He was some sort of Indian garden gnome. In his glassed-in office on the third floor of the Hong Bay branch of the Hong Kong Telephone Company, the gnome said, "Hmm." He had smooth skin and pupil-less brown eyes that looked like they had been painted in. He was the voice you got when the operator told you your time was up, you told her to get the supervisor, the supervisor came on the line and—guess what?—your time was up.

So was Chi's. There was only one chair in the office. V. K. Ranganathan was sitting in it. O'Yee, standing up, said very clearly and slowly so it got through, "He's running out of money. If I don't get him today he'll be out of money and he won't be able to call me and he's got a very large gun he doesn't know a goddamned thing about and he's liable to shoot himself with it—if he doesn't shoot someone else." He smiled. It was a very thin smile. O'Yee said, "What I want is for you to put a trace on my line so I can get him." Clear? Clear.

V. K. Ranganathan said, "Hmm." He had no hair. He was portly. He needed a red hat with a point on it and a bell. He had a good job. He liked it a lot. It fed and clothed his family.

O'Yee said, "I can't get a court order because I haven't got any evidence that anything he says is true! I can't get a Juvenile Bureau waiver to a court order because Juvenile hasn't got the power to tap phones unless the offender is an adult and—"

V. K. Ranganathan said, "How old is this alleged person?"

The alleged person was ten or eleven. O'Yee said, "I'm not asking you to tap his phone, I'm asking you to tap mine."

"A police phone. . . ?"

O'Yee said, "Yes."

Ah. Click. V. K. Ranganathan said, "No problem. You can get a court order because you're an adult!" He smiled. He looked like he had painted lips. Problem solved. He could go back to his garden of circuits, wires and flashing lights. V. K. Ranganathan said, "No problem. We'll hook into your phone and the instant it's used, we can tell you where it's located."

It was located in the Detectives' Room of the Yellowthread Street Police Station, Hong Bay, third desk from the right. O'Yee said, "I want to locate his phone."

"Private or public?"

"Public."

"Which area?"

"If I knew which area I could saturate the area with cops and I wouldn't need you!"

V. K. Ranganathan said, "Hmm." He thought. He asked, "Any Security implications?"

"Yes!" O'Yee, nodding, said, "Yes! Yes, it's a big spy thing!"

V. K. Ranganathan said, "A request then from the Governor's Standing Security Committee on Electronic Surveillance will do it."

O'Yee said, "He's running out of money." O'Yee said, "He's got a gun."

Oh, that was nothing. Forget it. V. K. Ranganathan said, "A formal request to the company to approach the union to negotiate the appropriate danger money for the technicians will take care of that."

"Can't you just tap into the phone for me on a personal basis?"

V. K. Ranganathan said with concern in his voice, "Are you applying to have your calls monitored?"

O'Yee said, "Yes!"

"That's a police matter."

"I am the police!" Out there, somewhere, a little at a time, Chi was dying. Sooner or later, either he or someone else was going to take the gun out of the satchel or it was going to fall out of the satchel or— O'Yee said, "Look! Do you watch TV? I'm one of those cops who doesn't go home at night. I'm one of those cops who gets involved, who gets personal, who takes it personally, who doesn't give up until the end like—like—" He tried to think who.

V. K. Ranganathan said, "Like Dirty Harry or—"

O'Yee said, "Right!"

Easy one, that. V. K. Ranganathan said, "Great. Bring me a personal request from you, a notarized statement from the police surgeon that you're completely sane, a personal insurance policy indemnifying the company from any action arising out of gunfire, wrecked cars, smashed-up school buses, stress, fear and terror and—"

O'Yee said, "Please help me."

V. K. Ranganathan said, "I can't."

O'Yee said, "He keeps calling me and he's terrified and he's got a gun and somewhere, somewhere, there's a dead man." O'Yee said, "Do you have children?"

V. K. Ranganathan said, "Three."

"What if he was your child?"

"—all girls."

*"He'll die out there!"* O'Yee said suddenly, "How about I hold you at gunpoint? How about you say I held you at gunpoint in the office here while you—"

V. K. Ranganathan said, "While I go down three floors, see seven or eight supervisors, go down into the garage to get a trace team together, set it all up, come back to my office to oversee it—"

O'Yee said, "Yes!"

"—while you go eight blocks away and sit at your desk by the phone waiting for a call." He wasn't made of cement. He could put two and two together. V. K. Ranganathan said, "No. Won't work."

"There are worse thing in the world than losing your job over concern for a fellow human being in trouble!"

V. K. Ranganathan said, "I can't think what they are."

*"Human rights!"*

V. K. Ranganathan said, "One reason why we aren't permitted by law to tap telephones without a court order." He glanced at an enamel sign over his door. The enamel sign read, TELEPHONE SERVICE IS PROVIDED ACCORDING TO THE TERMS OF THE TELE-PHONE ORDINANCE (NO. 18 OF 1951) AND AMENDMENTS THERETO AND TO THE CONDITIONS CONTAINED IN THE SUBSCRIBER'S HIRING CONTRACT. COPIES OF THE LATTER AND INFORMATION ON THE FORMER MAY BE OBTAINED FROM THE SUPERVISOR V. K. RANGANATHAN, 3RD FLOOR, BELL BUILDING, 678 LOWER KAI YUEN STREET, HONG BAY. It was him. It had taken a long while. V. K. Ranganathan said, "I'm sorry."

"Why don't you just change my number and I'll probably never hear from him again."

"The change of number of a public utility or emergency-service facility has to be advertised three months in advance in at least three demonstrably effective electronic-media outlets plus no fewer than two printed daily media in at least three common languages for at least seven consecutive—"

"Make a goddamned exception! This poor bastard kid is running around loose with nothing!"

V. K. Ranganathan said, "My three poor bastard kids are running around with something! That something is my job!"

"Don't you give a *damn*?"

V. K. Ranganathan said tightly, "No."

"He's going to die."

"In India, where I was born, people die all the time."

"In the United States, where I was born, people *care!*"

V. K. Ranganathan said, "No, they don't."

"Well, I do!" He had lost. He knew it. O'Yee said, "For God's sake—"

He wasn't a gnome, he was a man. He was a man who had his name in enamel. He had come a long way. In India, his father had not even had his name on a grave marker. One of his girls was in her first year of medicine and doing well.

O'Yee said, "For God's sake, man, *what the hell do I do?*"


He pissed. Sitting on the toilet seat holding himself in position with his left hand on the wall, in the adjoining bathroom, Fan pissed hard and long.

He pissed. Breathing hard, he felt the relief flow out of him.

He pissed. He pissed until there was nothing else left in him and he sat there after it had all gone with tears running down his face, breathing hard, sucking in air with his bandaged stump held hard across his chest.

They made it easy for you. They gave you a nightshirt like a shift that tied at the back and, because it was old and frayed, ripped when a grown man leaned forward in it. It was a shroud, a rag for a beggar.

His body was still alive. He pressed a little at his chest with the bandage and felt his heart beating.

He needed a cigarette.

It was not allowed and they had taken them away with his clothes.

He needed a cigarette.

He did not need a bedpan or a bottle. He needed—

He sat quietly, holding in the pain, trying to keep his eyes open so he could be a person.

He needed a cigarette. He needed—

He hurt. He *hurt*.

On the toilet seat, Mr. Fan, trying to stay away from the pain said, "Fan! Fan Chi Hung—*Lewis Fan!*"

It was his name. It was who he was, what he had reached in his life. "*Lewis Fan, age fifty-one!*"

It was him.

He got up, pushing hard at the seat with his good hand and thrusting with his legs and feet, to find a telephone.

It was 8:47 A.M. by the gold Omega wristwatch on the bedside table he constantly worried some eighteen-year-old nurse would take for her boyfriend while he was asleep. At the side of the bed, swaying, he almost went to pick it up with his stump to put it on his left wrist.

The watch was heavy, expensive, the reward of living long, working hard and being someone.

It was him. It was what he was.

He swayed. He forced himself to plan out the long walk down the corridor to the telephone at the end of the ward.

Carefully, minutely, one step at a time, he planned how to get to the telephone so he could call someone.


He unnailed.

Ginger. Good.

Onion essence. Right.

Spiders' skins. Of course.

Rhino-horn powder, monkey nuts and lotus leaves. Mr. Wah, alone in the shop, unnailing, clawing, throwing his door open to prosperity, reward and a dumb dog, said, nodding, "How pathetic."

Poor bastard. The master sounded in a pretty bad way.

Sea-horse dessication. Ginseng. Dinosaur dust.

Sea-sparrow meal. Wet squid ink. Burned watermelon ash.

Phoenix skin, pig's liver, snake bladder, beetle dung, slough of sea louse—all, all just too, too simple.

Odors, smells, scents, fragrances—all, all just too, too simple.

And there was probably a big cash reward in it.

There was probably a huge reward in it.

He unnailed. He hummed. He whistled as he worked.

He wondered not at all, in the panstereorama of pharmacological passementerie what on Earth or anywhere else—to a dog—a wind chime could possibly smell like.

\* \* \*

He found a doorway in an alley where he was safe and he counted his money.

There was hardly any left. All he knew was the six-times multiplication table—it was as far as he had got in school before his parents had abandoned him to his grandmother and she had died.

He counted. He counted. He did his tables.

In the alley, moving the weight of the gun in his satchel on his back to settle it, Chi tried to work out how many more times he could call the number.

It was his wife. At the other end of the line Fan's wife said urgently in Cantonese, "*Hai?*—Yes? *Hi been wai*—Who is this?" and he saw her standing there in the main room of their house by the black lacquered antique table the telephone stood on with her head crooked to one side listening. He pictured her face and her eyes—he pictured her eyes darting around the room to see that everything was in order.

"*Hai?*—Yes?"

He was silent. He hurt. He *hurt.* "Huei-Mei? *Alice?*"

"*Hai*—yes." In the room, at the table, in the silence of the still place, Fan Huei-Mei said anxiously, "Yes? Yes?"

Fan Huei-Mei said with a sudden, anxious tone in her voice, "Yes? Yes? Is something wrong?"

He couldn't concentrate. Driving back to the station, twice in the middle of the street he almost ran someone down.

He noticed not at all.

Driving through the streets, not watching, all the way back to the telephone on his desk, O'Yee tried to think what—what in God's name—there was left to do.

Outside in the street Auden's car was still there, but it was locked and neither he nor Petal were anywhere to be seen.

In the street, listening with one ear to the sounds of Mr. Wah readying his shop for Dalmatian and denouement, Spencer, looking worried, walked up and down the sidewalk peering into alleys and looking in shops and doorways.

"Petal? Fang? —*Phil?*"

He whistled.

He wondered where they had gone.

# 13

In Victor Leung's Imperial Palace Restaurant on East Peking Road the table was by the window, covered with a disposable paper tablecloth. It was 9:10 in the morning—too early for yum cha—and the restaurant was closed and Mr. Leung and his wife not needed in the kitchens for an hour. On the table, the menu holder was empty and the little glass vase and toothpick-holder tray unfilled. Above the eighteen other tables in the sparsely decorated place there was only a single fan turning about the red paper lanterns hung from the ceiling. Mr. Leung and his wife sat opposite Feiffer at the table. Between them was the folded newspaper with all the pictures of the dead in a row like a strip of film negative. Mr. Leung said, "They sat here, where we're sitting now." He was in his shirt-sleeves, wearing an expensive gold watch. He wore heavy horn-rimmed glasses for reading. He touched at the pictures in the newspaper one by one. He looked at Feiffer over the glasses, reading the names, "That one, Lau; that one, his wife; that one, Hang; and that one."

Feiffer said, "Tin."

"Yes."

All the windows and doors in the restaurant were closed. They were made of armor glass for security. In the street outside, through the windows, people and traffic went by silently, as if everyone inside watching were deaf. The restaurant was a place during the day for yum cha: tea and talk. It was a fishbowl, neutral in color with all the colors and movement outside—a mass, passing like figures in a landscape on a magic lantern slide of Hong Kong—remote, transitory, otherworldly, *out there*.

She was in her late fifties, lined, with gray hair pulled back into a bun. She glanced at her husband. Mrs. Leung said, "They were husband and wife, those two?"

Below the row of pictures in the folded newspaper you could just see the barrel of the little silver gun.

"Yes."

"He killed her with the gun?"

Feiffer said, "Yes. We think so."

She glanced again at her husband. Mrs. Leung said, "We never knew them by name. We always kept the table reserved for them, but if they ever told us their names the first time they reserved the table I don't remember." She touched at the edge of the tablecloth with her fingers. Her nails were clipped back and the skin on her hands was lined and wrinkled. She was a woman who had worked hard all her life. Her body was thickening. She was a woman who had had children.

"How often did they come?"

Mr. Leung said, "Every Thursday. In the evening."

"For how long?"

Mrs. Leung said, "Since we opened. Eighteen months. We moved here from smaller premises in General Gordon Street eighteen months ago and they started coming perhaps a week or two after we opened." Mrs. Leung said, "When we first opened we had other staff we brought with us from the old place and maybe one of them took the booking." Mrs. Leung said, "They've all gone—moved on or opened their own places or—" Mrs. Leung said, "Sometimes, when they paid the check the woman smiled at me"—she had a name— "Mrs. Lau, but I never spoke to her. They came at exactly 8:30 and left at exactly 10:30—that's our busy time."

"Together."

"Yes."

"By car or—"

"They just came. And went."

"What did they talk about amongst themselves?"

"Nothing." Mr. Leung said, "Nothing." Mr. Leung said, "They didn't talk." He put his hands flat on the table for support. His hands were shaking. He looked down at the photographs.

"They must have talked about something. People don't just sit in a restaurant for two hours and not say a word to each other—"

"They talked about nothing! They sat there, one of them ordered food—whatever was the special of the day—they all had whatever was given them and they sat in silence and they didn't say anything!" Mr. Leung said, "Sometimes one of them went over to the phone and made a call."

Feiffer said softly, "All these people are dead."

"I know all these people are dead!" Mr. Leung said, "I'm telling you all I know! They were in here every Thursday night for eighteen months, they sat there opposite each other, they ordered food, they ate it, they said, so far as I or my wife had time to notice, absolutely nothing at all to each other, sometimes one of them made a local phone call from the coin box, and then they paid for the meal and they left!"

"Together?"

"Yes!" Mr. Leung said, "And they paid in cash!"

"You never saw anything change hands? Money? Or packages, or—"

"Do you mean drugs?"

"I mean anything."

"No."

"They must have done something!"

Mrs. Leung said, "They were ordinary. They were ordinary. They were just ordinary people! Ordinary people often just sit and eat and—"

"And you never once spoke to them in all that time?"

Mrs. Leung said, "I said, 'Good evening.' I said, 'It's a hot night.' I said, 'It's raining.' I said—" Mrs. Leung said, "I said, 'What would you like?' and one of them—one of the men said, 'The special,' and sometimes the woman, Mrs. Lau, looked up and smiled." Mrs. Leung said, "They sat looking. They looked around waiting for their meal, and when it came they ate it and then, when it was cleared away they drank tea and they—" Mrs. Leung said, "They drank their tea, they got up, they paid, and then they left." Mrs. Leung said for confirmation, "Victor?"

Mr. Leung nodded.

"We think Mrs. Lau was driving the van. The van was loaded with plate glass—"

Mr. Leung said, "It's all in the newspapers—"

"We think, a second before the van collided with the truck, a second before all the glass disintegrated and cut everyone in the van to shreds and all their clothes into rags—we think Mrs. Lau's husband, who was sitting behind her, put the barrel of his revolver against the base of her skull and—"

Mrs. Leung said, "We don't know anything! We called you! You didn't have to find us—we called you!"

"They must have said *something* to each other! Just once, just once in eighteen months, just once you must have overheard—"

"It's our busy time!"

"Once, they must have been carrying something!"

Mrs. Leung said, "If it rained, umbrellas! And if it rained and they were carrying umbrellas, I may have said, 'It's wet tonight,' or 'It's getting heavier,' or 'The bureau didn't forecast this' or—" Mrs. Leung said, "And one of them, whoever turned to hear what I said, may have nodded and said, 'Yes.'" Mrs. Leung said, "Or the woman may have smiled." Mrs. Leung said, "She had a nice smile! That's all!"

Mr. Leung said, "They were punctual. They were always here at 8:30 and they always left at 10:30." He touched at his face. "We—we could always book the tables around them because they were so—"

"If you booked around them you must have made some reference to them in your reservations list—"

"We wrote, 'Table six: 8:30 P.M. to 10:30 P.M.'"

"Surely to God it must have occurred to you that—"

Mr. Leung said tightly, "No, it didn't. Whatever it was that should have occurred to us if we were detectives, didn't occur to us. We run a restaurant, we didn't go up to them and demand to know why the hell they weren't talking to each other and we didn't—" He was shaking with anger, "And we didn't—we didn't—" Mr. Leung said, "And when they were in here—" Mr. Leung said, "Then, they weren't dead! They weren't in the newspapers! They weren't—"

Mrs. Leung said, "They were ordinary!" Mrs. Leung said, "They were ordinary! They were just—they were ordinary people! If they were dealing in drugs or—or money or—"

Feiffer said, "They weren't dealing in drugs."

"Or—"

"They were dealing in nothing. They were a marine electrician and his wife, a lens grinder and a gardener." Feiffer said hopelessly, "They came six miles down the wrong side of a freeway in the middle of the night with a tape cassette blaring music at full blast in a van loaded with glass we can't account for, one of them drew a pistol we can't trace and shot his wife in the back of the head for a reason we can't fathom, and then—"

Mrs. Leung said, "You saw it. You saw the van after it hit?"

Feiffer said softly, "Yes."

Mr. Leung said, "I promise you, there isn't anything else we can tell you!" He looked at his wife. He touched at the table. Mr. Leung, dropping his voice, shaking his head, trying to remember, said hopelessly, "There isn't anything else. I can't even remember how they dressed. I can't even remember how they—" Mr. Leung said, "They—"

"Yes?"

Mr. Leung said. "They—they—" He touched his face, trying to remember, "They—"

"Did they always take the same places at the table?"

"No. They—" Mr. Leung said hesitantly, "I—once or twice I—" Mr. Leung said with a dismissive half shrug, "Sometimes I suffer from insomnia and I—" He looked at his wife, "And I, myself—" He looked up and out through the thick window into the street, "And I myself, I—" Mr. Leung said, "Sometimes, I—they—" Mr. Leung said curiously, "Yes. I saw it—I did!" He looked at his wife's face and nodded. He was sure. Mr. Leung said to his wife, "Perhaps you'd get some tea." He smiled. He was still thinking. He looked over at Feiffer and frowned, remembering, wondering. He raised his hand up with the fingers outstretched and held it there, moving it slowly toward the window.

Mr. Leung said slowly, remembering, remembering all his own nights, "Yes. For some reason, each of them—each of them, depending on where they were sitting at the time, I saw each of them—not on the same Thursday night, but over a long period of time . . ."

It was something, for some reason, he did not want to talk about while his wife was beside him.

Mr. Leung said curiously, "I saw each of them reach out and touch the window with their hand. Each of them. I saw each of them touch at the window with their hand, with their fingers as if—"

Mr. Leung said, "They looked out. All the time they sat here, they all looked out through the window as if they were looking at something. I saw—I saw—each of them—" It had never occurred to him until now. Mr. Leung said, "The glass in the window—each of them, absently, while they were staring out into the street, at one time or another each of them—each of them reached out and very carefully, gently, tested the thickness of the glass in the window." Mr.

Leung said, "They were alone. They were thinking about something past. They were in here together—all together, but they were all alone and they were thinking about something past and they were—" Mr. Leung said suddenly embarrassed, smiling quickly at his wife, "If you could get the tea . . ."

Mr. Leung said, "In here, together, alone, I think each of them—" He looked not at all at his wife as she rose to get the tea, "I think each of them—" Mr. Leung said, "*I think they were thinking about their lives.*"

There was nothing in the address book and all the names and phone numbers were of ordinary people or utilities or shops or businesses. In the Translation Unit of Headquarters on Artillery Road, Hansell looked down at the carefully typed transcribed list of all the entries from all the three books from all the three apartments or rooms and saw—nothing.

There was nothing. What there was, was a set of four thick-black-plastic body bags on trays in the Mortuary with all the bits and pieces wrapped in thick white paper like butcher's meat. What there was, was flecks of white frost forming on the zippers of the bags and what there was inside was meat going hard with the cold.

*Night Battle.* It was a smashed and broken tape cassette from the van, of a Chinese opera he had never heard of. There was nothing. Altogether, everywhere, there was absolutely, utterly *nothing.*

*Night Battle.* All that was left of the box the tape had come in was a single strip of clear plastic in a glassine envelope. The sleeve of the box describing the opera was shredded paper with little blobs of red and white and yellow where once there had been a picture or a painting of some character from the story or a distributor's description of the quality and clarity of his product.

There was nothing.

Copies of all the photographs of the dead were laid out in a line in front of him on the reading desk in the section, all the blurred, indistinct, silent faces.

There was nothing.

Putting the typed transcription to one side, alone in the big, filing-cabinet–filled room, Hansell, against regulations, lit a cigarette and, gazing out, out into nowhere, wondered.

He wondered somehow, because of them, idly, straying into it, about his life.

\*　\*　\*

"What were they waiting for? Did it ever come?"

Mr. Leung said, "They weren't waiting."

"They must have been doing something. They can't simply have appeared out of nowhere!" Feiffer said, "There has to have been some sort of reason, a common purpose. As far as their families knew, they didn't even know each other. They obviously knew each other! They knew each other well enough to meet here every Thursday night like clockwork and they must have had some end purpose in mind— something they were waiting for or expecting or—"

Mr. Leung said, "I don't know!" It was impossible to do everything for everyone. You did what you could for your own family and that had to be enough. He brushed his hand across his face. Mr. Leung said, "I didn't go up to them and ask them what the hell they were doing because they weren't doing anything. I didn't know they were going to die!"

Outside the window, there was traffic and people passing. There was nothing. Across the street there were shops and offices and buildings. From the table, Feiffer counted the buildings he could see. From right to left, there was a small family-run supermarket, an electrical-goods shop advertising special bargains in duty-free minia-ture televisions, a fashion shop, two stalls in a single divided shop-front selling God only knew what from socks to sewing machines, all secondhand—the shop or business next to that was not even in business but boarded up, a newspaper stall, a small ivory shop selling probably fake ivory, and at the limit of his vision, the entrance to a bulk-rice merchant's. There was nothing. Whatever they saw or looked at or waited for or hoped to see, it was not there. Feiffer said, "North Point isn't my precinct. What else is around here?"

"What do you mean?"

"I mean, what else is around here? Is there anywhere they could have come from? Is there anything around here like, like—"

"Like what?" From the table, Mr. Leung looked at his wife. She had the tea on a tray, ready. She stood with it in her hand by the kitchen door. Mr. Leung shook his head. Mr. Leung said again, "Like what?"

"Like—anything! Like—" It was hopeless. "What happens around here on a Thursday evening? Is there an open-air market? Meetings? Union gatherings? Special buses or trams—*anything?*"

"No."

"*Think!*"

"This isn't my fault! They were respectable people! If I should have done something, then everyone should have done something!" Mr.

Leung, being threatened, starting to get up, said so his wife could hear, "We're good people. We called the police. We're ready to help. They were ordinary, respectable people—*what they did had nothing to do with us!*" He was finished. He wished he had never called.

"What were they thinking about?"

"*How should I know?*"

"Please sit down."

Mr. Leung said, "No. No, what I know I've told you. I'm not a criminal."

"I know that." He saw, for an instant, Mrs. Leung start to come forward. He saw her husband, protecting her, shake his head for her to go back. Feiffer said softly, "I know that. I apologize to you. I know you've told me everything you think you know." Feiffer said so quietly Leung had to strain to hear him, "There's nothing. We can't find out anything about them. Lau, the marine electrical contractor, was a man like you. His wife was like your wife." He paused, gazing for a moment out the window. Feiffer said quietly, "I keep looking to find out something about Lau and his wife, about Tin or Hang, but there's nothing. They were like you and your wife; they worked, they lived, they brought up a family—and they died out on the freeway in the dark cut to pieces by a load of glass in a van I can't explain, and Lau, with a revolver I also can't explain, shot his wife stone cold dead at the wheel for another reason—or maybe the same reason—*that I can't explain.*" He saw Mr. Leung sit back slowly in his chair and look at him. He felt tired, on the edge. Between the time he had looked into what was left of the van and now he could not remember sleeping. Feiffer said, "It came out of nowhere. If it can happen to them—if there's no reason for it—then, anytime, for no reason, it could happen to—"

Mr. Leung said, "Honestly, I took so little notice of them . . ." Mr. Leung said, "It was always our busy time—"

"What's around here?"

"I don't know."

"What were they thinking about?"

Mr. Leung said, "I don't know." Mr. Leung said, "There's nothing around here. There are streets and businesses and cars and people and roads and—" Mr. Leung said, "I can't think!" Mr. Leung said, "I can't think!" He touched his hand to his face. He saw his wife, looking worried, start to come over to protect him. He could have wept; she was a good, good girl. Mr. Leung said, "Honestly, I—"

Mr. Leung said, "Wait! Wait!" Mr. Leung said, "Wait. I'll get the local area *Business Directory*—" He got up and motioned Feiffer to stay where he was with the palm of his hand. He thought suddenly of bicycles wrapped up as presents in crackling red paper. He had no idea why he thought it.

Mr. Leung, shaking his hand hard to keep the man where he was at the table, said as an order, "Wait." Mr. Leung, in a week fifty years old, a man who thought he was pleased with his life, said, almost pleading, "Wait! *Please*, wait!"

He had nowhere to put the ash from his cigarette on the table except for a matchbox he carried in his pocket. The box itself was half full. In the Translation Unit reading room, Hansell emptied out the matches and tapped the end of his burning cigarette into the little cardboard drawer of the box. *Double Luckiness Matches, Shanghai*. The shops gave them away with packets of cigarettes. They were tiny, half matches that usually snapped when you struck them on the phosphorous paper on the side of the box. Even if they lit, they flared or fizzed and in any sort of slight breeze you could not keep them alight long enough to light your cigarette.

Everything, all the photographs and files and address books and all the speculation was worthless. There was nothing.

Putting the cigarette on the edge of the table, Hansell, one by one began arranging the little, cheap matches into patterns. There were no patterns and all he did, like the photographs, like the body bags, like everything, was merely lay out the little bits of uselessness in a single straight line.

He wondered.

He touched at the matches with his fingertip and moved them. He changed them. He moved them back and forth.

There was nothing and they were never going to know anything.

He was alone in the reading room. Taking up the cigarette, he pushed back and forth at the matches with his fingertip, staring at them.

He wondered. The Laus, Tin, Hang; he wondered who they had been.

He pushed the matches into little patterns that meant nothing at all.

He was alone, he had never married and, he supposed, he had no one.

Pushing at the matches, he wondered what his life, seen by someone else, under investigation, would come to.

He wondered what clues he had left to it, or if, indeed, he had left any clues to it at all.

He looked down at the matches by the photographs and books and transcriptions.

He wondered, when he too was dead, what people, maybe for some reason searching, would think, would find out, would believe of him.

It was a privately printed publication for the local businessmen's and shop-owners' association. It was like a police beat book: a small blue bound volume the size of a pocket notebook with a flip-open cover embossed with the colophon of the North Point Business Association and its motto in Chinese, *Prosperity Through Community*. On each page, a little section of one or two streets and lanes and alleys was reproduced with all the names and natures of all the businesses neatly inserted in tiny printed Chinese characters, together with the fraternal and business organizations and charities their owners subscribed to. They had waited there in his restaurant for two hours each Thursday night—there was no reason to look much further in the book than around East Peking Road and the streets and alleys and roads around Mr. Leung's Imperial Palace Restaurant. Mr. Leung, reading it off to him, said, "On this side of the road, east to west: an attorney's; a freight and passenger-information service for the CP Rail service; a garment factory above; an assembler of small engines for pumps; below that a shop, doing badly, selling a range of skin and leather products—" Mr. Leung said, "—they're selling off the last of the legally imported skins from Africa. The owner is planning on going into the rag trade with a partnership in the garment factory two doors back—; the Hunter watch company; below that a real-estate office for office and shop rentals; here, my own place, and above living quarters and above that, storage for the watch company, and, next to me—"

"In the next street?"

"Ice House Road. The main thoroughfare. Hong Bay. Your precinct." It wasn't in his book. Mr. Leung said, "Everything. Anything."

"In the street parallel to this?"

"Nanking Alley." He turned a page. "All redevelopment."

"East of this street?"

"Thompson Road." He turned a page. Mr. Leung said, "An open-air market—closed on Thursdays; a car park; bus terminal; three general-goods stores; a small tea room; a firm that makes brooms and brushes; above, another garment factory; a block of apartments for the employees of the bus company—" Mr. Leung said, "*Nothing.*" He had sent his wife away. The tea had not been brought. Mr. Leung said, "North of that, Kam Wa Street: a jeweler's; above that the workshops for the business; next to it—on the southern side—an electrical-goods shop; above it: housing for the owner and his family, more storage above; next to that an undertaker's; a shop selling funeral Hell Bank money and paper funerary objects; next to that a small hotel, three floors; a camphor-wood chest-making business; a picture-framing shop; a small restaurant specializing in Fukien cooking; a newspaper and magazine stall; a paper-lantern business; another small tea shop; another wood-carving business specializing in carved buffalos; a tailor's; an Indian spice shop; an Indian restaurant and then—" Mr. Leung said, "It's Hong Kong. They're streets and businesses and people and—" Mr. Leung said hopelessly, "It's Hong Kong. *What else could it be?*"

It could have been four people dead on a roadway. He shook his head. In the restaurant, at the table where they had all sat, Feiffer looked out the window.

Mr. Leung said, "Thursday. Events." He had another page at the back of the little book. Mr. Leung, reading it off, said, "Movies: open every night—the Palace in Peacock Street, the Hung Yieh in Tsatsemui Road, the Dragon on the corner of Shouson and Barker. Restaurants: open all week. Thursdays: occasional meetings of the Tai Chi Association in the bus-station car park on Thompson Road; Indonesian puppet shows in Wun Sha Street during summer; in Wyang Street—" He looked up.

Feiffer said, "Yes?"

Mr. Leung looked down at the folded newspaper on the table.

Feiffer said, "What is it?"

What it was—Mr. Leung said almost in a whisper, afraid to ask, "*Night Battle.* Was that the name of the opera?"

"Yes."

He felt an electric tingle run up his back. He sat at the same chair where all of them had sat.

Mr. Leung asked, "The opera, is it in Cantonese or Mandarin?"

Feiffer said, "Mandarin."

Mr. Leung, reading the entry in the little book, said with all the color draining from his face, "Wyang Street. Chinese opera house. Mandarin opera."

It was nothing. It was—

Mr. Leung said, "Performances every night."

It was nothing. It would have been playing while they were sitting there. It was nothing.

For some reason, as he did all the time now as he grew older, he thought of his wife's wonderful face and wondered as, like him, she grew old, why he never saw it.

He had done something. He had bought bicycles for his grandchildren and he had done something there, but it was for his own, for people he knew. He had known the people at the table not at all.

He wondered. He wondered.

At the table, looking hard into Feiffer's eyes, Mr. Leung, quoting the advertisement word for word, said clearly and firmly. "Hung I Kuan Chinese Opera Theater, Wyang Street, North Point. *Sole Retail Outlet for Quality Mandarin Opera Cassette Tapes in Hong Kong.*"

He looked. He watched.

He took off his thick, horn-rimmed glasses and, sitting there, he watched Feiffer's face.


At the phone in the Detectives' Room, O'Yee waited.

He put his hand to his face and closed his eyes.

At the phone in the Detectives' Room—

—he *waited*.

# 14

$\mathbf{T}$he Dalmatian was up against the rear delivery door of Victor Leung's Imperial Palace Restaurant where the trash cans were. On the ground around the cans there were burst-open paper sacks of rejected food and boxes and twists of unused rejected condiments, rice congealed in lumps that had gone cold and been thrown out, and, evidently scraped straight into an open can on top of the boxes and jars, the remains of a meal of beef and black-bean sauce and rice. The delivery door was shut. The Dalmatian did not eat the food. It stayed at the door with its head lowered, listening.

At the door, it listened. It heard nothing. It lowered its head.

All the smells were going. At the door, from inside, it heard nothing. The sounds were all going; it listened for wind chimes, but the memory of that sound was going and it shook its head and tried to fix the sound it was listening for.

It had not eaten for several days. There was water in potholes or in the gutters of the streets, but it had not drunk much from them. The ribs in its sides were starting to show and there was a weakness in its legs—the dog, pushing its head hard against the door, quivered, listening for a sound it was forgetting fast. It hurt. Its stomach had started to shrink and there was a long pain in its stomach that registered in its brain as a gray, wrong color.

The food on the ground had a strong smell. It was wrong. It was the wrong smell. All the smells were going and the Dalmatian, knowing only that something was wrong, did not know how to recall the right smells and charge them back into his nose and brain. It whimpered, but no one heard.

The smells in its brain were evaporating. Like flurrying clouds, they were passing, changing, vaporizing, turning to nothing as something bigger, something larger, sharper began to take them over and erase them.

The Dalmatian pushed hard against the door and felt no warmth from the metal it was made of—and heard nothing from inside where it was warm and like a cocoon.

The thing destroying all the smells, eating away at them, eroding them, turning the little clear white clouds of smells into part of itself was the smell of death.

Death smelled like blackness, like a heavy, ponderously rolling darkness in the sky before the sky closed in and it stormed.

It smelled like the pressure building up before a typhoon. It smelled like the smell of the world when the sky vaulted over with pressure and darkness and then the typhoon came.

The smell was devouring all the other smells of the spices and the herbs and the medicines and all the smells that had been so clear when the door had been—

Wah. Even the smell of Wah's fear was going. There was no triumph to it—the pictures in the Dalmatian's brain of Wah's shop and Wah's fear were all going, being overtaken—the grayness was moving throughout every sense in the Dalmatian's body and sapping all its strength.

It could not touch the food. It ached, but it was not for the food. It ached.

At the door, the Dalmatian, starting to shake from the weakness of its back legs, tried to get its breath. It was panting, gasping—it thought it saw in the air in front of its muzzle an insect, a movement, and it snapped at it. There was nothing there.

It listened. It hurt.

It ached.

There was froth starting at the side of its jaws, and as it ached, it quivered and thought it saw insects in the air that were not there.

It snapped.

There was nothing there. It tasted the taste of froth in its mouth. It hurt.

It smelled, gray and pungently, overtaking all the other smells, the smell of death.

At the door, it listened.

At the door, lost, alone, hurting, becoming mad, it ached for the sound of a human voice.


It had a human voice. The human voice—Auden's—asked, "What do you usually get for breakfast?"

Mush. You could tell from the look old Fang gave him that what he usually got was mush. Auden said, "This morning, at my place, you got a man's breakfast. You got liver."

The Alsatian made a sound. The sound was, "Yeah!"

They were somewhere safe, alone, secure. He was patting the dog on the head. Auden said, "Good, wasn't it?"

It was. He wagged. Fang said, "Yes, sir."

Auden said, "Call me Phil." Half the time you said to people, "I know what you're saying," and you didn't. With dogs you did. You knew what they were saying. They said whatever you wanted them to say. The Alsatian said, "Thanks very much, Phil."

Auden said, "Farmers eat mush. Hunters like you and me eat red meat with blood still dripping from it."

It had been good liver. The Alsatian, nodding its head, said, "Yeah." It was the old primeval blood lust. The Boss, Sir, God—Phil—had been right, of course: we'd all come from the caves. The dog, looking up into the face he idolized, said, "I ate two portions."

"You spend too much time on laps and not enough time out in the streets being dominant!"

Fang said, "My mistress is a sort of nun. Your mate out there doesn't have any luck with her at all. They sit around with me on the sofa and they listen to music." Disgusting. Fang said, "He usually brings me little chocolate doggie-treats." At the time it had seemed perfectly normal. Fang said, "They don't taste like liver." Fang said, drooling with idolatry, "You're the first person who's ever given me a decent meal I could get my teeth into."

For a German dog born in Hong Kong it spoke pretty passable English. It sounded just like Auden's English; basic but definitely The Law. It looked up and worshipped. It wagged. It would have killed for another pat.

Auden said, "Do you see a lot of action with women around your part of the world?"

Fang said, "Not much."

Auden said, nodding, "No, me either."

"I never get out, Phil. I can't even get out to crap on a nice piece of sidewalk or near a tree—I get a John Dog cardboard john and she sweeps it up with a little silver spade before I even get a chance to—"

Auden said, "My mother was a bit like that. She thought I was sickly. When all the other kids were out playing in the street she kept me inside because I'd had measles and she thought the light would damage my eyes." Auden said, "What I always wanted was an air gun."

Fang said, "It would be nice sometimes to bite someone."

"—a big .22–caliber Webley air pistol with a leather holster and a belt with lacings on it and my name on the buckle." Auden said, "There was a big kid up the street—he had a leather kit. He used to put your name on the leather or his dad used to engrave buckles with something on it." He looked down hard at the dog. Auden said, "*Death before Dishonor.*"

Fang said, "The locks in the car were stuck, Phil! I wanted to get out and kill someone, but the locks in the car—"

Auden said, "*The coward dies a thousand deaths, the brave man only one.*"

Oh, God. "Phil—!"

Auden said, "Great gun the old Webley air pistol. If you put a drop of oil in the barrel before you cocked it, you got a hell of a bang and clouds of gray smoke when it went off." Auden said, "Every kid in the street wanted one. All they ever got were crappy little Gem pistols with barrels you pushed in to cock like a sort of air pump and when they went off they made a sort of 'blurk' noise." Auden said, "I had the money saved! One of my uncles used to give me money on my birthday and at Christmas and I had it all saved! If my mother had let me out I could have simply gone around to the High Street and bought one!" Auden said, "The old Webley—by God, it didn't go 'blurk'—it went 'Crack!'"

". . . I went 'blurk,' didn't I, Phil?"

Auden said, "Civlized, that's what my mother wanted me to be." He shook his head. Auden said sadly, "God rest her, she was a kind woman, but she didn't know anything about men."

"No." Fang lowered his head. Funny, they both had the same voice. Fang said, shrinking, "No."

"—real civilization for a hunter isn't staying inside and crapping into John Dog john boxes or pressing your face up against the window while the other kids are out there shooting sparrows or crows or anything that moves! Real civilization is the companionship of men, the sweat, the blood, the striving, the going on together, fighting them on the beaches and in the streets and in the—" Oh, how it rankled. Auden said, "Real civilization is not to let down your mates— to be loyal and trustworthy and battle till the last bullet and, if need be, throw your life into the breach in defense of a wounded friend!"

"Right!" They were alone, hidden, together. Old Phil, he smelled of—he smelled of—he smelled of *power!* Fang, quivering, standing by his friend said, "Kill! Mutilate! Eviscerate! Disembowel!"

Auden said, "I just—"

"I know, Phil!"

"—she was a good kind mummy, but I just—"

"She was a woman, Phil—"

"She was." Auden said gaily, "And what would we do without them, aye? God bless 'em, but—"

Right. But. Fang, German shepherd, police dog, slayer of nations, said, "Yeah! But—" Fang said, "Ha, ha."

"—but you can get sapped of all your—"

"You can't even get out and crap in the street because they think you'll get run down by a car!" Fang said, "Me? Run down by a car? I *eat* fucking *cars!*"

He patted the dog. Dogs were nice. You could talk to a dog. It wasn't a bad dog. It had slept at the end of his bed all night. And it was house-trained and it was—well, it was company. Up high above Peripheral Street, safe, together, mates, Auden said softly, "Sometimes, thinking back on that old Webley, I—" Auden said, "After I joined the cops here, I went back to England on leave. I went home and I—"

"Was the air pistol still there in the shop, Phil?"

Auden said, "No."

Right. Life could be a real bummer. Fang said, "Once I—when I was a puppy, my mistress took me out to the airport to meet someone and I saw, getting out of a plane—"

Auden said, "We used to live near an airfield—"

Fang said, "It was a military plane—"

Auden said, "You know, an air-force field where they used to train—" He patted the dog.

Fang said, ". . . my old mate . . ."

Auden said in a long, sad sigh, "Ahhh . . . well, whatever . . ." He looked down at Fang.

Fang said with tears in his eyes, "She calls me Petal, Phil! That's a girl's name!"

Auden said, *"Chicklet."*

*"You?"*

He nodded. Auden said, "Me."

Fang said, "No!"

Auden said, "Yep."

Fang said, "Friends forever, Phil."

He nodded. His eyes glistened. Auden said, nodding, patting, "Friends forever."

There was a silence.

Auden said quietly, intimately, "Fang—"

Fang said, "Phil . . ."

Auden said, "Fang, I—from the time I was old enough to see them after school at the airfield—from the time I was old enough to look over the fence there—"

Fang said, "I saw dogs out on that airfield that day! They were shepherds like me. They were—"

They had warmth. They were together, hidden. They had the smell of each other. They were men together out on the plains. They were hunters, they were— Auden said suddenly, letting it go after a long time, "God help me, Fang—all I ever wanted to be in life—all I ever wanted from the first time I saw them training—all I ever wanted to be *was a paratrooper!*"

"God!" They had the same voice. If you didn't know, you would have thought both the voices were coming out of Auden. Fang said in a sudden, wonderful, awful recognition, *"God!"* Fang said, "The dogs I saw that day at the airfield—"

Auden said, "Paratroop dogs?"

"Paratroop dogs." He wagged. He nuzzled. *"Paratroop dogs!"*

There was a silence. In that silence, there was only, solely, stillingly, a funny, strange, strange feeling: camaraderie, friendship, loyalty, trust—some people would have said love.

Not paratroopers.

They were behind enemy lines.

Up high, waiting, a weapon forged to a single honed edged, like men, they kept their feelings to themselves.


"The dead man was halfway out of his grave!"

On the phone O'Yee said, *"Bullshit!"*

Chi said, "Mr. O'Yee—?"

O'Yee said, "Bullshit! Which particular X-rated goddamned video is this one from—*I Kill My Parents And Get Away With It Because I Tell the Cops I'm Fucking Crazy?*" O'Yee said, "Bullshit! There is no dead man! There is no goddamned Luger. There isn't any poor, pathetic bloody Chi—THERE ISN'T ANY YOU!"

"I—"

"You don't sleep in the streets! People don't thump you over the ear in phone booths—you live in a house somewhere with your parents and what you do is—" O'Yee said, "You don't know the address of the house where the dead man is, but I'll bet you know the address of the school you go to—which one is it? One of those ones where your parents pay a million dollars a year so you can buy dope and get hold of guns because you can pay for them? What's the trouble, kid? Rich mommy and daddy living too long? *Or are you just so fucking bored you thought you'd like to bump them off and get away with it just for kicks?*"

"It isn't a house where the dead man is—it's a shop!'"

"Sure it is! Which one—Tiffany, Abercrombie & Fitch? Harrods? Bloomingdale's? Lane Crawfords?" O'Yee said bitterly, "Poor old dead man halfway out of his grave—all he had were a few coins for phone calls . . . *Didn't he have any paper money?*"

"It doesn't fit in phones!" Chi said, "Mr. O'Yee—"

O'Yee said, "Go to hell."

"I—"

O'Yee said, "Go to hell." O'Yee said, "Fuck you."

"*Mr. O'Yee—!*"

O'Yee said, "You won't get away with it because I'll make sure you don't get away with it. You think playing at being a poor little street kid is tough? You wait until you start playing poor little kid in juvenile detention—that'll make tough look like cakewalk!" O'Yee said, "That is, if you are a kid!" He dropped his voice and became full of malice. "Because if you're not a kid you're going to rot! You'll find a new meaning to rot! You'll rot so hard and so deep, you won't even rot, you'll turn to goddamned dust!" O'Yee said, "Get off my phone line!"

There was a silence.

O'Yee said, "Well?"

There was no sound at all on the end of the line.

O'Yee said, "Well? Is that it?" O'Yee, shouting, demanded, "*Well?*"

It became mad.

At the door, snapping at the air, the Dalmatian, becoming mad, frothing, began pushing at the door to the restaurant.

It began barking, snarling. It pushed and threw itself against the metal door and howled.

All the smells were going—the smell of death was taking it over, cloaking it, eating it up—it had nothing in its nose but the smell of death and dying and it threw itself against the door and did not budge it.

It bayed. It bayed, not with its head up in the air, but lowered, and it bayed at the step and the sidewalk and the smell of death seeping in everywhere and overtaking it.

It had become mad with the hurt, with the ache.

Snarling, snapping, running then stopping, snapping at something invisible that pursued it, the Dalmatian, shaking its head to hold in the last wisp of all the smells except the smell of death, got down the alley and, without pausing, running, trying to escape, ran from the smell of the thing that smelled of death.


"*Commandos Strike at Dawn!*"

Fang said, "*Silent Killing. Death by Canine Windpipe Ripping-Out!*"

"Soldiers we—"

"Pals and mates!"

"'When all the world is young, lad, / And all the trees are green; / And every goose a swan, lad, / And every lass a queen; / Then hey for boot and horse, lad, / And round the world away; / Young blood must have its course, lad, / And every dog his day.'"

The man was a prince! Fang said, "God, that's good!"

"I learned it at school."

What a friend he had in Auden. He was lost for words. Fang said, "Gosh!" And he got a pat on the head. Fang, touched to the soul, said, "—*gosh!*"

"Fang . . ."

"Phil . . ."

Auden said, "The Dalmatian—"

Fang said, "Ah! Ha! The what?" Fang said, "Oh, ho, ho, ho, ho. *HO!*"

Death, destruction, murder, ruin, rapine, sparrow shooting.

Fang, just waiting for it, said, "Heh, heh, heh, *HEH!*"


Chi said softly, "I don't know what to say—"

"Say the goddamned address if it's true!"

"I don't know the address!"

"You can read! You can read the words on a goddamned Luger so you can read the name on a street!"

"I didn't go in the front way! I went there at night! I went through an alley and I—" Chi said, "I called you because—"

"I know why you called me!"

"I—"

O'Yee said, "Why don't you have a little blubber? A little weep? A sob. Get a catch in your voice—after all, I'm a daddy—it'll work on me!" O'Yee, his voice hard and brittle, said, "Why don't you say, 'I called you because I don't have anyone else in the entire world'? Why don't you say you live on the streets like a dog and all you want is a friendly voice? Why don't you say that—"

Chi said, "It's true! I don't have anyone!"

"Well, now you haven't got me!" O'Yee said, "You never had me! What do you think I am—some sort of pathetic dumb bloody cop who'll fall for anything? Is that what they teach you in your expensive private school? That cops are there as the blunt objects of the goddamned ruling classes and if you're a member of the ruling classes yourself you're immune? *Is that what they tell you?*" O'Yee said, "A dead man halfway out of his grave in an unnamed shop in the unnamed street with his pockets full of coins and a loaded Luger—is that really the best you can do?" O'Yee said, "You speak English—"

Chi said in Cantonese, "No—"

"Oh, yes, you do. I can hear it in your voice! If you want a really good one next time try reading Edgar Allan Poe—next time, try the premature burial or the razor-sharp pendulum bits—at least they've got a bit of style!" O'Yee said, "A Luger—is that the top of the line? Why not a goddamned Persian scimitar or a Philippino head axe or a goddamned medieval mace next time? How about a cased pair of quality eighteenth-century English flintlock dueling pistols?" O'Yee said, "*How about something with a bit of style?*"

He was sobbing. It was a strange sound, as if it was something he had never done before and did not know fully how to release. It was a soft sound. It sounded a long way away.

O'Yee listened.

O'Yee said softly, "Go to hell."

He hung up.

At his desk, with his hands shaking, he lit a cigarette and drew in deeply on it.

At his desk, looking at the hung-up phone, he put the cigarette carefully into an ashtray and got out of his chair.

He could not stop himself. He ran for the toilets in the corridor of the station just outside the Detectives' Room.

There, long and violently, until he thought his guts would twist and strangle everything inside of him, there, long and violently, he threw up.


All its senses were gone, and in its brain there were little sparking flecks of pain. It smelled only death; it was pursued by it—it remembered as a folk memory only the sound of a single voice. The voice was going, disappearing, growing fainter, being swallowed up. The Dalmatian was snarling, frothing, hurting.

It was lost. It had nowhere to go. All the smells it smelled now were a confusion, a maze, a kaleidoscope—they all, all meant nothing.

It ran, not knowing where it was going or what it was supposed to do.

It ran. It ran.

It ran, without knowing it did it, becoming lost over and over, in the direction of Peripheral Street.


### HUNG I KUAN CHINESE OPERA THEATER
*Sole Retail Outlet for Quality Mandarin Opera Cassette Tapes in Hong Kong*

It was painted in huge yellow and green Chinese characters on the entrance to the place, above a billboard of a stylized painting of a white-bearded Imperial court official in full brocaded coat holding up his hand, as a warrior wearing a jeweled headdress drew his sword to slay him. Behind the two figures there was a flat of willow trees and a Chinese arched wooden bridge.

*Now Playing, Evenings and Matinees*:

*LIEN HUA HU*! It meant Lotus Flower Lake.

The building had once been a movie house with fake marble porticos and steps—the swinging glass doors into the carpeted hallway were still there. Outside in the street, Feiffer could hear the sounds of *bianging* and *paixiao*—chime slabs and panpipes, and the rhythm of *shu* and *yu* percussion instruments as the orchestra inside must have been practicing or tuning up for the afternoon's performance.

## HUNG I KUAN CHINESE OPERA THEATER
*Sole Retail Outlet for Quality Mandarin Opera Cassette Tapes*
*in Hong Kong*

It was all he had.

Going up the imitation marble steps, only half listening to the sounds of the orchestra and their ancient instruments, Feiffer pushed at the center glass entrance door and went inside.

"Petal? *Fang? Phil?*"

Peripheral Street was full of trash cans and, strung across the road from all the buildings, early morning washing: sheets, shirts, linen, underwear, dresses—he could see nothing above the ground floor of any of the buildings.

He saw Mr. Wah standing by the open door of his shop. He seemed to be counting something on his fingers.

"Fang? *Petal?* Phil?" For the third time, Spencer looked into Auden's parked car and felt the hood. The car was locked and empty and the hood cold.

"FANG?"

"Petal . . . ?"

"*Phil . . . ?*"

In the street, Spencer looked at his watch.

He shook his head and wondered where they were.

# 15

It was the sole, single thing they had in common other than that they were dead. In the dressing room of the Hung I Kuan Chinese Opera Theater, Han Shou-Chen, the actor-manager of the place said in a raspy, throaty voice, "The names mean nothing to me at all." He was dressed in the costume of Ts'ao Ts'ao, the legendary villain of the Three Kingdoms in the opera *Ch'ang Fan P'o*—the Long Hillside. He towered over Feiffer. At least six-foot-four in his brocade gown with its padded shoulders, he touched at the long flowing black beard and then at the thick white death-mask makeup on his face. His eyebrows were penciled in: they were sharp stabs of blackness on the plaster-of-paris face. Han Shou-Chen, shaking his head, said, "I saw the pictures in the newspapers— I don't know the faces." He touched again at the horsehair beard, then reached back behind his ears and took it off. He shook his head, "No, nothing."

Outside on the stage the rest of the cast, the nobles, the princes, princesses and the peasants, were reaching a crescendo in a chorus. They were in front of a simple painted set showing willow trees and a bridge, like the pattern on old plates. Like the choruses or climaxes of all Mandarin operas, the crescendo was coming in high, screeching falsetto voices. In the orchestra, the chi—the side-blown flutes—and the pan pipes and jiangu drums were getting louder and louder, drowning out the singing, and he had to strain to make himself heard. Feiffer said, "What about the other members of the cast?"

He was watching them, checking on their rehearsal. Han Shou-Chen, starting to remove his brocaded gown, said, "No. We all saw the papers this morning before rehearsal. Everyone was talking about it, but no one knew them." He took off his heavy brocade coat with an effort and put it carefully on a bamboo valet framework where it hung down like a giant's shirt on a dwarf. His shoulders and chest and stomach were heavily padded. Han, undoing the strings that held the shoulder pads and removing them, becoming slighter, said in a thinner, more natural voice, "If they came here regularly—"

"Do you have a booking list?"

"No." He took off the layers of stomach padding and became thin. With the metamorphosis the husky voice of the character he played was also going. Han Shou-Chen said sadly, "This isn't the Tang dynasty in Imperial Nanking, this is the twentieth century in Hong Kong." He undid a massive quilted padding like a bulletproof vest from around his abdomen. "The only booking lists you'll find around this part of the world these days are for videos at the local video shop." Under all the padding he wore a vest and long, padded trousers. He seemed strange, misshapen, too tall for his upper body. He had, under the makeup, a small, delicate face. Han Shou-Chen said, "Very few people in the Colony speak Mandarin, even fewer can claim to have a love of the traditional form of Mandarin opera, and, as our audiences dwindle and our costs rise, even fewer of those can afford the prices we have to charge to keep the theater open." The dressing room had only one mirror. All the rest of the room was taken up with the bamboo valets for the gorgeous costumes. Han Shou-Chen, wiping at his forehead with a kerchief and at the same time removing his black horsehair wig, said sadly, "Here we are, the custodians of the ancient pre-Communist ways in the real China, anxiously awaiting the time the Communists take back Hong Kong so we can receive state grants from them to continue to show the way things were before the world changed and you had to have state grants." He wiped at the white makeup on his forehead. He seemed quite young. Han, going to sit in front of the mirror, said, pointing at the penciled slashes of the eyebrows, "False face. In Chinese opera all the actors wear false faces—even the men who play the parts of women still disguise their women's faces as other faces—"

Feiffer said firmly, "Lau, Hang, Tin . . ."

"—supposedly it stems from the legend of the Prince of Lan Ling whose face was so beautiful he had to wear a mask to frighten his enemies." Han Shou-Chen said to the mirror as he must have said to his cast a thousand times, "The Communists are pragmatic. They know that to encourage the tradition of ancient theater is to affect nothing in their grand scheme of things—on the contrary, it makes the people think they're not only pragmatic and unafraid, it makes them think that somehow Communism, one day, will also be in the great tradition of things Chinese." He wiped at his face in a single streak from eye to mouth. He was not listening to Feiffer; he was hearing, outside, the great climax of the opera, all the straining falsetto voices and the roars of the villains and the crashing of cymbals and drums. Han said, "They need us because the sort of modern operas they created—*Six Days on a Collective Farm* and *The Revolutionary Girl*—are garbage." He wiped away at his face. He was not young. Under his eyes there were lines and dark circles of tiredness. Han Shou-Chen said, "I can't help you, I'm afraid." He shrugged. "Maybe the cassette was just a gift from a friend. Maybe, like music to most people, it was just noise."

"There were two cassettes, one in each of the vans." Feiffer said, "Is there any sort of theater club that—"

"No."

"Or group bookings in maybe someone else's name that—"

He wiped off all the makeup. Han Shou-Chen, gazing in the mirror at the man who looked back at him, said, "No." Outside on the stage the maid was singing the virtues of her lover. She sang, *"Ta teng lung chao pieh—jen! To light one's lantern for another—Oh!"* Han Shou-Chen said, "I can tell you nothing at all."

The dressing room was heavy with the smell of makeup and the brocade. The brocade smelled musty, as if the cost of hand washing it were prohibitive or there were no time for it. At the mirror Han was staring at his own eyes, picking off the eyebrow slashes with bamboo tweezers. The padded white pantaloons tied around his waist by white strings must have been too tight. He undid the knot and exhaled a breath. Feiffer said, "The cassettes can only be bought here—is that right?"

"Of our current operas, no. Of ones we did when things were better, yes."

"*Night Battle?*"

"Yes." All the makeup was gone and the voice was of a middle-aged, sad man with very little future and a cast and orchestra to sustain.

Han said, "Yes, you can buy that." He smiled. "Do you want a copy? We've got about twenty or thirty of them left gathering dust in the office. Or *Tai Chen Wai Chuan*—we've got a lot of them too. Or even the opera the theater is named after, the *Hung I Kuan*, The Rainbow Pass—lots of them too." He was breathing hard, holding himself back. Han said tightly, "We're falling to pieces! We're in the middle of the new China—the pop music and the videos and the cheap fourth-rate and you ask me if—" Han said, "Go to the nearest video shop! See if they've got a spare copy of the latest sex and murder film! Listen to their answer!" Han said, "Yes, we sell them here! We're the sole outlet in Hong Kong! We're the sole outlet because no one else will stock them because—" Han, getting up, looming over Feiffer, demanded, "What do you want? I don't know why four people who are dead had our cassettes! The four people who are dead had one of them playing as they became dead! We're not part of that! We know nothing about it! We aren't dead, merely dying!" He was shaking a little. Outside on the stage there was a second long sad climax coming. The chime bells were ringing in a monotone and, as the heroine died and her lover cried to heaven, there was the soft thrum of a panpipe on a single, long, held note. Han said, "Once, the Hung I Kuan company was the greatest troupe in all of Imperial China!" He shook his head hard. "I don't understand the world anymore!"

He had nothing. He was getting nowhere. He realized under the padded pantaloons the man was wearing wooden Chinese boots with thick square wooden high heels almost eight inches tall. When he got up from his mirror and all the makeup was gone, he would be short.

Han said sadly, "All I can tell you about the people who are dead— if they came here to the theater, if they listened to the music and the singing on tape—is that, probably, they were good, ordinary, decent people!"

"They were."

"Then I know nothing." Han said, "Good, ordinary, decent people—who ever notices them?"

He stood up, undoing the strings completely on the pantaloons to go to one of the bamboo valets to get his own street clothes hanging there.

Han said softly, tightly, "No one! No one ever notices something good until it is gone!"

". . . Mr. O'Yee . . ."

O'Yee said on the phone, "Yes."

There was a silence.

O'Yee said, "Yes, I'm here."

Chi said, "It's not true."

O'Yee said, "No."

"I'm not what you said—"

O'Yee said, "No." O'Yee said, "Aren't you?" He was calling from somewhere on a main street. In the background, O'Yee could hear the traffic. O'Yee asked, "What sort of person are you?"

"The man in the hole was dead!"

"Sure."

"The gun was lying beside him and the money was—" Chi said, "I took the money to call—to call—"

"And you got me." O'Yee said, "And you're happy with that. Anyone would have done, but you got me." O'Yee said, "You got a dead man in a hole and you got a gun and you got money and you got someone yesterday waiting for the phone who clipped you around the ear and threw you out and, last night, you probably got a doorway to sleep in." O'Yee said, "You get a lot of things. You get a lot of people. You get all sorts of people and all sorts of things because they turn up or they appear by accident or you stumble onto them—" O'Yee said evenly, tightly, "Tell me though, when you're not getting things, when things aren't happening to you, when you're not just reacting to whatever happens or whoever happens along—what do you actually do for yourself?" O'Yee said, "What sort of person are you?"

"*All you want is the gun!*"

"Yes."

"You want the gun! If I didn't have the gun you wouldn't even talk to me!"

O'Yee said, "You talked to me. I didn't call you—"

"You don't even know who I am!"

"All right. Who are you?"

There was a silence. Chi said, "I don't know what you mean!"

"What sort of person are you?" In the Detectives' Room, he was perspiring. His voice was steady. O'Yee wiped at his forehead with his finger. "What sort of person do you think you are?"

"I don't know what you mean!"

"What sort of person do you think I am?"

"You're—you're a cop!"

O'Yee said, "And, as a matter of fact, I'm also Eurasian, a little shortsighted, married, a father, a great worrier over small things, an American by birth and Chinese by inclination, unsuccessful at probably almost everything; I'd like to sail away in a yacht to South America, I often think about dying and I'm also not as tall as I'd like and—" O'Yee said, "Game: pick the label. What sort of person is that in one word? What sort of person are you?"

Chi said, "I'm just a kid!"

O'Yee said, "All right." O'Yee said, "So was I, once. I forgot that in my description of myself."

*"All you want is the gun!"*

"What do you want?" O'Yee asked curiously, "What do you do? Not what happens to you, but—what do you do? What do you want to be?" O'Yee asked, "Who are you?"

*"Who are you?"*

O'Yee said, "I don't know. Is it one of the twenty questions you get to ask in the game?"

"Yes."

O'Yee said, "Give me a second to think about it."

Chi said, "Your time's up!"

O'Yee said, "I don't know. Do you want a quick answer—you know, the sort you give . . . or would you like a proper, truthful answer?"

"The proper, truthful answer!"

All his children were nearly grown up. They needed him no longer. They knew all the answers. He touched at his face. O'Yee said slowly, "I don't know. I'm a man in clothing with a face and I take up a certain amount of space in the world so I am, I guess, what you see . . ." O'Yee said, "I'm a cop. I'm a sort of body shell that I dress up with a face and an occupation and I guess that's what I am." Maybe, really, that was all he was. O'Yee said, "I'm something inside of that shell and under those clothes and not even remotely connected to that label that—whatever it is that isn't all the things I appear to be, maybe that's what I am." O'Yee said, "People think there is something else— everybody thinks that. Everybody thinks there's something hidden and deep inside them and different and that's what they are." O'Yee asked casually, "What do you think?"

Chi said, "You talk to people. Not many people talk—to people—"

O'Yee said, "Yeah, I like people. I like—" O'Yee said, "I used to like talking to my children, but they don't want to talk to me anymore." O'Yee said, "They know everything now."

"No one can know everything!"

"How about you? Do you like talking to people?"

There was a silence. In the silence O'Yee could hear the traffic. He could hear trucks. He was on a main street somewhere. He was not far away.

Chi said softly, "I like talking to you."

"Sometimes I used to hug my children, but they're too old for that too now." O'Yee said, "I used to think I did it for them, but it wasn't—it was for me." O'Yee said, "I guess you know what I mean. I guess you don't like being hugged either—"

He said nothing.

O'Yee said, "Do you?"

Chi said, "I don't know."

"Chi—"

Chi said, "Yes?"

O'Yee asked quietly, touching at the perspiration on his face, "Chi—?"

"Yes?"

O'Yee asked again, "Chi, what sort of person—for a kid—do you think you are?"


He heard it. In the street, coming from the receiver in his car, Spencer heard a single beep from the beeper unit.

In Peripheral Street, walking up and down, trying to peer behind all the washing up high and the lines of trash cans on the ground, he tried to work out where Auden and Petal and the beeper unit all were.

In the street, outside his shop, Mr. Wah was still counting on his fingers. He was smiling.

*Beep!*

He heard it.

"Phil— Fang? *Petal?*"

Walking up and down, watching for Dalmatians, he tried to work out where they were.


The washing smelled like parachutes. The paratroopers, dreaming their dreams, nuzzled their noses into a hanging sheet and dreamed of drops.

They wondered.

*Green light.*

*Hit the silk!*

*Go!*

They were silent. They wondered. Over Arnhem, their eyes closed, they pressed together in the confined space of their humming aircrafts—waves of them above a black and white cloudy sky—and wondered.

Maybe . . .

Maybe . . .

Mates. Mates never let a mate down.

On the second-floor balcony of the boarded-up and dank apartment block due for demolition eight doors down from Mr. Wah's, hidden by the sheet, the Airborne, shuffling slightly on their benches and sitting accidentally on the activated beeper unit, glanced at each other and wondered what, really, they were made of.

"Apache—!" It was a low grunt in the back of Fang's throat more than a word.

Auden said in a whisper, gently, "Geronimo."

Oh, right. Fang said, nodding a little, "Right, Phil."

Phil said, "Okay."

"Right."

They were silent.

They waited.

"*Night Battle*—what can you tell me about the opera itself?" He watched as Han, sitting on a camphor-wood stool beside the clothed and bearded bamboo valet, bent down to slip on his shoes. The great wooden villain's shoes were at the base of the valet, poking out under the brocaded coat like an intruder behind a curtain. He saw Han glance at them.

Han said, "It's a martial opera full of drums and rasping warriors' arias and great sweeping balletic movements." He seemed to be holding back tears held back a long time, "Flags and pennants and swords." There would be no relief in the tears; tomorrow, the world would be only another day older, going where it was going—there was no point to tears. Han said, "Not good. Not good for the tourists; too noisy, too fast to follow in the photostated translations the hotels used to give out. No girls in cheong-sams." He made a mocking sound at the back of his throat and tapped himself on the chest, "How old am I?" Han said, "No girls doing live sex acts with donkeys." Han said, "It's one of the cycle of Chinese operas from the Warring States period—it isn't popular."

"Who actually sold the cassettes?"

"The girl at the door." Han said, "There were, originally, two hundred and fifty of them—that's a minimum order."

"How many do you have left?"

"Twenty, maybe thirty."

"Would she remember who she—"

"No! Of course not." Han said, "And she's gone anyway. She—and she's gone anyway."

"Then who mans the door? When I came in there wasn't anybody."

"The cassettes are sold the night of the performance."

"How often do you do—"

"Never! It isn't popular." Han said, "It isn't a popular opera. We only do it—we only did it—" He wished he was not having this conversation. Outside, on the stage, there was silence. The rehearsal had finished and the cast knew who he was with and stayed away. He wished they would come in. They waited on the stage in semi-darkness, saving the lights. Han said, "We only ever did it once or twice."

"The cassette is your company?"

"Yes."

"And you had one or two seasons of it?" Feiffer said, "Is it one or two? How many performances did you do?"

"*We did it once!* We didn't do it once or twice, we did it once! And it wasn't a season, it was a single performance!" Han said, "And we sold maybe thirty cassettes of it at the door because we probably only had about thirty people sitting in the seats watching it! We do a lot of things once! We rehearse two operas at a time in case, after the first performance of one, the house is so bad—" Han said, "We have that in common with New York; if the critics don't like us, we close down the same night!" Han said, "We did *Night Battle* once! We never did it again!" Han said, "Why are you doing this?"

"You said the minimum order for the cassettes from the, I assume, recording company, was two hundred and fifty—"

"We had thirty people in. We have maybe twenty-five left." Han said, "The other two hundred or so cassettes—" Han said so softly Feiffer had to strain to hear him, "We have a special deal with the company. They let us return the unsold cassettes for erasure." He twisted his mouth. He shrugged. Han said, "We have to beg that in the name of culture."

"The two cassettes in the vans were sold here the night of the performance?"

"Yes."

"Have you sold any more since?"

"No."

He would not look up from his shoes. Maybe he was weeping. Feiffer said, "I'm sorry."

He said something, but Feiffer could not hear what it was.

Feiffer said, "I'm sorry. I'm very sorry."

He looked up. He shrugged. Without the great coat and the padding and the high wooden warrior's shoes he looked very small, like a child sitting next to his father's oversized clothing.

Other than that they were dead, it was the sole, single thing they had in common. Feiffer, pressing, said, "When? Mr. Han? When? When did you do the single performance of the opera?"


Chi said with alarm, "I'm out of coins! I haven't got any money left!"

O'Yee said nothing.

"Mr. O'Yee—!" Chi said in terror. "Mr. O'Yee, I haven't got any money left to call you!" Chi said, "Mr. O'Yee—?" In the background there was the sound of someone banging on the glass of the booth with a coin. They were in a hurry to ring and inside the booth all there was was a kid. Chi said, pleading, "Mr. O'Yee—what do I do?"

At last, all the coins were gone. He waited, perspiring. O'Yee said quietly, "I don't know. It depends on who you are and where you are and what you think you—"

"Mr. O'Yee—" In the background, the banging was becoming angry. If he didn't get out of the booth, he was going to be hit. Chi said in alarm, "I can't think of—of—"

O'Yee said, "Come in."

"*All you want is the gun!*"

"Come in."

"I—"

"Come in. Just hang up and walk and come in and—"

"*I'm afraid!*"

"Come in and—"

"I—" In the background, the banging stopped and there was a sudden silence.

"Come in and I can—" O'Yee said desperately, "I can help! I can help! I swear to God that I can help!" He swore to God that he could—his children no longer needed him to hug them. On the line, there was nothing. O'Yee, shouting down the line, ordered him, "Chi! Chi! I can—"

There was a click.

There was a click and it meant that the line had gone dead.

"*CHI—!*"

There was only the steady burring of the dial tone.

"*CHI!*"

In the Detectives' Room, alone, all the things he was and he thought he was and hoped he was and—maybe, possibly, all the things he really, truly was—O'Yee—nothing, just a man with a face, a little shortsighted, wearing a shirt and slacks and a tie—shrieked hopelessly at the top of his voice into the dead, black instrument, *"CHI—! DON'T GO!"*

O'Yee said softly, "Please, please, don't go . . ."

Please . . .

In the Detectives' Room, all his life, in the odd secret place where what he really was was hidden, alone, O'Yee, so close, put the receiver back down on the phone and touched at his face.

Outside his shop, grinning, Mr. Wah was putting all his wind chimes in the street. Good dog, rich dog. Dog with master-criminal master worth many dollars—nice dog.

Chinka-chinka-chinka . . . In the street, hanging from boxes, from ladders, from broken-up shelves and door boards, hanging from everywhere, the little bells went chinka-chinka-chinka.

Mr. Wah went, "Heh, heh, heh, heh."

"Phil? Fang? *Petal—?*"

*Beep!*

"Phil! Fang? *Petal!*"

He heard them. At the far end of the street, on his haunches behind a trash can, its muzzle all covered in froth, its fangs bared, the Dalmatian heard the bells.

It was sick, hurt. It was made of muscle and bone and terrible, unyielding obedience. Something inside its brain cord made the connection and all the bone and muscle tensed.

On their balcony, the chums dreamed of soft landings and fields of yellow daffodils. They dreamed their martial dreams.

Behind the trash cans, it began snarling. It tasted blood.

Behind the trash cans, the Dalmatian, rising, strong, listened to the sound of the bells.

Han said, "Two years ago. I don't remember the date or the month, but I can look it up for you in the office if that's what you want."

It was all he had. He waited.

Han said, trying to think, "I don't remember! Two years ago. I don't remember the month or the date, but it was two years ago when we thought we might try out unpopular operas just one night of the week—when we thought the people who were real fans might come and—" He touched at his face. He did not want to get up and walk with Feiffer along the back of the theater to the office in full view of his silent, waiting cast. Han said, "I don't remember—what does it matter? It was like all the operas—it ran, in its cut form here from 8:30 in the evening to 10:30 and it—" Han said, "It was about two years ago."

"What *day?*"

"What?"

"What *day?*"

He looked up. It seemed to matter so little. Han said, "Day?" He shrugged. He remembered that. Han said, "Well, it was—"

"It was a Thursday."

"Yes."

"It was a *Thursday!*"

Han, not understanding, said, "Yes, that's right. How did you know that?"

"A *Thursday*—8:30 P.M. to 10:30 P.M. exactly—on a Thursday—"

"Yes!" He couldn't understand the look on the man's face at all. It seemed, to him, such a little, unimportant thing. Han said again, "Yes."

He asked, "Why? Is that something important?"

# 16

Curse the steady droning of the C–47. It played havoc with men's minds. The sheets all smelled like parachutes. Jaws jutted. Worms of doubt crept in. You started talking to yourself. Dogs started talking to you. Whether it was nobler in the nerve to— He patted Fang on the helmet. Auden said softly, "When the dog comes down the street, you leap down and clobber it. If you freeze I'll be there to give you a shove."

"Thanks, Phil." Fang said breathlessly, "You're a very noble person." He was his mate.

Airborne was about nobility. He'd seen this movie once when the first guy out of a captive balloon for his first jump went out with a careless grin, pulled at his ripcord and, after the chute didn't open, went down like a rock. That wasn't noble. What was noble was that the next guy in the stick—the one they'd all thought was a coward— went out without a word to prove that the girl he loved in the chute-packing room packed good chutes. He couldn't remember what happened then. Auden said, "The coward dies a thousand—"

Fang said softly, "I'm not a coward, Phil. I've had a good breakfast.

A man needs red meat. Before—before—" Before he was a vegetarian. Fang said, "I don't want to talk about before."

It was a long way down to the street. The street was full of the sound of bells.

Fang said, "You stay here. I'll go."

It was a hell of a long way down to the street.

Fang said, "I won't need a push."

It must have been twenty feet onto the sidewalk and the sidewalk was solid cement.

Fang said, "My plans are far advanced and this time I shall not hesitate." Nobility. Fang said, "Phil, I appreciate you giving up your moment of glory and honor to see an old friend regain his self-respect."

You could get killed hitting that cement.

Fang said, "There are worse things in life than death." Going shopping with the nun. Fang said, nuzzling a little, "We dream our dreams, Phil, but few of us ever get the opportunity to see what we're really made of."

Auden said softly, "Maybe I should go . . ."

Fang said, "Airborne. Airborne puts a premium on nobility and self-sacrifice."

Auden said, "Maybe I should try it myself just to prove I can do it."

"You can do it!"

"I know." It was a hell of a long way down. The cement on the sidewalk looked like cement. Auden said, scratching at his face where his helmet chin-strap was starting to press in on him, shrugging, "What the hell does it matter if an Alsatian leaps off a balcony? Alsatians are always leaping off balconies. What counts is whether a man can leap off a balcony." Auden said, "The Dalmatian is probably as vicious as hell by now."

"I can do it, Phil!"

Auden said, "Maybe I should go—" The bells, the bells—they were getting to him. Auden said slowly, "I know I can go, but you, you've—"

"I was undernourished! I wasn't the dog I am now!" The kid was starting to beg. Fang, whining, pleaded, "Phil, I can do it! Give me a chance and I can do it!"

"I don't know." He'd often wondered what it would be like. It would be like cement. Auden, scratching, trying to make up his mind, staring deeply into the dog's eyes to see the weakness there, said, "I—um—I just don't know, Fang—"

"Phil, I can do it! Just gimme a shot!"

The Title—how many shots did you get? You got one. Maybe you never even got— He could do it: he knew he could. When he had been a kid he had jumped off his bed a thousand times. Auden said, "Maybe I should see if I can do it myself."

Oh. Nobility—he's wondered what it was. What it was was giving up your own chance to know and giving that chance to your mate and living the rest of your life not knowing—that was nobility. It was hard lines. He was an Alsatian, a noble breed. He tried noble. Fang said nobly with a lump in his throat, "Okay. You go." He was sitting next to his friend. He put his head on his paws. A single tear welled up in his eye. Fang said in a soft growl, "Yeah, I owe you. You go." He would walk the streets of cities the rest of his life a broken dog. Fang said, "All right, Phil, I give my chance to you."

"You're not a bad dog, but—"

Fang said, "But I failed. I failed twice." He knew. Oh, he knew all right. Fang said, "The doors in the car—I kept them shut because I was afraid."

"You bit the wrong guy!"

"Yep."

"You had two chances at it and you blew both of them!"

Fang said, "I did."

"Airborne—the paras—you either jump or die!"

"I died, Phil."

"The dreams you have when you're a kid—"

"Just dreams."

"—when the chance comes you have to see if—"

"You go, Phil. You know you can do it because you've done it before. Me—well, I could let the regiment down and—"

Auden said, "I've never done it before! *I've never jumped down from a balcony onto a vicious, snarling dog in my life!*" He looked at Fang. It was a good dog, old Fang, with soft brown eyes and when you patted it, it wagged its tail. Auden said, "I've never—" He fell silent. Auden said, "I don't know, maybe I'm afraid."

"*You Phil?*"

"Why not? Why can't I be afraid too?" He had the big .357 magnum. He wasn't allowed to use it. Auden, staring at the cement, said in a quavering voice, "God, if I miss the dog—"

"*You, Phil?*"

"*Me!*"

Fang said, "You go, Phil. You can do it." The droning of the aircraft was getting louder. It sounded just like Hong Kong traffic working itself up to the rush hour. The bells, the bells. Fang said, sucking in his chest, "Phil, you go, and if you hesitate, I'll give you a push!"

"I don't need a push!"

"A shove. A gentle nudge—"

Auden said, "If I were noble I'd give up my chance to see if I had the nerve to do it and let you do it to make a man of you!"

Fang said nobly, formally, "Phil, I give up my chance."

It made you ashamed—if he meant it. Maybe it was the cement.

Fang said, "I am not afraid of the cement. I welcome death, but, as your friend and your mate and your comrade in arms, I pass up my chance to die on the battlefield and I bequeath my place on the regimental honor roll to you." Nobody would ever know—maybe that was true courage. It was going to be hard to live with on a diet of mush. Fang said, "Take my place and leap into glory!"

The bells, the bells. "You're only saying that because you're too shit-scared to make the jump!"

"That, Phil, is a thought unworthy of you."

"You failed twice yesterday! Twice yesterday, *you failed*!"

"I failed because I had forgotten all my atavistic instincts." He was hurt, you could tell. Fang said tightly, "I had forgotten that we sprang from the caves, and to the caves we must all respring." Fang said with a lump in his throat, "My friend reminded me of my duty to my own basic, true animal nature and I now reward my friend with the opportunity for him to soothe his fears about his own manhood while I slink away ignobly through life branded as a coward and a cur in men's eyes."

"You go."

"No, Phil." Fang said, "I doubt your motives now. Now, you must go yourself."

Auden said, "I can do it."

"You can. You can do it."

Auden said, "I can." He looked down at the cement.

"You've had a good, hearty breakfast, Phil, and the companionship of a dog who worships you and now, now—"

Auden said, "I'll do it!"

"You won't be sorry."

He was sorry already.

Auden said, "You're a good dog, Fang."

"Thanks, Phil." There were bells. The traffic was swelling. Tears were welling up.

"I have to know, Petal—"

It was a whisper. The whisper said, "Chicklet—"

Auden said sadly, "Please don't call me that."

"Bye, Phil." Fang said softly, affected, "I fear we will not meet again in this world."

"You're a damn good dog."

"Give 'em hell, soldier."

"Okay." On the balcony, the sheets all smelling of parachutes, Auden said, "Fang—?"

"Yes, Phil?" Funny when you found a real friend how he sounded just like you.

Auden said, "Fang, you go! I am not afraid. I am noble! *You go!*"

"Phil?" His heart leapt. He heard bells. "Phil!"

He heard bells and bells and bells and bells. He heard someone call his name. It was Spencer on the street, but he heard bells and bells and bells and his heart leapt. He saw, also, coming around the corner of the street, a Dalmatian dog frothing at the mouth. His heart sank. He saw the cement.

Fang, his eyes wide in alarm, just like Auden's, said in a sudden gasp of alarm, "Who? *Me?*"

Auden said, "*Oh my God!*"


It was like coming out of an empty, darkened room into the light. Yellowthread Street teemed with people. There were cars, trams, buses, handcarts—it was the busy time of day and from the steps of the station, all O'Yee could see were people. They were all adults, men, women, pushing, moving, avoiding each other at the distance of half an arm's length—there was no room between them for a child.

He had never thought of it before—he had never thought what they looked like to someone small. They were giants, they were the colors of shirts and pants and dresses and slacks. They were shoes and sandals and rubber flip-flops. They were movement and chaos and perfume and sweat and mouths talking, making sounds, high up. The street was full of hoardings, of unlit neon lights, of signs and stalls and paper scrolls advertising wares or calling on the gods for protection. He could not see the sidewalk. He could not see anything of it other than that it was the repository, the ground floor, for the trash of the giants, for the dust they carried on their shoes, the cigarette butts they threw down—it was a gauntlet of swinging paper shopping bags.

He had never listened to the noise. It was deafening, a hum, a cacophony of engines and movement and sound. Down there, low, there was the sound of shoes on the cement—from the step, he followed with his eyes two tee-shirted men carrying rolls of carpet and heard—actually *heard*, isolated—the sound of their bare feet on the pavement. He smelled the fumes from the cars and trucks and buses. The fumes were down there, low, swirling, invisible, *there*, down *there*.

On the street, there was no room for a child at all and if he was there O'Yee could not see him.

He watched.

He stood on the steps of the station in his shirt-sleeves, his gun and shoulder holster in the Detectives' Room in a drawer. He stood there with his hands by his sides, moving his head from side to side, trying to see.

He could see all the street.

If the boy was there, he could not see him.

He waited. Pursing his lips, all the muscles in his neck tight and hurting, O'Yee, silent—in all the street the only truly silent thing there—O'Yee, kneading his thumbs against his fingers in fists, waited.


*South China Morning Post.*

In English.

*Oriental Daily News.*

In Chinese.

*November 16, two years ago.*

There was nothing. In the newspaper reading room of the Hong Bay Public Library, both the newspapers were on the same microfilm strip for Chinese/English comparison. They were side by side, page to page.

REFORMERS GAIN CLEAR ADVANTAGE IN TOP-LEVEL PEKING SHUFFLE.

It was political news from China: it covered the front pages of both newspapers and ran over, continued, into the next two pages with pictures of all the personalities involved and, just so no one would have any doubt, a stock photograph of the Gate of Heavenly Peace to show what Peking looked like.

It was nothing.

At the screen Feiffer clicked up the next few pages.

FORTY-SEVEN CMB EMPLOYEES ARRESTED BY ICAC.

It was about corruption in the Hong Kong Bus Company.

LOVERS LEAP OFF MOUNTAIN TO MARRIAGE IN MIDAIR.

It was about a pair of fading TV stars who had abseiled down the Peak to a marriage ceremony conducted by a mountaineering priest and a barrage of cameras and journalists from the fan magazines. It was a Hey-Martha story. It was garbage.

There was nothing.

CONSENSUS ON 1997 COURTS REACHED.

OLD-TIMERS AND "WINE-GHOSTS" HAUNT TIAN'S CHERRY TEAHOUSE.

It was rubbish. It was trash. It was all forgettable. On that day nothing had happened.

WING LAI CALLS THE TUNE.
WONG CONSIDERS HONG KONG RETURN.
SING TAO SPOT ON IN VICTORY.

There was nothing.

—*END OF FICHE. PRESS BUTTON TWO FOR FOLLOWING DAY*—

He had thought, he had hoped—

There was nothing.

He pressed the button and brought up the front pages of the next day. He pressed not for what happened that day, but what had happened that night. He pressed up, on both front pages, a single two-word, two-character headline.

He pressed up, because the words and the characters were put up close together, a single character, a single word.

He pressed up with a photograph below it of a Toyota Hi-Ace smashed to pieces in the front window of a shop somewhere—

*GLASS STORM!*

He pressed up, below it, on both front pages of both newspapers, all around the van, pictures of people in the street in the night.


"*Oh my God!*" At the car, listening for beeps, he saw Wah in the center of the sidewalk festooned with wind chimes and a club. It was a very big club. It wasn't some sort of cut-down baseball bat or lathe-turned truncheon, it was a club from the same cave the dinosaur bones came from. He was dripping wind chimes. Wind chimes hung down from his outstretched arms. He was calling. He was chinkling. He was calling and chinkling to the Dalmatian stopped under a sheet-covered second-floor balcony, The reward. What reward? The dog was frothing, snarling, tensed—Spencer, starting to reach for his gun, saw drool and death seeping from every bicuspid in the dog's mouth.

"Here, doggie . . . here, doggie . . . come to Uncle Wah . . ."

Chinka, chinka, chinka.

The dog was stopped, tensed, frothing. It tightened its muscles and all the ribs showed. It coiled. It frothed. Its eyes were going funny—it listened to the bells.

"Phil! Fang! *PHIL!*" There was no one around. "*WAH!*"

"*Fang!*"

"*Phil!*"

He heard yells, cries. They seemed to be coming from up high, from an aircraft. Spencer yelled, *"Wah!"* He saw the Dalmatian coil to kill. He saw the club come back. He saw—

*"FANG!"*

*"PHIL!"*

There were voices calling to each other. They seemed to be trying to decide something.

*"WAH!"* At the car, starting to run, Spencer got his gun out and, going for the dog and the dolt, aiming for the Dalmatian, began squeezing at the trigger for a quick kill shot to the head.


He wondered.

On the steps of the Station, touching at his glasses, O'Yee wondered what he looked like standing there.

He wondered.

He wondered, to a kid—

His mouth was dry and he could not seem to swallow.

He wondered what he looked like.


*North Point Police are investigating the deaths of four people late last night after a stolen Toyota Hi-Ace van apparently went out of control in the street, mounted the pavement and crashed through a plate-glass window, demolishing a family shop and living quarters in North Point.*

*Killed in the incident were the owner of the shop, Henry H. L. Lee, age 63, his wife and his two younger sons, John S. L. Lee, age 22, and Lester C. Y. Lee, age 14.*

*A third son, William Y. L. Lee, age 32, was not at home at the time and returned to find the badly mutilated bodies of his entire family still in the front of the shop and on the street.*

*Police believe the driver and passengers of the stolen van had been drinking prior to the incident and they have taken possession of various items from the van as evidence.*

*It is believed that the driver and passengers of the stolen van fled following the incident, which occurred at approximately 11:00 P.M., and police have appealed to any witnesses to come forward to assist them in their enquiries.*

*(More details, pictures, page 3.)*

The address.

At the machine, Feiffer pressed at the buttons for page 3 for the address.

\* \* \*

*"Don't shoot the dog!"* They came down, the first stick of the best and bravest the paras had, locked in a terrible, grinning embrace that struck fear into the craven hearts of the enemy. They sank to their knees as bondsmen and stood up again as heroes—then they sank to their knees again, wondered why the cement was so soft—wondered why the Great Death was nothing but the Great Death—and thanked God they missed the dog and landed on Wah and he, being sprung like a concertina, kicked the Dalmatian full in the face and laid it out—and then up again. They thanked God they hit not the cement again, but Spencer—and Spencer, convulsing like a coil spring, lashed out with his gun butt and knocked the half-stunned recovering Dalmatian senseless again.

They were not dark days, they were great days—the greatest the boy on the bed and the dog in the shopping mall had ever known.

*"Phil!"* It was the war cry of a comrade and a friend. They had come through together. All around them on the battlefield were the bodies of the vanquished and the moaning. They heard bells.

*"Fang!"* Liver—it was the breakfast food of champions.

*"Phil!"* What a friend he had in Auden.

*"Fang!"* Bet you five dollars he was a good dog too.

Chinka-chinka-chinka—the bells.

Beep—the beeper. Get the beeper on the Dalmatian.

"Bill, get the beeper on the Dalmatian!" Auden, rising up, standing straight as a gun barrel, giving a few words of command, looking down at Wah trying to crawl away to get his club—ignoring the pathetic creature—said as an order, "Bill!"

Fang gave old Spencer a few licks on the face.

Auden said, "Bill—"

He didn't give a damn about Bill. Auden, reaching down and embracing him, said with martial fierceness, "Fang—old friend!"

Their eyes met. Phil, old mate—

"Fang—"

The Alsatian, now—in public—only made a soft grunting sound. It meant, *"Phil . . ."*

It meant—

Never to submit or yield—

*Veni, vidi, vici*—

It meant, it meant—

In the world, unknowing of their secret, together, they only growled.

Auden said, "Heh."

Fang, nodding, said, "Heh, heh, heh." They worked while the world slept.

In the street, on that terrible sidewalk—that nothing, that *cream puff!*—they, together, carefully fastened the beeper collar around the awakening Dalmatian's neck and, with a careless flick of a paw and a finger, set it beeping.


What he looked like, waiting for a kid for whom nobody had ever before waited, was like a man waiting for a kid for whom nobody had ever waited before.

What he looked like was a man, not so tall, slightly built, a Eurasian who was a little shortsighted and had to wear glasses.

What he looked like was a man with a voice who was saying nothing with his voice to any, to all of the people passing him by on the street, but was keeping that voice, that private part of him, for the person he was waiting for.

He kneaded his thumbs against his fingers in his fists—he was nervous, he was hoping the person he waited for would come.

All the street was full of people and movement. In the street, coming from a doorway, in a gap in the movement, Chi saw only him.

What he looked like— For an instant O'Yee put his hand behind the lens of his glasses and wiped at his eyes. For an instant, Chi thought perhaps—

What he looked like was— He was a man waiting. Faces in the crowd, giants—through all the giants and the faces, Chi began walking. All he wanted was the gun.

He saw the man waiting touch at his face. He saw him wait. He heard, hidden in him, his voice. The satchel was on the boy's back. He took it off and carried it by the straps in his hand. Giants, sound, noise, all the effluvia the giants dropped to the ground—he saw O'Yee waiting, watching for him and he went forward.

He saw him see him and start to come.

He saw his face. He thought it, then, with the look it wore, a wonderful face.

He thought—

"Mr. O'Yee?"

O'Yee said in a voice that no one else heard, ever, "Yes."

O'Yee said in a whisper, nodding, "Yes." All he wanted was the gun. He touched at the satchel not at all. O'Yee said, "Yes."

They were giants. All around, they were giants.

"All my coins are gone."

All he wanted was the gun. O'Yee said, nodding, "Yes." He looked at the satchel not at all. He was a very, very small boy. All his own children were nearly grown up and they needed him not at all. O'Yee said, "I'm very pleased to see you." For a moment, he almost put his hand out to touch the boy on the shoulder. O'Yee said in a whisper, "Thank you. Thank you for coming."

In the street, he almost put his hand out and touched the boy on the shoulder.

In the street, with all the giants around, he almost knelt down and took the boy in his arms. Almost. But he did not because, perhaps, he was afraid and he did not know what the giants would think.

He was a very, very small boy. In the street, he almost took his hand to lead him into the Station, but he did not.

Almost. But he did not.

"Thank you for coming." He looked into the boy's face and smiled and there, then, for one almost-captured instant, just touching on the edges of it, just, by a fraction, missing understanding it, in all his life, wondering, O'Yee almost—but not quite—almost, for once, knew what the secret part of him was, what its name was.

Almost. But not quite. Almost.

In the street, together, they saw all the giants and heard all the noise and chaos not at all.


He knew it. He knew it before he found it. It was opposite the table by the window in Victor Leung's Imperial Palace Restaurant, and once, it had been a shop, and what it was now was a boarded-up, derelict, darkened room behind plywood and planks to keep it secure.

Once, before the stolen van had hit it, it had been a shop and a place where a family lived. It had gone, all that—them—in a shower of glass.

It had happened two years ago.

It had happened on a Thursday.

It had happened two years ago on a Thursday. On each Thursday, for two years, they had sat there, silently gazing at it, looking at what they had done.

They had done it—the Laus, Tin, Hang—it was them. They had done it.

*Night Battle.* They had come from there, been drunk, taken a van for God only knew what reason, maybe because they had their new tapes and the van had a cassette player, and they had done it.

It was them.

It was the sole, the single thing they had in common other than that they were dead.


"There." In the Detectives' Room, standing on a chair, Chi working the streets through on the wall map with his finger, said, "There."

On O'Yee's desk was the unloaded gun and the satchel. He had a call in to Katy Wing Ho at the Samaritans. O'Yee watched the phone, waiting for it to ring.

Chi said, "There." He pointed out the street where the dead man was.

East Peking Road.

Katy Wing Ho would call.

East Peking Road. In the Detectives' Room, O'Yee nodded.

Watching not the map or the gun, O'Yee waited for the phone.


It ran. Beeping, registering on the receiver on the dashboard of Spencer's car, the Dalmatian, going home, ran. It was going northeast, toward North Point. It was going hard toward the main feeder road there.

It was sick, dying, maddened. It ran fast.

It ran fast for home, for its place where all the wind chimes and the smells were.

It was all that was left in its brain; everything else had gone or been destroyed.

It ran hard and fast for home.

It ran for East Peking Road, North Point, where once, when it had been a puppy and happy, it had lived with all the people it had loved.


It was a Chinese apothecary's shop. It was opposite Victor Leung's Imperial Palace Restaurant. It was there. It was them.

It was Number 268, East Peking Road, North Point.

It was there, on that night, in that instant, everyone—even those who had survived to live another two years—had suddenly, torn to pieces by the glass, *died*.


It ran.

Through the streets, the Dalmatian, crazed with fear and sickness, ran for the dead man in the grave.

# 17

It was the same man who had come to their restaurant. It was the policeman, Feiffer. Across the street at the boarded-up shop, there were cars and vehicles everywhere. There were two traffic policemen in uniform starting to divert the traffic around the vehicles. At the door of the restaurant Mrs. Leung saw that one of them was limping. She saw Feiffer at his car giving orders to two other Europeans. In their car there was an Alsatian dog. There was another, a Eurasian, by them, in his car a woman and a small boy. She saw an ambulance coming down the road and behind it a marked police Land Rover with ACCIDENT INVESTIGATION in Chinese and English on its side. There were more people in uniform in the vehicle. She saw Feiffer see the vehicle and flag it down to stop by the marked traffic car the two uniformed cops had come from.

The restaurant was full of diners. They were watching. At the doors to the kitchen, Mrs. Leung saw Victor come out carrying trays of food. He saw the street and stopped. She saw him look at her.

In the street, all the traffic had been stopped. There was a siren coming from somewhere: another traffic vehicle to close the street or an ambulance or a fire engine—she didn't know. She saw Feiffer, for an instant, glance across to the restaurant and she saw him say something to the uniformed European cop getting out of the accident-investigation truck. She saw him point to the boarded-up shop.

There was a small boy in one of the cars, with a woman. He looked afraid. Mrs. Leung thought she had seen him somewhere, on the street, somewhere. She saw the woman in the back of the car with him put her arm around his shoulders and call out something to the Eurasian. Under his coat, for a second, she saw the Eurasian's gun in its shoulder holster. The Eurasian, looking at the shop, shook his head. The dog in the back of the other car was locked in. It was starting to move backward and forward on the seat, trying to get out. She saw her husband's face and all the diners watching. She glanced back and the two European cops were going down the side alley by the shop. She saw the two traffic cops move into the center of the road. There was an ambulance coming. She heard the siren.

At the door Mrs. Leung said, "Victor—?"

They were gone. They were down the alley. There were sounds—creakings, bangings as if they were trying to get into the boarded-up shop. She heard, in the sudden absence of traffic, an order shouted. She could not make out what it was. Mrs. Leung said, "Victor—?"

In the back of the car the dog was starting to go mad, running back and forth on the seat and barking. She heard a voice shout out an order from down the alley and it stopped.

All the diners in the restaurant were watching.

In the alley, there was a crash as a door went.

She was shaking. At the door, she was shaking and she could not stop shaking. "Victor—?" All the diners in their restaurant were watching.

"Victor—?" From the door, her eyes wide in alarm, Mrs. Leung called out in English so the customers would not understand what she said, "Victor—those people who came here—*who were they*?!"


It was them. They were the ones. In the shop, all there was was rubble. They were the ones. They had done it. In the front room and living areas of the shop everything was torn up or destroyed. Their stolen van had come in off the street in midair and gone through the twenty-foot-long plate-glass window and what had happened in there had been an explosion, a detonation, and everything in that instant two years ago had smashed, become shrapnel and shards and, like bullets, ripped everything animate and inanimate in the place to shreds. The floor had gone and the cement under it. The van had come in nose-first and hit the floor and lifted it like piano keys and then, its motor still roaring, all the wheels spinning for purchase as the tires blew and the rims showered sparks, lifted up, slewed and spun around on its axis and scythed everything in that room in half. Against the back walls there was nothing but rubble and cold, broken timber, the masonry above it broken through and cracked down to the brickwork. It was them. They were the ones. They had done it.

In the room, Hansell, with the folder he had brought from Records in his hands, said, looking at the boarded-up window, at the fragments of glass still in the frames held together by plywood and sheets of cardboard and nails, "Henry Lee, age sixty-three, his wife and his two younger sons, John Lee, age twenty-two and Lester Lee, age fourteen." Hansell said, "They all died instantly." Hansell said, "It was traveling south on the other side of the road when the driver lost control and it skidded across the full width of the street, mounted the pavement and became airborne." They were looking for something. He saw Auden and Spencer and O'Yee looking for something in the rubble. He saw Auden stop and listen for something. Hansell said, "There were no witnesses. The officer in charge got nowhere with his investigation."

It was them—the Laus, Hang, Tin—it had been them. They had gone to the opera, bought their tapes and then they had stolen the van and they had—Feiffer said, "Why? Why did they steal the van? They were ordinary people. They were—" Feiffer said, "Where was the other son, William? What happened to him?"

"He was out. He didn't come back until it was all over. He was the one who found his family. By then, the driver and the passengers were—"

"What was he doing?"

Hansell said, "He was walking his dog, a Dalmatian. It was the shop watchdog. He—" He saw Auden start. Hansell said, "He was—"

"Why the hell did they steal the van?"

"They were drunk."

"The newspapers said you took items from the van—"

"Bottles." Hansell said, "They were drunk."

"They were ordinary people! Why the hell, drunk or sober, did they steal the van in the first place? All they had to do was get a cab and they—"

Hansell said, "It was raining, Harry. There weren't any cabs. The van lost control on the wet road and—" Hansell said, reading the file,

"Harry, all the fingerprints were smudged in the passenger seats and in the back—everything was wet, but—" He saw Auden and Spencer testing the walls, knocking against them looking for something. He saw O'Yee listening, watching. He saw Feiffer's face. Hansell said evenly, "Harry, according to Scientific, in the van, when it came through here, there weren't four people, there were five." Hansell said, "Only one set of fingerprints Scientific lifted were good. They don't belong to the Laus or Hang or Tin—it would have shown up at Records. They belong to—"

"Who?"

"The driver." Hansell said, "We got his prints from the steering wheel. In the rain and after all this, none of the other prints were any good. All the bottles were smashed and the door handles covered in glass and—" He looked into Feiffer's face. He had no idea how the man had even got this far. Hansell asked mildly, closing the file in his hands, "The driver. The fifth man. Have you any idea—any idea at all who he might be?"

It had been an apothecary's shop. Like Wah's in Peripheral Street it had been a Chinese apothecary's shop. Against the boards and the plywood on the window frame, bracing it, there were parts of camphor-wood boxes, just broken sections of them, with the Chinese characters for medicaments written on them in paint. It had been, like Wah's, a Chinese apothecary's shop. In the car, the beeper had stopped there. He listened. Watching Spencer tapping at the walls, looking for cavities, Auden stopped and listened. He listened. He heard nothing. O'Yee was at the doorway to the living quarters, looking down at the floor, looking for a way down. Auden listened.

He listened.

At the window Hansell said softly, "Harry—?" Auden turned to see Feiffer's face.

Auden saw Spencer push at a wall. There was nothing. It was solid. The stairs to the rooms upstairs had gone and in the back room where O'Yee was there was nothing but broken steps and newels and no way down.

Through the floorboards O'Yee could see only darkness. There was nothing down there.

Auden listened. Through the smashed-down side door where they had gotten in, there was the sound of a wind. It was a breeze coming down the alley, getting in amongst the splintered wood and making it whistle like pipes. Auden listened.

It had been raining. That was all. They had gone out and maybe met that night for the first time and because it was raining and all their children were grown up and they hardly ever went out, they— all of them, the Laus, Tin, Hang—finding new friends—they had gotten drunk because it was raining and they had no one at home waiting for them. And they had killed a family. And they had watched each Thursday night from that Thursday from across the road and said nothing. And they had—

*He heard it.*

O'Yee said, "Here!"

*He heard it.*

In the room, listening, O'Yee heard in the breeze, just once, the sound of—

O'Yee in the next room said in triumph, "Here! Stairs down to the cellar!" They were each of them fighting their own separate battle. O'Yee said, "Here, goddamit it—*here!*"

He heard—Auden heard, from down there, just once, singly, the little clear sound of a wind chime.

He heard, he thought—he *knew*—the sound of the Dalmatian move it.

He had recreated it, but it was no good. He had recreated the place he had lived in with his master, but it was no good because amidst all the smells of the medicines and the herbs and the specifics he had taken from Wah's shop because the smells were the same, there was no smell of his master and it was no good. The Dalmatian, on the earth floor of the cellar, lay in one corner of the dark room and all the smells were sour and old and not smells of happiness and running and wagging, and they were all no good.

The little glass things that had hung down from the ceiling of the place where he and his master and his master's family had lived had smelled of sand, of glass, of paint, and they had made sounds and he had sometimes jumped up to snap at them and set them ringing, but the wind chimes from the other place where he had got everything his master had had to make him happy—to change things—were different and they did not hang up and they only made sounds when they fell and they were not the same things and smelled wrong.

In the cellar, by the dead man in the grave, the Dalmatian pining, sat back into the dark corner and did not listen to the sounds upstairs, to the breaking of wood and stone. There was a long, hurting pain behind the dog's eyes. He had stopped frothing at the mouth and now there was a dryness and his tongue was beginning to hang out as if he were a dead thing.

He could smell the increasing smell of death on his master. In the hole in the ground, he did not move. It was a face. The Dalmatian had tried to dig him out when the smell of life was still there, still warm, but it was only a face and the look in the eyes was different and it was a dead thing.

In the half-dug open grave in the floor of the cellar there was a dead man with the side of his head and part of his face blown away by a gunshot.

It was something dead, gone. All the wind chimes and all the smells were not the same and they were wrong and the dog had not pleased and there was no one to pat him.

In the corner, squatting down, the Dalmatian put his head on his paws.

There were noises, sounds, voices, but they were all the wrong noises and sounds and voices and the Dalmatian did not listen to them.

All the smells were wrong and they did not stop the smell of the increasing death, of the corruption, of the turning from life to something dead and repulsive.

The wind chimes, lying all around the grave with all the strings of herbs and all the roots and sachets of powder and dust and twists of fish and animal extract surrounding the grave like amulets, were silent.

Upstairs, getting in, voices were coming—the Dalmatian heard them.

He had not pleased.

All his life, from the time he had been a puppy, he had done nothing but love the man in the grave and the man in the grave had loved him.

He was his. The smell of too-late was increasing, and he had not— for the only creature he worshipped in the world—he had not pleased.

He hurt.

In the dark corner of the cellar, the Dalmatian hurt.

In that corner, with his head on his paws, not listening to the noises, the Dalmatian, smelling the too-late, too sick and tired to do anything more, waited with all his world lost as if, briefly, he was sleeping.

\* \* \*

There was a dead man half out of his grave. Like the dog, Chi had gotten in through a hole in the wall and crawled down. With the door down, at the top of the stairs, shining a flashlight, O'Yee saw him. He saw a dead man half out of his grave.

He saw by him, amidst all the potions and wind chimes and herbs and strings of ginseng and everywhere white bone dust from dinosaurs long dead eons ago in caves, a single, dull, green corroded cylinder a little under an inch long.

He saw in the light from the torch the face of the dead man. He saw where the bullet had gone in.

He saw the single, empty, ejected shellcase from a German 9-mm. Luger automatic pistol.


It was William Lee. In the basement, as Spencer at the top of a flight of wooden stairs got the back door open to the street and filled the room with light, Feiffer, shaking his head, said to Hansell with no room for argument, "No, they didn't do this. It wasn't them." He was bending over the body in the half-open shallow grave, feeling for the ID card and wallet in the man's shirt pocket. He saw Auden with the dog, ready to hold it. He saw the dog, too weak to resist, bow its head. Feiffer said, "No, it wasn't them."

"Who else?"

"It wasn't them!" He had the ID and wallet out. It was Lee. He had an address in the New Territories, dated back two years. Feiffer said, "He hasn't been back here since the accident—" He read the details, "Lee, William, age thirty-four, occupation clerk, employer Hong Kong Railways, Lo Wu office." He had been shot once. The bullet had blown out all the right side of his head and half of his face. He had been shot once with a Luger. The fired shell was on the ground next to him. O'Yee was circling it with a pencil. Feiffer said, "They didn't do this. They died the same way his family died. They loaded glass into their van so that when they hit it'd slice them to shreds and deny them all their chances of heaven the way they had denied it to his family. They did it for him—to show him they atoned. What the hell was the point of it if they'd already killed him?"

"The Lau woman—the driver—was dead before the van crashed." He saw O'Yee gazing at the bills in Lee's open wallet. He seemed somehow relieved. Hansell, wanting to close the file, said, "He shot her. Her own husband shot her!"

"He shot her so she would be dead before the glass went! He shot her to gain her admission to heaven—so she would be dead before her body was cut to pieces." Feiffer said, "In Chinese theology, if you don't die entire—"

"I know about Chinese theology!" It was Lee, the last one left. Someone had met him in here, come in the back door to meet him in here and, coldly, probably without speaking a word, raised the pistol and killed him where he stood. Then they had dug a shallow grave with something they had brought with them, a fold-up entrenching tool, and then they had taken the tool away and closed the door behind them. It all came together. It made sense. It made sense of all the things he thought about. Hansell said, "Harry, he must have recognized one of them—"

"He wasn't there when the accident happened!"

"—then he must have found out somehow and—"

Feiffer said, "They sat across in the restaurant in open view every Thursday night—every anniversary of what they'd done—for almost eighteen months. If they'd—" Feiffer said, "Maybe they wanted to be recognized. They weren't."

It wasn't such a bad dog. He liked dogs. Dogs, sometimes, liked him. In the corner of the room Auden, squatting down beside it, stroked the dog gently on the head. It had stopped frothing. It felt weak and tired. He thought, from time to time, it dozed off.

There was no one watching. At the body, bagging the fired shell, O'Yee—with no one noticing at all—dropped a few coins from his pocket into the grave. He thought it was the right amount. He bagged the shell and put it in his pocket.

Feiffer said, "They were ordinary. They were four people who met for the first time on a rainy night and they—" All the bone and brain matter from the head, when the single round had been fired, had exploded across the basement floor. On the walls, with the light from the open door, it had dried hard and caked in streaks. "Keith, when they got into that van two nights ago and started off down the freeway, they—"

"*If they were atoning, who the hell were they atoning for if he hadn't recognized them?*"

"*If he had recognized them and they'd killed him, why the hell did they do it at all?*"

He saw O'Yee stand up. Hansell demanded, "Have you got a witness?"

O'Yee said, "No." O'Yee said, "I've got the gun, but there's no involvement and no usable prints."

"They didn't do this, Keith."

"How the hell do you know that?"

"Because I know them! If there was a fifth man in the stolen van then he—"

"The second van was for the fifth man!"

"He didn't take it! He took it a quarter of a mile out of the glass-factory parking lot and then he brought it back again and reparked it and then he—"

Hansell said, "What? What did he do? Come back here and kill Lee? If everyone was going to be dead anyway why did he do that?"

Feiffer said, "I don't know." He had no idea at all.

"Harry, they did this. They did the thing to the shop upstairs and they did this."

"The thing with the shop upstairs was an accident!" They must have known what happened to William Lee. They must have known where he was. All they had to do was look him up in the telephone book. All they had to do any time in the last two years was— Feiffer, not giving in, said, "No, they didn't do it. They didn't kill this man." Feiffer said suddenly, at the end of it all, "For Christ's sake, Keith, they killed four people by total, pure accident and it destroyed their lives—surely to God they couldn't then go on and slaughter someone at point-blank range in a goddamned cellar! It isn't them! They were—" They were ordinary. Feiffer said slowly and clearly, "*They couldn't have done it!*"

"They did do it, Harry. They loaded the vans with glass and they set off down a public freeway at night going the wrong way with all the goddamned lights off and they—"

"That was to kill themselves!"

"And one of them, Lau, got a pistol from somewhere and—at point-blank range, *in the head*—he shot his own wife stone cold dead!"

"He was dead himself an instant later!"

"So, almost, was the goddamned man in the truck! So could have been any poor bastard who happened to be on the freeway when they were!" Just once, just once, he wanted it all to make sense. Just once, he wanted a reason. Hansell, starting to shake, said, "Harry, you haven't seen what I've bloody seen! You haven't seen entire bus loads of schoolkids slaughtered by fucking maniacs on the road. You haven't seen the fucking maniac survive and get a year's probation! You haven't had to stand there while the parents come in cars and taxis to sift through to see if their child was among the dead. You haven't seen the look on their faces and you haven't goddamned—goddamned— heard them scream!" Hansell said, "People will do anything! They did this! If they were such good, ordinary people, why the hell couldn't they just have driven their van off a fucking cliff or into a goddamned wall? *Why the hell did they take off down a public highway into the goddamned darkness hoping they might hit something?*"

"They thought they were going to hit the second van!"

"*Why?*"

"For their children! To protect their children!"

"From what?"

"From being shamed by what they'd done here!"

"You said nobody knew! Nobody recognized them!"

"They knew!"

"Bullshit! Then why didn't they do it straight away?"

"I don't know."

Hansell said quietly, "And if they didn't do it, who killed this man here?"

"The fifth man."

"We don't know who the fifth man is." Hansell said, "All we've got are his fingerprints." Just once, just once, he needed a reason. Hansell said softly, "Harry, all the other prints are smudged. We don't even know if the other four passengers were them."

"It was them." In Victor Leung's restaurant, sometimes, they had gone to the telephone to call someone. Whoever it was, he never came. Whoever it was . . .

## WRONG
## WAY
---
## GO BACK

They had gone six miles down the wrong way of the freeway at night with all their lights off and the music blaring with the van—with the exact same type of van—loaded with plate glass and they had, at the exact moment—

*At the exact moment.* There was a fifth man. The fifth man had started off from the parking lot with them in the second van and he had driven until they were out of sight, going in the other direction so they could collide at a specified point, and then he had driven back and left the van and then he had—

What if they had not hit anyone? What if they had driven all those miles in the darkness and, in the darkness, at that time of the morning, they had met no one—there had not been a single vehicle on the freeway—and they had completed their run and then they had—

What if they had hit nothing? What if they— Someone had called Lee in the New Territories and got him here and then he had— In the corner, Auden said softly, "You poor bastard, you poor, poor bloody . . ." Spencer and O'Yee were with him. He lifted up one of the dog's paws. There was almost no pad left. The dog had come a long, long way. He had come, when his master had not returned, from the New Territories. It was a pretty good sort of dog. It was a para's dog. Squatting down by it, Auden put its head in his lap and stroked it.

Feiffer said, "The fifth man. It was a sort of club. Meeting there in the restaurant, for the four of them, it was a sort of club—it was a sort of huddling together." Feiffer said, "They were ordinary. They were just ordinary people and they—" *But the fifth man wasn't.* The fifth man wasn't ordinary, a nobody. He was someone. He never came. All there was left to their lives was what they had done. There was more to his. There were more things to be done. There were places to go and— Feiffer said slowly, "But, his fate tied to them, with them, the fifth man was just ordinary. With them, he was just—" William Lee had not recognized anybody. The fifth man had sought him out. The fifth man had, thinking about it, not meeting each Thursday in some awful memorial, but *thinking about it*, working it out, sought him out and he had—

Hansell said, "Harry?"

He knew. He knew them. He knew what they were. The fifth man—the one they telephoned in the restaurant when they were alone or afraid together, he had— Feiffer said, "Keith, I think what the fifth man did was tell them that Lee knew who they were." They had children, families. On a night two years ago they had gotten drunk because it was raining and their children had grown up and they were not needed and then, because it was raining, they had stolen the van and they had killed, they had killed—

They had killed a family of people just like them.

Feiffer said, "I don't think Lee knew anything. I think the fifth man told them Lee knew who they were and he demanded an atonement. I think he told them that Lee demanded that, like his family, they—" Feiffer said, "I think they were good people. I think Steven Lau loved his wife and I think he killed her a moment before the crash so—" Feiffer said, "I think they did it for their children. I think—" He looked at Auden and the dog. Feiffer, hardly believing it himself, said, "I think they went to hell—literally—to save them." Feiffer said slowly, "I think the fifth man told them William Lee was going to kill their children for revenge if they didn't atone, or even just reveal to

their children what their parents had done. Death wasn't enough for
him. Like his family they had to die with no hope of heaven." Feiffer
said, "I think, for their children and what they wanted them to think
of them, I think they gave up all their eternities." They were
ordinary. He fell silent.

"Harry." His voice was soft, gentle. Auden said, "Harry, I think I
might take this poor old dog outside into the car if you don't
mind . . ." He patted the dog. He saw Spencer's face looking down
at the dog and, picking it up, he almost offered it to him. Whatever
you said about old Spencer, dogs liked him and he liked dogs.

O'Yee said with a shrug, "In my car there's a kid who, um—" O'Yee
said, "I'll show you where he is."

All anyone needed were reasons. He almost touched Feiffer's
shoulder. Hansell said gently, watching the dog go, "Harry, one of
these days, when we get him for something else and match his prints,
maybe we'll find the driver." Hansell said, "Maybe one day we'll—"

*"God in heaven!"*

*Endless, endless night. His hands were covered in blood and tiny
shards from the van.*

*Macarthur, working himself out backward from the cavity, opening
it, setting it from* Beam *to* Diffused, *held the flashlight up in the cabin
section of the van so Feiffer could see clearly what was inside.*

*"God in heaven!"*

*Endless, endless night. His hands were covered in blood and tiny
shards from the van. Everywhere there were lights and vehicles and
unhuman, washed-out figures moving about in uniform.*

*All they had had to do anywhere along the six miles of the freeway
was pull over and stop.*

*They had had their headlamps off. They had their music going full
blast and at the last moment, at the last moment—*

The fifth man had not been ordinary. He had thought, he had
planned—he had murdered them and, if, at the last moment, if there
had been no last moment, if the van had met nothing on the road, if
the fifth man had not been there, approaching them, aiming at them,
then all that would have happened was—

Feiffer said softly, "He was there. The fifth man was there!"

Endless, endless night.

"He was there: the fifth man." He saw Hansell's face. He reached
out and took him by the shoulder. Feiffer said, "He was there. He
thought about it, he planned it—he killed Lee—and, to make sure—
*he was there!*"

It was him. He was not ordinary. He was going to America to join his children. He was there. It was him and, as he had murdered all the people in the shop one night when he was drunk—when he was driving the van—he had murdered Lee and then, aiming for them, not in a van with glass, but in a truck!—he had murdered them all. It was him. It was Fan. It was the antique dealer. It was the man in the truck fifteen feet off the highway inside his armored cabin—it was him—*it was him!* Proof, all he needed was proof. Fingerprints. They had his fingerprints from the steering wheel of the stolen van from two years ago.

Fingerprints.

In the cellar, in that awful place, with the light streaming in from the open basement door, Feiffer, his fists clenched hard together, pushing Hansell away, said in triumph, "Goddamit, Keith—now, we've got his fucking *hand!*"

# 18

"*A* is an enclosure or lake—"
"*B* is a ridge ending in a downward direction—"
"*C* is a ridge forking in an upward direction—"
In close-up through the fluorescent-tube–lit magnifier the print of the index finger, right hand, was an out-of-focus blur of contour of broken fuzzing lines. At the pathology table in the Morgue office, the Fingerprint Man, bending down to peer through the lens, ticking off the similarities or lack of them, said, ticking, "*D* is a ridge forking in an upward direction. *E*—" He glanced up and saw O'Yee and Auden and Spencer looking at him. The Fingerprint Man said, "They're composites. Arches or loops or whorls are straightforward—these are composite prints." He had Hansell's file with the impressions taken from the scene of the accident two years ago. The Fingerprint Man said, "They're not clear. The prints were taken off a steering wheel which isn't a flat surface and they were taken when it was raining and everything was wet. Latent prints are made by the sweat of the papillary ridges of the finger." All there were on the sheet of paper were smudges. The Fingerprint Man said, "I read about the accident on the freeway. This is it, isn't it?"

They had helped the Fingerprint Man take the prints from the severed hand in the Morgue. It had been cold, like ice. There had only been two fingers there and part of the thumb. O'Yee said expressionlessly, "Yes."

"If the hand in there was too bad for microsurgery it may not be any good at all for prints." All he had were smudges. The Fingerprint Man, not being attacked, defending himself, said, "The tissue from something dead is different. It distorts because the flesh isn't elastic." The Fingerprint Man said, "I just don't want to get it wrong!" The smell of death in the Morgue had been a smell of coldness. It was the coldness of the dead, mutilated hand as he had reached into the plastic bag that held it and taken it out not knowing what part of it he had hold of. The Fingerprint Man said, "It's frozen tissue! It's like taking an impression from a flat stamp—none of the rolling characteristics are—" They were all watching him. They were waiting. The Fingerprint Man said, "I have to do it slowly contour by contour or I might—"

"Take your time." O'Yee said quietly, "Take your time." He looked first at the Fingerprint Man's face and then down at two sheets of black smudges on the table and the magnifier lying between them. There was a comparison sheet to one side of the file prints and, on top of it, a pencil to check off the similarities and an eraser in case— O'Yee said softly, "Take your time."

He waited. He watched the man's face. The usual Fingerprint Man was away on leave. This man was his assistant. He looked about eighteen years old. O'Yee said quietly, "It's all right." The white dust-coat the man wore was brilliant white, hand washed probably by his wife. It had not a mark or stain on it.

The Fingerprint Man looked down. "E—" He looked down through the glass. "E is a ridge ending in an upward direction."

O'Yee said, "Thank you." The man was only on the first set of prints from the steering wheel. He was listing all the features for comparison. He had yet to start the comparison itself. He had yet to look through the lens at the prints from a dead, mutilated hand he had touched.

O'Yee waited.

"F—"

In the Morgue, they waited.

"F is a short independent ridge or island—"

In the Morgue, they waited.

\*   \*   \*

In the hospital, at the nurses' station, there was no one. He knew where the room was. He knew where Fan was. He needed a witness. At the station, Feiffer pressed the buzzer for attention and waited.

There was no one. On the wall behind the counter there was a light flashing for room 7 on the *Nurse* panel and whoever was supposed to be on duty was there, in that room.

It was not Fan's room.

NO SMOKING. At the station, waiting, Feiffer drummed his fingers on the counter. The notes and files and patient clipboards were there in a pile waiting to be annotated or sorted or checked and he touched at the side of the top file and moved it.

There was no one there and on the panel the light was flashing as the staff on duty attended to someone who needed them. All the doors to the rooms were closed. Perhaps they were giving medication or bed baths.

Fan. He knew which room was his, but he needed a witness.

The light was flashing, flashing. He had pressed the bell. Someone had heard.

At the station Feiffer drummed his fingers on the counter and waited.

He was on the second set of prints, the ones from the hand.

"*B* is a—"

By the table, Auden said, "*Well?*"

"*B* is a ridge ending in a downward direction—"

"*Well?*"

"*C* is a ridge forking in an upward direction—I think."

Auden said, "*Jesus!*"

Spencer said, "Wait. Wait, Phil. Let him do it."

He went back. His hands were shaking. "*C*—" He swallowed hard. His wife had washed and pressed his dust coat. It was only his first week out on his own. He looked at O'Yee and could not read anything at all on his face. All he read was that he waited.

"*C*—" The Fingerprint Man said definitely, "*C* is a ridge forking in an upward direction."

He made a mark on his sheet in pencil and ticked it.

He was weakening, drifting in and out, wavering. He was teetering, almost going over, swaying with the demon staring at him not from somewhere outside, but from the lenses on his own eyes.

The demon had no body, it had only a face and the face was stark white like an opera mask and it stared unblinkingly at him with round expressionless eyes, staring through to inside him.

The stump of his hand was throbbing—he felt the phantom hand there and it was throbbing, losing something, going away, draining out—he was swaying, dissolving, going over.

He wept.

Swaying, blurring, almost going over, falling, everything blurring and merging and dissolving as, through it, the demon's eyes watched him without blinking, Fan wept.

He felt the tears running down his face.

Banging, banging, banging, banging—he heard it.

Banging, banging, banging, banging—he wept. He heard it.

Banging, banging, banging, banging—he was dying, going away, dissolving into the demon's face.

Banging, banging, banging—

Fan, weeping, teetering, going over, his stump throbbing and throbbing, trying to raise his good hand to his face to hide it, said, "No—!"

The demon. Banging, banging, banging—he heard it.


He was on the last few lines. "D—D is a ridge forking in a downward direction. E—E is a ridge ending in an upward direction." The Fingerprint Man said, "I've got it. The focus has to be set differently and then you can get the three-dimensional character you lose when you—" He looked up. The Fingerprint Man said, nodding, "I'm getting it."

O'Yee said tightly, "The two sets of prints—the one from the hand and the one from the steering wheel—is it the same man?"

"I'm getting it." The Fingerprint Man said, "I'm getting it. E—E is a ridge ending in an upward direction." He hadn't written it down on his checklist.

He did that first.

Bending over the table, he peered down into the glass for F.


Banging, banging, banging, banging—it was the demon. It was the demon staring and banging at his eyes and merging into him, taking him over, and his hand was throbbing, pulsing with pain and washing the pain over him as he swayed and lost his focus and all the time there was the banging, the noise, the sound, the hammering.

He saw, for an instant, a bright light. He saw, for an instant, Susan Lau's face. He saw her head. He saw the bright light a second before the van and the truck hit and he saw her head jerk back and he saw her face explode onto the windscreen and he saw—

Banging, banging, banging, banging.

Fan Chi Hung, Lewis Fan, banging, banging, banging, shrieked, "NO!"

"*NO—!*"

No one heard.

Banging, banging, banging.

In his room, alone, going, swaying, dying with the pain, Fan shrieked to the demon, banging, banging, banging, "No, *it wasn't me!*"


"Harry?" It was Hansell. He was coming down the corridor. He saw Feiffer starting alone for one of the rooms in the ward.

"Wait there!" He could wait no longer. The light on the nurses' panel was still flashing. It was going to flash forever.

Going for Fan's room, motioning Hansell back with his hand to wait there, Feiffer, starting to run, ordered him, "Wait! Wait there!"


In the Morgue, O'Yee said finally, "Well?" He saw the Fingerprint Man finish and go back one more time for a gross comparison and to check his list. O'Yee said tightly, "Yes or no? Is it the same man?"

It was his first week out on his own. One more time. He had to check just one more time.


*"No! It wasn't me!"*


It was his first week out on his own. It was his first, his very first moment.

In the Morgue, finished, sure, looking up, the Fingerprint Man said with no doubt in his mind at all, "Yes, both the prints match. The man who drove the stolen van into the shop two years ago and the man who lost his hand on the freeway—yes, it's the same man."

\* \* \*

## "*IT WASN'T ME!*"

He was gone. The room was empty. At the end of the bed, ready for collection, was the clipboard with his records on it.

He was gone.

He had discharged himself.

*Prognosis at unadvised self-discharge: Extremely Poor.*

In the corridor, running for the phone at the end of the ward, seeing Hansell's face, Feiffer shouted, "Goddamit, he's gone! He's gone!" He got to the phone and began dialing the number for the Morgue. So simple, so easy. Dialing, getting the numbers wrong and starting again, Feiffer, losing him, as the shouting woke people and all the lights on the nurses' panel starting flashing at once, yelled, "Goddamit, his wife came and collected him and he just—goddamit, he just went *home!*"

William Lee, the son. The last one left alive. The last one. The one dead with a bullet in his brain in the cellar of the shop on East Peking Road.

In his room at home, swaying, with the banging and banging echoing inside his head as the demon got closer and closer to him, Lewis Fan, swearing it through all eternity, shrieked, "I didn't kill him! It wasn't *ME!*"

# 19

"**M**y God, it's a goddamned mansion!" He had known Fan lived on Hanford Hill. He had not known how he lived. At the entrance to the house on Hanford Hill Avenue, driving hard through the open main gates onto the gravel driveway that led up through an acre of trees and lawns to the two-story, Chinese-style stone house, Feiffer said in a gasp, "My God, it's a goddamned *mansion*!" Fan: there was a single stone character above the stone archway at the gate. He had known he was a wholesale antique dealer. He had thought he drove a truck. The place was deserted—there was no one, the main gates wide open and on the house, all the curtains gone from the windows and all the panes glittering in the sun. It had been sold. He was selling it. The double glass doors to the main entrance hall at the top of a flight of carved stone steps were open. He was—Auden and Spencer and O'Yee were in O'Yee's car seconds behind him. Feiffer, braking the car at the bottom of the stairs and looking up, ordered Hansell, "Tell them to go around the back and stop anyone getting out!" He heard, inside the house, a banging. He was doing something. He was getting out. He saw O'Yee's car stop by the edge of the gravel drive on the lawn and

Auden get out carrying a shotgun and he ordered O'Yee, "Christopher, get around the back and find his car and disable it!" Christ, he probably had six cars. Feiffer yelled, "Anything you can find—disable it!" He saw O'Yee start for the side of the house with Auden and Spencer a little behind him. The glass doors to the main entrance were open. There were no curtains on any of the windows—

"Harry—!" Hansell said, "Listen! Listen!"

He heard from inside the house, banging, banging.

Hansell said, "Harry—what the hell's that sound?"


Sitting, Fan said to the demon, "I see their faces. I see all their faces in the flash the gun made." He was swaying, his stump on his lap. He was looking down at the blood. Fan said, "I see the flash and then I can't remember anything, but I see their dead faces laid out side by side and I see their faces and I—" Far off, he could hear sounds, movements. He could hear the banging. Fan said to the demon, "I see the shop in East Peking Road. I feel the loss as all the wheels on the van leave the road in the rain and I feel—I can *feel*—" Fan said sadly, "It wasn't me: William Lee—that wasn't me." Fan said, "I see the flash as Lau shot his wife in the head to spare her suffering through eternity!" Fan said, "I see them outside the glass factory, getting into the van and I see—I see her holding his hand and I—and I—" Fan said, sobbing, "He must have hidden the gun all the way and sat behind her and made her think that, at the end, he didn't want to sit beside her because he didn't care for her anymore, but it wasn't true because he had the gun and he wanted to kill her a moment before her body was torn to pieces and it must have been, for him, all that way behind her—" Fan said to the demon, "It was such a little thing, but I—" Fan said to the demon, "AND IN THAT INSTANT WHEN I SAW THE FLASH I KNEW THAT WHATEVER I WAS DOING WAS NOTHING COMPARED TO IT!"

The demon was on the lenses of his eyes. It was an expressionless white-painted mask from an opera. It moved across the lenses of his eyes and stared into his soul and the expressionless staring beads of eyes were like needles. Fan said, "I SEE THEM LYING SIDE BY SIDE DEAD!" He heard the banging. Fan said, weeping, sobbing, watching the blood, "I HEAR YOU! I KNOW YOU'RE COMING!"


"He did it for his goddamned kids!" Everywhere in the entrance hall there were packing cases and crates and boxes and tea chests ready to go. He was going. He was going to America to be with his married children. On all the tea chests and crates there were framed photographs of them, three girls and a boy. They had been laid out, placed, arranged—they started from the doorway where the largest crate was with photographs of all the girls with their American-Chinese or European husbands and all the grandchildren by them or in their arms. All the frames were gilt or carved wood. All the cartons were marked to be picked up and stacked and taken on board ship or containerized in order. Feiffer, taking up a photo of one of the girls with her husband smiling, outside what looked like some landmark in Los Angeles with the Pacific behind her, said to Hansell, "He did it to get away so he could be with his kids." He remembered. Feiffer said, "He told me he had a residence visa for America—he did it to get away from the four of them who knew what he did to be with his kids!" Feiffer said, "And William Lee—maybe he recognized one of them and maybe he didn't, but Fan told them he did and he was going to tell and destroy everyone's life—" He heard the banging. All the house must have been empty. It echoed against walls. It was hard, insistent, like someone wielding a hammer on wood. Feiffer said, "They all did it for their families—all of them! They went to hell for them—they went to hell, cut to pieces, so Lee could be revenged, satisfied—" He heard the banging. He saw Hansell look up to the balconies on the next floor. Feiffer, throwing down the photo, said, "But this bastard had already killed Lee and this bastard didn't intend to go to hell—he intended them to go to hell!" The back door must have been locked. He heard a blast as Auden used the shotgun and blew the lock off.

He heard banging, banging. The house was a goddamned mansion. It was huge. "Where the hell is he?"

He saw Hansell trying to listen for the banging.

It was everywhere, in all the pores of the house. All the carved doors leading off from the entrance hall were closed.

Feiffer, reaching for his gun, going for the first door ready to shoot open the lock, yelled as Hansell stood listening, "Keith! Take the next door!" he heard the banging, banging. It could have been coming from anywhere. He heard O'Yee shout an order to Auden out in the servants' quarters at the back of the house. He heard Spencer say, "It's empty! It's all emptied out!" and Feiffer, pushing on the door and finding it unlocked, yelled, "The cellars! Check the goddamned cellars!"

He heard the banging, banging.

The room off the entrance hall was empty and he could not tell at all where the sound was coming from or what it was.

"Bill? What the hell's that sound?" It was down in the cellars, it was in the walls, it was everywhere and he could not tell where it was coming from or what it was. It was the house. It was the house itself. In the cellar, Auden, coming back up the stairs and shaking his head, said, "What is it?" He saw Spencer with his gun out at the open door to what looked like a servant's bedroom. Auden said, "There's nothing down there." There was a small kitchen off from the bedroom with just a hot plate and small bar fridge. It was empty. It had been used, but there was nothing in it now except a few bowls on a rack drying and what looked like the remains of a light meal in a plastic trash bin.

Spencer, coming out shaking his head, said, "Nothing. There's no one there." He heard the banging. It was in the walls. It was coming from the cellar. It wasn't coming from the cellar. It was coming from the ground floor and then it was not. It was moving. It was echoing, vibrating. It was the house itself. It was like—

Spencer, cocking his head, trying to listen as O'Yee came in from a room along the corridor, asked Auden, "What is it? What the hell is it?"

"Empty!" O'Yee, holstering his gun, glancing back down the corridor to make sure he was right, said, shaking his head, "No one. The whole place is empty—there isn't anyone here—"

Photos. He found more of them in what had been a reception room or library off to the right of the main entrance. It had been a room built by a man who had had money, a man whose business had prospered. The walls had been lined with carved camphor wood and there had been tables against the lining with, probably, wonderful objects displayed on them—he could see the marks where over the years the sun had not lightened the color of the stained wood.

The room was full of packing crates and each of the crates had photographs of the children set out on them, in order, the three girls and the boy, not this time in Los Angeles, not this time with their children, but somewhere else, somewhere in the Midwest, smiling with their new wives or husbands. There were no photos of the children at their colleges—that would be next.

He saw Hansell in another of the rooms to the right of the hall, looking at the photos. It was them—it was the college pictures. It was their history. It had been laid out like exhibits in a museum on top of the cartons and crates and cases. He saw Hansell come out. He saw him look up to the next floor. Up there, if there was anyone, there was no way out.

He heard the banging. He thought it was coming from the back of the house.

Feiffer, slamming the door to the camphor-wood room shut and nodding hard in the direction of the back of the house, said, "There! Keith! Check all the rooms there!"

It was a maze. All the rooms in the back of the house ran off corridors and it was a maze.

They were getting into them one by one.

There was no one, nothing. The house had been sold or was under contract and everything the servants or whoever lived in the rooms had had had been cleared out and taken away and there was no one and nothing.

They heard the banging.

In the corridor, Auden and Spencer and O'Yee, listening, stopping, trying not to breathe, tried to work out where the sounds were coming from and what they were.

"They would have talked." Explaining it to the demon, Fan said sadly, "They would have talked because they were, I thought, just ordinary people." He was watching the blood from his stump. He shook his head. Fan said softly, "I was wrong. They weren't ordinary. I thought that they were just ordinary and—" Fan said, "All they had were their children. I thought—" Fan said softly, in a whisper, "That evening, at the opera, I was feeling a bit—"

Fan said, "They seemed nice and they—" Fan said, "It was raining so we got drunk and we—"

Fan said, "And we played one of the new tapes we'd got and we—" Fan said, "And all my life was destroyed."

Fan said, "And I told them William Lee had found out who they were and I— But I didn't kill William Lee and I—"

Fan said, "AND I DIDN'T THINK THAT IT WOULD LOOK LIKE THAT!"

Fan said, "I thought—"

Fan said, "I DIDN'T THINK THAT LAU WOULD LOVE HIS WIFE THAT MUCH AND I DIDN'T THINK HE MIGHT HAVE A GUN—AND I DIDN'T THINK THERE'D BE A FLASH!"

The demon watched him.

Fan, swaying, drifting, coming in and out of a blur, a mist, yelled to the demon, "I DIDN'T THINK THERE'D BE A FLASH AND I'D SEE THEIR FACES!"

Fan said quietly, "I hear you." Banging, banging, banging, like something slamming shut in the wind.

Fan said quietly, "I hear you—"

Fan said quietly to the demon in the closed room, "I hear you coming."

*"God in heaven!"*

*Endless, endless night. His hands were covered in blood and tiny shards from the van.*

*Macarthur, working himself out backward from the cavity, opening it, setting it from* Beam *to* Diffused, *held the flashlight up in the cabin section of the van so Feiffer could see clearly what was inside.*

*"God in heaven!"*

*Endless, endless night. His hands were covered in blood and tiny shards from the van. Everywhere there were lights and vehicles and unhuman, washed-out figures moving about in uniform.*

*Endless, endless—*

He heard the banging. It was coming from upstairs.

He heard the banging. It was coming, coming. It was in the house he had built, it was in all his life, it was in the walls and the floors and it was coming, getting louder, coming for him and he heard it.

He was sitting in the corner of the room with the stump in his lap. He was looking at the blood and it was all over his legs and groin and, where the bandages had been, all the stitches had broken and the blood was flowing out of his body and he made no effort to stop it.

He had never thought, in all his life, that such a little thing—

He had never thought in all his life—

Banging, banging, banging. In all the rooms in the house, in all the rooms there had been wonderful objects. All the rooms once had been full of children and his children's friends and the children of servants and—life and sound and color and faces—and in all that time he had never thought—

Fan said to the demon, "I thought, always—I thought that one day, rich and old and—" Fan said, "I thought that—" He heard the banging, the banging—he heard it coming.

Fan said quickly, "I never thought that I'd sit here like this, like a dog and I'd find out that all my life, everything I'd planned—"

He heard the demon come.

Fan said, "I never thought that it'd all come to nothing because of people like them!"

He heard it stop outside his door.

Fan said, "I never thought I'd see something happen in an instant that went beyond all the things I'd always— I never thought—"

He heard the demon make a single banging sound.

Fan said, "I NEVER THOUGHT ANYONE COULD LOVE SOMEONE SO MUCH THAT THEY'D GO TO HELL FOR ETERNITY AND BE ALONE THERE FOR THEM!" Fan said, "I never thought anyone would do that for their children!"

Fan said, "I did it all for me! I did it all to be with my children in America so they could admire me!"

He saw the demon standing there in the doorway looking at him. He saw, not on the lenses of his eyes, but there in the doorway, the demon's unblinking, staring face.

Fan said, "It wouldn't have been them—it would have been *me*! I would have been the one who told! It would have been me! I couldn't go to their restaurant—I couldn't be with them because it would have been me! I would have been the one who told!"

He saw the demon raise its hand.

Fan said quietly to the demon, "I never . . . I never . . ."

The demon's hand was on the door.

Fan said, crying, "I never loved any of my children as much as they did. All the things in my life were for me."

Sitting in the corner of the room with his stump on his lap, he watched the blood flow.

Fan said to the demon, "I'm sorry. Everything I ever did in life was for me."

Fan said, "I never thought there'd be a flash and I'd see all their faces."

He saw the demon's hand on the door. The demon's eyes were dead. The demon did not hear anything he said.

He was bleeding to death. He had taken off all the bandages and opened all the stitches and he was bleeding to death and blurring in and out of consciousness.

The demon's hand was on the door.

The eyes were black and like beads.

\* \* \*

Fan said, "I—" He shook his head.

Fan said, "I thought—" He tried to look up, but his head was heavy and he had no strength in the muscles of his neck and he could only look down into his lap where the stump was.

At the door, the demon had a knife.

Fan said softly, evenly, finally, "I would have told, in the end. In the end, it would have been me . . ."

"Keith!" At the bottom of the stairs Feiffer saw Auden and Spencer and O'Yee link up with Hansell at the door through to the rear of the house.

"Keith!" He still had his gun in his hand. Feiffer, looking up the stairs toward the maze of rooms leading off from the landings and walkways of the carved, oiled teak steps, yelled, "It's up there! Whatever it is, it's up there!"

Banging, banging, banging.

At the entrance to the room, the demon was banging the door closed and pulling it open and banging it closed again. It had opened all the doors in the house and then closed them, door by door, room by room.

Banging, banging, banging. The demon, at the entrance to the room, watched. The knife, hanging down, was a long, heavy-bladed packer's knife used to cut and trim and lever the reinforcing tape on cartons and crates.

Banging, banging, banging . . .

Fan, dying, blurring out, shrieked to the demon, "Lau was ready to suffer through eternity for his children because he was ordinary! They all were!" He could not look up at the demon's eyes because there was nothing there in them to see. They were merely, only, black glass beads.

"I—"

Banging, banging, banging.

"I—"

He lowered his neck because he had no more strength left.

*BANG!*

He heard the demon slam shut the door.

He heard the demon come.

He thought, in that instant, as he felt the blow, of his children not at all.

"It's a goddamned *door!*" On the landing, pausing, they heard another, a second, a louder bang. On the landing, pausing, they heard—
They heard nothing.
They heard only
. . . silence.
The corridor was full of photographs along all the floors, on both sides, everywhere.
"Harry—?" On the landing, listening, O'Yee said in a whisper, "Harry—?"
He listened.
From the room at the very far end of the corridor, behind the door—to one side of it, maybe in another, a second corridor, a servants' passage—somewhere—briefly, faintly, Feiffer heard a second sound, a whisper, a rustle.
From under the door at the very far end of the corridor, he saw the blood.
He listened. He heard the rustle.
Feiffer said softly to O'Yee, nodding to the door, "There. Fan. He's in there."
All the house was full of photographs of the children.
All the house was empty and echoing and silent.
Feiffer said to them all, nodding to the far door, "Go!"
He listened to the sound.
Turning, he began walking very slowly with his gun held down by his side in the other direction along the corridor, paralleling the rustling sound of the demon as it moved.

He had bled everything away. In the corner of the room, everything had bled from the opened sutures in his stump and the wound from the knife at the junction of his neck and back was only an open, bloodless, single jagged line.
It had been a death thrust. It had been a heavy, rigid-bladed knife and it had severed his spine. In his pajama pants, his chest naked, Fan sat in the corner of the room with his head fallen forward like a fat boy asleep after too much food. The blood was everywhere. There was a double bed in the room, unmade, and the blood went from there where the torn bandages were as a river to the corner. From the corner, it radiated out in pools, in puddles, dark and sticky and

smelling of death. The carpets were up in the room: it had soaked into the wooden floorboards and run in little trickles along their joints and, striking butt joints or cross-lays, formed in perfect circles. It was on the wall behind him where he must have reached up or steadied himself. It was on his lap, about his groin. At the open door to the room, Hansell said in a gasp, "God Almighty . . . !"

There was no sound at all in the room, nothing.

Moving carefully inside with Auden and Spencer and O'Yee behind him, treading carefully, Hansell looked for the knife.

In that room he knew Fan would be dead. In the corridor, moving away, Feiffer listened for the rustling. It was paralleling him, moving quietly, almost on tiptoe. Somewhere behind the rooms in a parallel corridor, there was another passage: he heard the rustling, the tiptoeing.

There were more photographs of the children—photographs of the children as children in Hong Kong—he recognized the backgrounds. The photographs were on the floor of the corridor, dropped as they had been sorted through and found wrong. Like the sound, they were moving, diminishing in the age of their subjects as he went with the rustling sound away from the main bedroom.

"Harry! There's another door in here!" In the bedroom O'Yee found footprints in the blood. Set into the wall, almost invisible, with only a shallow concave cut out of the panel to make a handle, there was another door, a service entrance. It went behind the walls into a passage. O'Yee, pulling at the door, losing his grip on the concave and trying to get his fingernails into the joint with the wall, called, "Harry!" He had no idea where the man was.

He pulled.

The door came open.

O'Yee, drawing his gun and going inside, listening, said in sudden alarm, "I hear them! I hear someone moving about in there!"

It was not him. He had not been the one. In the corridor, moving, looking down, everywhere Feiffer saw the photographs. He heard the sounds.

It had not been him. Fan. It had not been him. He was like the others. He had not been the one who had lured Lee from the New Territories and there, in the cellar, drawing from nowhere the Luger, shot once for the head and dug a shallow grave.

It had not been him. The photographs were of his children, but all they were were his children and it had not been him.

He listened. He heard the rustling.

He heard, very faintly, the sound of a door somewhere click.

It had not been him. He had died. He had discharged himself from the hospital to die and he, in that room, was dead. *"God Almighty—!"* He had heard Hansell's voice. He knew Fan was dead.

All the photographs had been taken from a carton somewhere, broken open or cut free and then, carried, they had been looked at and sorted and discarded. It was not him. He heard, closer, the rustling. He heard someone walking on tiptoe softly, so as not to disturb the children and it was not Fan. He had not been the one. He had not been the one who had killed William Lee. It was the same sound William Lee must have heard in the cellar. The Laus, Ting, Hang—they had all decided to die. All that was left was William Lee. He had known nothing, had no idea of their names at all. He was only a small risk. It was enough—he had been killed.

Fan had been free. He was going to America to his children. It was all for that.

Slippers. The sound was of someone very light and small walking quietly in slippers. He heard the sound.

He heard it coming closer, somewhere in the maze of parallel rooms.

In the corridor, stopping, standing still, listening, Feiffer, his arm down by his side holding the gun, listened to the sound.

It was a servants' access passageway to all the rooms on the upper floor. There was hardly any light. The only light came down from angled skylights let into what looked like an eave above a balcony and all any of them could see in the passage were doors.

Footprints. Leading away, fading as the blood was walked off or scuffed, there were the bloody footprints of shoes with no heels.

*"Fun-gau la . . ."*

He heard it.

It chilled him to the bone.

*"Fun-gau la . . ."* Sleep now . . . He heard it.

It chilled him to the bone.

*"Fun-gau la . . ."*

It was behind him.

In the corridor, Feiffer heard it. He heard the voice.

He knew who it was.

It was behind him.

It was the person who had killed Fan for his weakness. It was the person who had never wavered. It was the person who, for the children, had murdered six people and, unlike Fan, uncaringly, had lived with it.

In the corridor, Feiffer heard it. He heard the voice.

He knew who it was.

In the passageway O'Yee said, "My God, it's the wife! It's Fan's wife!" They stopped. The footprints stopped. In the center of the passageway there was a pair of women's embroidered bedroom slippers. They were hers. They were covered in blood. Everywhere in front of the slippers, there were doors to the maze of rooms and all the footprints had stopped.

They had found no knife.

O'Yee, in the corridor, said, "It's the wife!"

Everywhere there were doors.

He could hear, now, no sound at all.

"The doors!" In the corridor, O'Yee, trying to think, ordered them all, "The doors—check all the rooms behind the doors!"

"Harry!" In the passageway, going for the first door with his gun out, O'Yee yelled at the top of his voice, "Harry! It's the wife! She's got a knife! *She's in one of the rooms coming your way!*"

*"Fun-gau la . . ."*

He looked and saw the face of a demon.

"Harry—!" The rooms led to other rooms and there seemed to be no way out of them into the corridor as they led into other rooms and then toward balconies and mazes of other rooms and—

"Nothing!" O'Yee heard Spencer banging as he went from room to room and there seemed to be no way to get through.

"Nothing!" Hansell, moving fast, slamming at doors, banging, banging, banging, yelled, "O'Yee, where the hell are you?"

Nothing. All the rooms were empty, cleaned out. He heard it. He heard a woman's voice.

*"Fun-gau la . . ."* Sleep now. He heard it as a whisper. She had the knife.

"Nothing!" He heard Spencer, going through the rooms calling, finding nothing.

"HARRY!" In the passageway, out again, running for the doors farthest away, O'Yee, in all the banging, banging, yelled in alarm, "Harry! It's the wife! *She's coming your way with the knife!*"


The eyes were beads. Inches from his face, they looked through him with no expression and looked through him and looked through him. They were a nightmare. They were gone, clouded over, filmed, merely reflecting what light fell upon them and seeing nothing.

It was her. He had only seen her once at the hospital and she had said nothing, merely stared out the window looking down at the Morgue and she had said nothing, but merely been there.

She was there. She was inches from his face. In her hand, he knew she had the knife. He could not take his eyes off her face. Her hair was pulled back in a bun above the black blouse she wore and he knew, there, by her side there was the knife.

"*Fun-gau la . . .*" There was no expression on her face.

"Oh my God . . ." He felt the butt of the revolver in his hand, but he could not lift it and it was too heavy and he stood there through eternity looking at the face, with her hand turning the knife and moving it or making it glitter by her side as whatever happened inside her head, behind those dead eyes, happened, and he could not lift the gun to protect himself.


"HARRY—!"


He thought, in that instant, that he was going to die. He thought, in that instant, that everything he had ever done or been . . . He thought, in that instant . . .

"*Fun-gau la . . .*"

He could not form a single word.


"*HARRY—!*" He could not get through. In the room farthest along the passageway, O'Yee, finding a door to the corridor, finding it locked, putting his shoulder to it, shrieked, "Harry—!" He knew she was out there. He heard Auden and Spencer and Hansell.

O'Yee, smashing again and again at the thick, locked camphor-wood door, not breaking it, shouted, "Help me! *Help me with this goddamned door!*"


\* \* \*

She listened. She cocked her head and listened. Muffled, far off, in a room somewhere there were sounds, noises, and she cocked her head and listened to them.

Mrs. Fan, bringing up the knife, looking down at it, said softly in Cantonese, "*Fun-gau la . . .*" She looked into his face and did not see him and smiled. For a moment, the film cleared on the eyes and she saw him.

His hand was paralyzed on the gun.

Mrs. Fan said softly, "Shhh . . ." She brought up the knife. She took a single step back and looked carefully at him, deciding, as she had decided everyone was going to die in the van, as she had decided everything about the truck, as she had decided to wait for William Lee in the cellar, as she had decided to cock the gun and, pointing it at his head, she had decided to—

She was the one who had driven the van back to the glass factory after her husband had gotten into the truck. She was the one who—

She was the one.

Mrs. Fan said softly, as an order, "Shhh . . ."

She was no more than five-foot-four. She was a woman in her fifties, gray, alone, with her children all gone away to America.

Her husband had not loved the children as she had loved the children. He had wavered, failed. She had killed him too. She had done it for the children.

She was the demon. The demon's eyes came back.

"Shh . . ." She had gone through all the house, sorting all the photographs and discarding them. She had gone through the house looking for her children.

"Shh . . ." In her hand, she held the long, rigid-bladed knife.

"Shh . . ."

The eyes were not human. They stared at him and through him, deciding.

She listened.

She heard far off, muffled sounds.

"Shh . . ."

Mrs. Fan, standing stock still, tensing with strength, said as an order, "*Fun-gau la—sleep now.*"


Like a dying person, she was sorting through all the moments of her life searching for the one, the single moment, the single day when everything, everything had been wonderful and right and—

He saw it in her eyes. He saw her cock her head and, listening, try to hear something that was not there. He saw the knife in her hand.

He saw her smile. *"Fun-gau . . ."*

Mrs. Fan said suddenly, "There." She pointed to a door. Mrs. Fan said, "There."

Maybe once it had been the nursery.

Mrs. Fan said, "There—" Mrs. Fan, the eyes changing, changing, said, starting to tremble, *"Fun-gau—fun-gau—"*

Mrs. Fan said softly, slowly in the voice of a small girl, *"Diem gai ngoh,/Joong-yee nei?/Yun wai nei ho liang."*

Once, the room behind the door had been the nursery. Once. Perhaps. Or perhaps it had not been in this house at all and she could no longer find it. Perhaps, the children were all she had ever had. Mrs. Fan said softly to whoever it was she spoke to, "No, they're still there." Mrs. Fan said softly, not to the room, but to the moment she had found, to all the children, to everything she had ever been, to a moment that, now, would never pass into another moment, Mrs. Fan said, growing old, needed, softly as to a child, to all her children together, to her family, to what she was and all she had ever been, *"Fun-gau la . . ."* Sleep now . . .

She smiled, at that moment, perhaps the way the Lau woman had smiled at the man in the rental yard, for some reason only she knew, wonderfully at him.

> *"Diem gai ngoh,*
> *Joong-yee nei?*
> *Yun wai nei ho liang."*

Gently, he took the knife from her hand.

It was a child's lullaby. It meant, *Why do I love you? Because you are so beautiful.*

Smiling, sitting down in the empty carpetless corridor in that house, smiling, she looked at the closed door to the empty, gone room and, in that once wonderful moment from so long ago, sang the words to her children in the room to lull them gently, softly, warmly off to sleep.

Dogs, children, family.

Sometimes, sometimes it seemed so clear.

Places in the heart.

It was all, somewhere, deeply, secretly, all to do with something no more complicated than love.